Lucky Seven Goes Hawaiian by F. Kalaukoa & S. Cook
A great PI story set in the late 80s Honolulu:

I am so proud to be able to help my mom, who never got a chance, to publish this great book. I found this manuscript 15 years after her death. While reading it I was fascinated at how she told such a good store of private investigation, the workings of a police family and was still able to show her love of Hawaii. While the lead character, Lucky Gregory, is introduced to Hawaii, so is the reader.
-=Stan Cook=-

I0687288

Lucky Seven Goes Hawaiian by F. Kalaukoa & S. Cook

.

Lucky Seven Goes Hawaiian

By
Frances Kalaukoa

and

Stan Cook

Lucky Seven Goes Hawaiian by F. Kalaukoa & S. Cook
Lucky Seven Goes Hawaiian

Printed in the United States of America
ISBN: eBook   978-0-9888126-4-2
          Paperback 978-0-9888126-5-9

Learn more information at:
www.BooksBy-Cook.com

Lucky Seven Goes Hawaiian by F. Kalaukoa & S. Cook

ACKNOWLEDGMENTS

This book is dedicated to the Author: Frances Cook King Kalaukoa, my mother. She wrote this book in the late 1980s and never got around to publishing it. In those days it was near impossible to get a book published by an unknown author. She passed away in 1998 without her dream of this book and one other every getting published.

After completing my first book, 1920,Shots Fired, Officer Down, I was looking for an idea of another book to write when it hit me. I went through her things that we had saved for all these many years. I found this manuscript as well as The Patchwork Mystery. I made up my mind to edit, add to and see that both these books get published.

Thus this wonderful detective from the 1980s is published in 2013. Then, as well as now, this is a really good story about a couple of PIs solving cases and discovering the Hawaii that Frances loved so much.

Enjoy and thanks mom for a great story.

Stan Cook

Book cover background and Chapter logo backgrounds are from a painting by Steve Paschal of Hawaii. Used with his permission.

Chapter 1

The staccato bark of gunfire and the hysterical screams of a woman broke the silence of the street. The young police officer in the unmarked car sucked in his breath, then opened the door, as running footsteps approached.

"Just where in the hell do you think you're going, Gregory? Get back in there!" Sergeant Brayton came running across the street, hurried around the car and climbed in behind the wheel, breathing fire. He stared angrily at the younger man. "Well?"

"But Sergeant, the shots, the screams--I thought--"

"You're not paid to think--not yet. We're on stakeout. I told you to keep an eye on that warehouse and nothing else!

Now get this and get it good. You're just a trainee in my department; and when I give an order you better obey it to the letter. Detective Division is no playground."

"But--"

"But me no buts, Rookie. Now report. Any action down there?"

"Nobody left the building; but two men and a woman entered--arrived in a big Lincoln. Here, I logged the license number. It pulled into the alley." Sergeant Brayton grunted. The sound of sirens fractured the air. Swearing, he started the car and pulled away swiftly. Gregory eyed him curiously, but kept silent. Obviously, they were on their way to the waterfront.

Stopping the car next to Pier Forty, the sergeant turned to Lucky. "You're in a whole new ballpark when you ride with a detective. What I say goes, no questions asked. Can you dig that?" And at Gregory's nod, he added, "It's safer for both of us that way. I don't want you questioning my orders, or failing to follow them. What happens in this car is no one's--no one's business but ours. We'll be okay as long as you remember that. Now, we'll get back to the warehouse and see what's going on."

An ambulance was pulling away, by the time they got there; and four squad cars were in the alley. Walt grunted satisfaction. "Everything under control. We don't need to stop."

Eight months later, Gregory was in the Hell Seat, outside the Captain's office, awaiting an appointment he had sought. Emanating from behind that closed door came the sounds of angry voices; and then the door burst open and a red-faced, plainclothes-man rushed past him and out into the hall.

Lucky Gregory had a sudden urge to follow him. Sounded as if Old Stoney was on the warpath. But he took a deep breath and walked into the office. The captain was on the phone and waved him to a seat.

"I was just trying to locate you," he said. "That's some kind of timing! I went over your files this morning; and I've got a proposition for you."

"A proposition, Sir?"

Tapping a file on his desk, he said, "I see by this that you have ambitions to become a detective. Are you still interested?"

"Yes, Captain. I came in to find out how soon I

can qualify. The scuttlebutt is out that there's going to be an opening." Captain Stone smiled wryly. "The guy that just left here is being replaced. He's tried to rewrite the rules. Now then, Detective Lieutenant Squires and I have come to the conclusion that you are the right man for that post. Your record is excellent and you've shown us some rare investigative talent, as well. "Plus, you passed your sergeant's test with high marks last September and a raise in rank comes with the territory. Squires will see that you get the manuals to read."

"Oh, I've studied them all. Captain. If my break came, I wanted to be ready."

"Good thinking. Now take this file to the lieutenant--and good luck to you!"

"Everything went smoothly for the transition. Then the lieutenant told him, "One thing more. You'll be partnering with Walt Brayton. Know him?" Struggling to hide his dismay, Lucky said, "Yes, I know him. I rode with him a few times during my indoctrination."

"Well, Walt is a strange man, a difficult one, but he's a seasoned detective and you can learn a lot from him. Has a mean streak, though. Don't let it bother you."

It was just small, unsettling things that troubled him at first. Brayton ran tabs at restaurants, never cash for anything and sneered when Lucky insisted on paying. Then Walt began sending him on pointless missions, while he "worked the streets for awhile." At such times, he would smell of alcohol when he returned to the car.

Their assignments went very well, however and the lieutenant seemed pleased with his progress. But

3

Lucky learned that, although they respected Walt's work, other men in the department disliked him intensely. He'd been through half a dozen other partners; and some of them warned him to "watch that guy." From the beginning, he had insisted that Lucky do the driving; and frequently he would say, "Stop! I've been trying to catch up with that bastard." And he'd hop out, hustle his prey out of earshot and there'd be a lot of gesturing and word tossing before he returned, looking pleased with himself. And contrary to procedure, he would simply add the time it took to an existent case, rather than logging it properly.

Once, when Lucky asked if that wasn't against division policy, he snapped, "My God, man, it saves paper-work. No sweat, Kid."

God, how he hated to be called "Kid!" And he was getting more and more uncomfortable with the situation. Still, he had to admit their cases were solved well within their time frame and the investigations of felonies and murders were going well. Perhaps he was being too critical--a new broom trying to sweep too clean. But he didn't have to like it.

Those tabs Brayton insisted on running bugged him as well.

"How do you keep them all straight, Sergeant? So many different places and all."

"You putting me on, Kid? When we go in their places, owners feel they're getting their money's worth with the show of police support. They don't expect us to pay for a little food now and then. You don't get a damn thing, paying cash the way you do. Hell, I've even heard you turn down offers. They just figure you're a dope."

It all fell into place one night, when Walt called for a stop and hurried across the street to talk with an over-dressed man who had "pimp" written all over him. Lucky watched closely. The two were arguing in front of a lighted store window. The pimp reached in his pocket. Lucky tensed and started to draw his gun--then relaxed, as he could see a large wallet in the man's hand. Holding it up to the light, he extracted what appeared to be a wad of bills and held them out to Walt, who shook his head. More were added and this time they disappeared into Walt's pocket; and he returned to the car.

With a smug smile Brayton told him, "If I've told The Fox once, I've told him a hundred times to keep his foxy ladies out of this district. He ought to remember this time. I really read him the riot act and--"

"Can it, Walt. I saw you take the money." Lucky pulled back into traffic.

"The hell you did! Well, it's time you learned the facts of life, Kid. Money talks down here. The quicker you learn that the better off you'll be. We have to play their rules; hit 'em in the pocket where it hurts the most."

Lucky nodded, noncommittally. Walt stared at him angrily. "You think you're so damn pure, you make me want to puke, Gregory. For God's sake, wise up! Join the real world!"

Lucky struggled to control himself. "If we can't follow the rules, we're in the wrong business," he said quietly.

The next morning, Lucky was back in the Hell Seat, when Captain Stone arrived. "Come on in," he said gravely. "You look like hell. Sleepless night?" And at his nod, added, "I see you know."

"Yes, Captain, I do know. I was hoping you didn't." Stone flinched. "I had that coming," he said, bitterly.

"You see old Walt is a pretty smooth operator. I kept hoping we were dead wrong about him; but I knew from your record that if he were dirty, you'd nail him and do your duty.

"The canny bastard would have caught on, if you had known why we were putting you with him. He would have made some excuse to get rid of you. Nobody ever lasted this long with him before. I'm sure you figured out that we set you up--Internal Affairs Investigation, of course. Had to be done, but I sure as hell didn't like being part of it. Brayton isn't the only one involved, but he's the ringleader; and when he falls, so will the others. I simply had no option."

"Neither did I, Captain. I figured that out during the night. And the bottom line is I've had enough; I'm out of here. Being set up as a pigeon makes me damn mad, Sir."

"I don't blame you. I must ask you to hang in on this, for the good of the department, though. IA is ready to interview you. And I'll sit in, of course. I know you hate to be in the position of being an informer, but it's for--"

"Don't bother to explain, Captain. Call them in."

6

It was a rough two hours; and the searching questions elicited information that even Lucky didn't realize he had. Then he was assured that his resignation would be accepted; and that his record would be cleared in due course, so that he could continue his career elsewhere.

And after the Internal Affairs men left, the captain still had another blow for him. "You'll have to ride a couple more nights with Walt, till IA's ready to move. You can handle that?"

"Yes; but then I'm going to get out of town. I'll be ready to roll on Wednesday. That's my day off anyway."

The captain extended his hand. "Good luck to you, Son. Damn, but I hate all this. You're good! Perhaps when this is all over, we can--" Don't say it, Sir," Lucky interrupted, shaking his head.

"I think it's time I moved on."

Just three months before these events had transpired, Pualani Kanai graduated from the Police Academy and she too was assigned to South Hills.

The exotically lovely daughter of Keoki Kanai and his English wife Mary hailed from the island of Maui, Hawaii. From her mother, she had inherited her slender figure and delicacy of facial contours. Her Hawaiian ancestry had blessed her with smooth, golden skin; her dark eyes, luminous in their fringe of long lashes; and in the cascade of satiny black hair that now curved softly just to the collar-line of her police uniform-- the longest regulation-length permitted.

She sometimes found her physical attributes more of a liability than an asset, however. Her new colleagues, predominantly male--had a tendency to overlook her intelligence and her stubborn determination to function effectively in her chosen profession. Her response to their amorous and/or protective approaches was to tighten her firm little jaw and set the record straight in polite but definite terms, eyes flashing a warning to lay off. After a few such encounters the word got around and she began to get, from her fellow-officers, a modicum of the respect she craved.

From her earliest memory, her father had been a police officer and to her, he was nothing less than a knight in shining armor. Her mother was sweet and fragile and she loved her very much; but it was her father who stirred in her the ambition to do him proud. To her, that meant following in his footsteps.

When he was transferred to the detective division of the Honolulu Police Department and the family moved to Oahu, young Pualani thought it the most wonderful time of her life. She remembered every detail of the ceremony, when he became a Lieutenant; and the one that followed, when he made Major. Sitting there in the small audience, she vowed that some day she would excite in him the same bursting pride she felt on those very special occasions.

At college, she majored in Law--not that she had ambitions to become an attorney, but in order to get a well-established knowledge of the law that would make her a better police officer. After she received her degree, she was accepted at the Police Academy in Los Angeles, graduated and was thrilled to get her rookie assignment at South Hills. There she was destined to meet Lucky Gregory.

Before that meeting occurred, her rosy dream crashed with a vengeance. She found herself doing paper work, paper work and more paper work. She had little taste for the desk jockey they were making of her; and was beginning to believe that she would never achieve her goals.

Even her transfer to the radio room was painful. Taking calls and transmitting instructions to officers who were out there where things were happening, only added salt to her wounded ego. And finally, in despair, she called her father from the pay phone outside the station.

Chapter 2

"Honolulu Police Department, Sergeant Kea speaking."

"Hi, Kea, this is Pua. I need to talk with my father. Is he in?"

"Aloha, Pualani. Hold just a minute. He's just coming in. "

"Major Kanai--"

"Dad," she blurted, not even waiting for their usual mutual greetings. "Oh Dad, I've got such a problem. Things are awful here. They won't assign me to a car, or give me a partner, or let me do a thing but log and type reports and I'm miserable. Things just aren't working out. I'm doing--"

"Baby," he interrupted. "Slow down a minute. Now listen to me. I'm not surprised to get this call. I've been expecting it. This has been the problem women on the force have had to face, since they were first accepted for duty. Maybe we should have talked more about this earlier on. You are going to have to be patient and keep on watch for the first opportunity to serve in the areas you want. It's as simple as that. I know how you must feel, though, kuuipo."

"But Dad," she wailed, "they keep me so busy on the desk and phones and computer that I haven't the time to take advantage of an opportunity even if one bit me."

"Honey, I tried to warn you that it was no easy career you'd picked for yourself. We have the same difficulty here. A few women are assigned under-cover

10

work, but even those few are treated more as decoys than operatives. I don't know what else to tell you, except to hang in there and somewhere along the line you'll get your break. Of course, you can change your mind and take a crack at that bar exam. It will only take you—what, one more year of college? Mom and I can spring for that."

"Gosh, Dad, I don't want to be an attorney. Those months of tough training at the academy just whetted my ambition. Now I'm impatient for some action. Thanks for the offer. I guess I'll just have to tough it out--right?"

"That's my girl! For now, accept the fact that you are serving, by doing just what they assign you--and do it so well, that when an opportunity arises, you are the one to get the nod."

"I suppose you're right," she sighed. "Maybe it was dumb to get into police work in the first place. But I hate to give up, even though I just don't feel I'm ever going to get anywhere here. Well, I guess I'll give it a few more months. Give my Aloha to mom--you too--. I do feel a little better now. Mahalo, Dad. I love you.

"We love you, Pua and don't you forget ever, your mother and I are here for you whenever you need us, whatever you decide to do. Okay?"

As she hung up, Pua felt tears coming and, determined that nobody at the station should see her cry, she made tracks for the locker room--but she wasn't quite quick enough. Blinded by the unwanted tears, she bumped headlong into the handsome young detective sergeant known to all as Lucky.

"Why don't you watch where you're going?" she stormed; and then as he reddened under attack, she covered her face with her hands and in a choking voice told him, "I'm sorry--I know it wasn't your fault."

The tears were falling fast now and feeling a little awkward, he put his arms around her and held her gently for a moment. "Look," he said, soothingly, "I'm off duty. Let's go talk somewhere."

"I can't," she sobbed. "My break is over and I have to get back to that--that--that miserable desk."

"You just wait here for a minute," he answered, "and I'll take care of that. Wait right here. Promise?"

She nodded, wiping away with her fingertips the tears that still brimmed over onto her cheeks.

When he returned, he said, "All right. You're covered for an hour, but it means hour overtime for you to work.

I have a feeling you need to talk to someone, so why not me? Now let's see a little smile--I don't want anybody around here thinking I picked on you."

In silence, they walked to the little park across the street and found a secluded bench. Seated, he turned to her and asked, "Now then, what is this tragedy all about?"

She gave him a small, shame-faced smile. "Oh, it's not a tragedy, I guess; I'm just so damnably discouraged." And she poured out to him her frustration and disappointment.

When she began to run down, he said softly, "I

12

disagree with you in a way. I do think it is tragic. You have gone through all that rigid training and the work you're assigned seems more demeaning than a stenographic pool. There's a lot in the system that is unfair and needs working over--and your situation is certainly one of them.

"Tell you what, I'll talk to a few people that might be able to work an active assignment in for you. The trouble is, you look so young and you're so attractive, that everyone from the Captain down wants to protect you, keep you out of danger."

She sputtered with indignation. "I'm a trained officer, not a sex object, for Heaven's sake! I want to work at my craft, because I'm good at it, not for any other reason. I want so very much to prove myself and they won't even give me a chance. I can't take it much longer."

"Believe me, Officer Kanai, I know just where you're coming from. It seemed to me I was never going to get anywhere, when I began, either. Tough it out for a little while, Pua and let's see what happens. I have to tell you this business has disappointments for all of us. You are not alone. Now, we'd better get back."

As they reached the station, she turned to him, "I do appreciate your taking this trouble for me. Just letting it out helps. Thank you, Lucky. I just can't--"

He held up a hand. "Don't thank me now. How about making that speech over dinner tonight?"

"Eight-thirty? I have that extra hour to work, you know." She managed a teasing smile.

"Eight-thirty it is," he agreed. That was the beginning of a good many dates whenever their duty hours didn't conflict. Three weeks after her first encounter with Lucky, Pua finally got her chance. She rode traffic detail and park detail and learned a lot from the veteran sergeant who showed her the ropes. And then came the day, when she was assigned an under-cover operation. Delighted, she went in for briefing, only to find that she was assigned to a downtown department store in a stakeout at the jewelry department, which had been the target of a series of costly robberies. Her briefing revealed only that the robberies were apparently the work of a gang working in pairs, but even that was still a matter of conjecture. It was up to her to sort it out. It wasn't the assignment of her dreams, but it was a challenge.

In spite of surveillance by both the store detectives and plainclothes men, the store had been ripped off, time and time again, without the thefts being detected. It was Lucky's idea that a woman, under cover as a salesperson, might make all the difference. He suggested they use Pualani Kanai.

It was an opportunity at last to prove her. For cover, she sold scarves at the adjoining counter, neatly dressed in the basic black affected by all of the regular employees. It wasn't a particularly busy counter, so she had time to observe closely, but unobtrusively, the area of the previous thefts.

The first day, she went over to the jewelry department to introduce herself as Lani; and the two women identified themselves as the manager, Jean and

14

her assistant, Lila.

"Where's Melissa?" Jean asked.

"She has a bad virus, I understand. She'll be out for a week or two," Pua told her. "I'm just filling in for her. Well, I'd better get to work." And she walked back across the broad aisle, to busy herself at her counter.

During the very first week, the thieves struck again, this time a costly emerald ring and Pua had seen nothing amiss. After a second undetected robbery, she spotted a fellow officer moving around the department, observing her and she was furious-

Returning to the station that evening, she marched up to the Duty Officer's desk, eyes flashing with indignation. "Look here. Sir," she told him, "I don't need a baby-sitter. I know what I'm doing. That officer will break my cover, for one thing--he's so painfully obvious that all the clerks are onto him--some of them warned me to be on my best behavior, of all things! If you've got to have me observed, at least tell him to keep his distance. No thief in his right mind would chance a heist while he's there."

"But Officer Kanai," he began and got no further.

"Besides, you know there've been two more robberies since I've been on this case--and don't think I haven't taken a ribbing about that around here. But I have a theory about what's going on and with half a chance; I can crack this thing and catch them in the act. I'm convinced these are inside-outside operations. Now, am I going to get a free hand or not?"

15

Lucky Seven Goes Hawaiian by F. Kalaukoa & S. Cook

"All right, all right!" He held up both hands and shaking his head, went on, "You're a real spitfire, aren't you! You'll get your free hand, but watch yourself. They've struck the store for over a million in jewelry already and they aren't about to roll over easy. Go to it, Officer Kanai."

So Pua sold scarves, draped scarves over the display racks, polished the glass of her showcase, sold more scarves--at the same time keeping close watch. Nothing. Yet she had a hunch about how it would go down.

On Wednesday, a well-dressed, but very nervous woman entered and went directly to the jewelry counter. Jean waited on her--but she seemed very angry about something.

"I assume my bracelet is ready," the woman said timidly.

"It certainly is," Jean told her, glaring. "It's been ready since Monday. Wait a minute." And she turned to Lila, holding out a paper.

"Take this list up and check it with incoming stock, Lila." And as the girl left, she turned back to the customer. "I've had it with you!" she hissed. "You may have screwed things up, being late this way; but here's your purchase. She opened a blue velvet box, exposing a shimmering diamond bracelet. "Your check has cleared; so return the sales slip to me."

Pua finished a sale she was making and knelt down to rearrange the scarves in her counter--all the while peering through the glass, her pulses racing.

16

She couldn't see Jean, who seemed to be having difficulty retrieving something beneath the cash register. When she stood up, she was slapping what appeared to be a label on a white paper-wrapped box. Then she slipped it and the bracelet box into one of the store's distinctive carryall bags.

Handing it to the waiting customer, she told her, "Ma'am, that bedside-clock you ordered for your husband came, so I've put it in here, rather than mailing it to you."

"What bed--yes, oh yes, the er--beside clock. Thank you." And she began to walk toward the door.

Pua toppled a scarf arrangement she had made and said, "Oh blast! I'm going out for a breath of fresh air— fresh air is just what I need. I'm all thumbs today. You don't mind keeping an eye on my counter, do you? I won't be gone long." And at Jean's grudging nod, she picked up her shoulder bag and walked out, following her prey to where she had left her car and was in the process of unlocking it.

Drawn gun in one hand, her badge in the other, Pua said, "Stop right there. And put your hands on top of your car. You are under arrest."

The woman took a startled look at the slim girl in her simple black dress and cried, "You can't do this! You're no policeman."

Pua displayed her badge. "I am a police officer. Now raise your hands above your head."

Stark terror in her eyes, one upraised hand still clutching her package, the woman pleaded, "Please don't shoot me. I've never been arrested before. It's all a mistake."

"Yours, I'm afraid," Pua said, securing the handcuffs around her prisoner's wrists and taking possession of the evidence.

At that moment, the store detective rushed up. "I got your 'fresh air' message, Ma'am," he said, panting, "and the patrolmen are on the way."

Together, they examined the contents of package and sealed it into an evidence bag.

"Hey, what do you think you're doing?" the woman protested. "I bought all that stuff!"

"Oh?" Pua asked. "May I see your sales slip?"

"They--they--forgot to give me one," was the response. "Oh, come now. No sales slip for jewelry?" And Pua turned to the store detective. "Give this evidence to the patrolmen--I have more business inside. Tell them to read her, her rights and keep her here until I return. I may just have another bird for the cage."

Entering the store again, she smiled at Jean and told her, "Oooh, that was refreshing--better than a coffee or coke anytime. You ought to try it. It's so nice out."

"Oh, yeah? Here comes my relief--maybe I'll follow your lead, at that. On second thought, though, a cup of coffee would go good right now."

"I think you'd better take the walk," Pua suggested.

Then she stepped closer and speaking softly told her in firmly uncompromising tones, "You are under felony arrest. Don't try anything; I am a police officer and the gun in my pocket is trained on you right now. Just walk ahead of me out of that door. Move quickly and quietly."

"You're insane, I didn't take anything," the woman snarled, "and I have my rights." But she was walking.

"There are a couple of officers outside who will read you list of what those rights are," Pua responded. And minutes later, her first assignment was completed; and for once, she was feeling good about her job. "You handled that real well," the store detective told her, as they watched the police car move away. "I'll bet not one customer knew what was going down. It's bad for business to have a confrontation inside there and you cleared out both of them without a hitch."

"With your help," Pua smiled. "Wiring me was your idea, you know and when I gave our 'fresh air' code the first time, I wasn't sure you'd be listening."

"Oh, no problem. I've had you tuned in all along-- heard it both times," and he tapped an earpiece.

"Well," Pua sighed, "I guess I've lost my job at the store. I'd better get going."

"Need a ride? Mr. Robison, the store owner will be going down to headquarters in a bit and--"

"No, thanks. My car is right over here."

"Okay. I hope we get to work together again. I like your style."

As she drove away, Pua could hardly contain her

glee. "I did it, Dad," she whispered. "I did it. Things are looking up. "

Chapter 3

Pua found the paper work not half bad, when it was her own case she was writing up; and she took her time making it complete in every detail. She had returned to find the detectives already interrogating her collars and had gone right on by to finish her part of the case. While she was typing, the captain came in to congratulate her.

"That was a sweet piece of work today, my dear," he began. Pua scowled at him, half-teasing, but obviously not too pleased. He hesitated then laughed aloud. "I'm sorry. Let me change that. You did a damned good job today, Officer Kanai."

"Thank you, Sir," she said, beaming with pleasure. "Bet you thought I was a bit touchy, but it's uphill work for a woman to get the professional treatment in this business."

"I know it is. We men get in the habit of patronizing the women here and I'm glad you caught me up on it.

Forgiven?"

"You bet."

"How come you're not at the interrogation? It's your collar, you know."

"I know that, but I wanted to get my report ready while it was fresh in my mind and not cluttered up with what they're saying in there. My dad always told me that procedures before the actual arrest can blow a case, if they're not reported accurately-and I don't intend to blow this one. It's my first."

21

"But not your last, I'll wager. You showed yourself to be cool and professional through the whole thing and you'll be in demand from now on. There are times when patience and determination, plus keen insight, are just what's needed to crack a case. And this was one of those. Oh, yes, you'll be filing plenty of those reports. I'll let you get back to that one now."

"Thank you, Sir."

A jubilant Lucky was waiting for her when she stopped at the desk to file her report. "Hey, you really have the whole place jumping," he grinned. "Everybody's talking about the good job you did. And on the subject of talking, those two babes did their share on the way in, according to the patrolmen. They blew their cool. The gal with the goods told the head clerk, 'So much for your sure thing. No chance of us getting caught, huh? You're a clumsy cow!' And Jean yelled back, 'Oh, yeah? If it was my fault, how come the other jobs went so smooth--so which one of us is clumsy? I should never have taken you on. That's where I went wrong.' Can you beat that?"

"Had their rights been read to them by then?"

"You'd better believe it! They waived them until the preliminary interrogation was well under way and suddenly decided they'd better have an attorney present after all. "They called one and after spending about fifteen minutes with them, he came out shaking his head. "'My God,' he said. 'After confessing to everything and ratting on everybody in the scam, including the Portland fence, they now want to cut a deal. And when I asked them what they had left to deal with, the Jean woman looked blank and then offered the fact that they'd been so cooperative. Can you believe that?

Anyway, Jean even gave names and addresses of other women she'd used as mules to cart off the gems. Neither one of them had any notion you were anything but--nor this is a quote--'a nosey saleswoman'. Neat, the way you made your arrests, too. You handled it like the pro you are."

Pua flushed, pleased and proud. "Barney, the store detective, was a big help. We had a code worked out for when it came down. I was wired and all he had to hear was 'fresh air' and he called for police back up, alerting them to our location, out in the parking lot. It all worked even better than we'd planned. Wish you could have seen the expression on Jean Mason's--that's the head clerk's name--face, when I took her--and not a customer in the store was the wiser, as far as I could tell."

"How did you figure it to be an employee, in the first place?"

"There never was any diversion activity or the confusion I had been led to expect. And yet I missed on two items, stolen practically under my nose. To be strictly honest, if that woman hadn't made Jean so angry by being late, I might have missed it again. That was no way to treat a customer in a store of that quality--it didn't make sense. And Barney had shown me his file on each robbery. Jean had been the one to report the discovery of every theft. I'm still puzzled about one thing, though. She reported jewelry missing three days ago--that was the second robbery after I started working there--the one the guys have been teasing me about. But the woman picked up a boxful today. And for some reason, Jean made her return her sales slip for a bracelet she apparently purchased.

"You know, Lucky, I have a hunch she was taking the pieces out of inventory before they ever got to the showcase and stashing them some place until she could pass them on. She was playing a game of strategy. What do you think?"

"You've got it nailed, Pua." She bragged that it was easy, since the inventory was her sole responsibility.

She'd select apiece when she was re-stocking and put it in one of the other storage cases in the safe. In case of a spot check, she would be the one to find it accidentally misfiled. Sometimes she'd report an article stolen days, even weeks, before it ever left the store.

"She bragged that she'd sometimes come in after her day off and pretend to be stunned that some valuable jewel had disappeared the previous day, when actually it had been taken out of stock days--sometimes weeks, before."

"No wonder it was all such a mystery--so hard to spot!" Pua gasped. "She'd been there so many years, no one would suspect her. If she had just been satisfied, they could have gotten away with it. Tried it once too often-- that's greed for you. And how did the others come into the picture, do you know? Were they pros?"

"Pros? Hell no. That was the beauty of her plan. A customer would come in, one of the jewelry-mad kind and after all her years there, she could read them like a

24

book. She'd boost the price on something her mark craved, so that she couldn't afford it; and then suggest a real deal on it, if her customer would come in when she was told to and pick up a package, pre-addressed to Jean Mason and mail it to her; and once or twice she had them addressed directly to the Portland fence.

"She boasted that she never had to use the same woman twice. Claimed most of them were wives of some pretty well known public figures. We still don't know all the ins and outs of the scam, but it worked."

"Those women must have known what they were doing was illegal, though. Getting that kind of a 'deal' for mailing a package?"

"That's for sure. And the irony of that 'deal' on the piece each one bought, is that it was actually sold at the store's regular price, so the sales books showed no discrepancy."

"Up to then, she was clever all right, but I can't figure out why she would keep doing it to a store where she'd worked so many years and had been given so much responsibility."

"Wouldn't have worked any other way, honey. Having that responsibility was the key to her success. When the storeowner Jay Robison came in to identify the jewelry in the white box, which by the way he evaluated at over $250,000, he asked her the same question.

"She turned on him and told him in a crazy-wild voice, 'It's all your fault. You put me in charge. You promised me raises and for twenty years I got nothing but peanuts--not even enough to keep up with the cost of living. You're a cheap, lying old man, J.R. and you owed me!'"

"The whole thing makes my head spin," Pua said. "Let's get out of here, as soon as I drop this off at the desk. She stopped suddenly, chuckling. "Wonder what will happen to the customer's bracelet--after all she did pay for that. Suppose they'll let her wear it in jail?"

Lucky laughed. "Somehow I doubt that. Besides, she doesn't have a sales slip for it. Now, how about a celebration dinner?"

"Great. I'll find us a special place."

"Nope," she laughed. "Tonight, it's on me and I'm cooking. Besides being the world's greatest investigator, I am also a super cook. Tonight, I prove it."

"Terrific!" he answered, "But I'm bringing the champagne."

It was an unforgettable evening. Her coq au vin was perfect and the salad crisp and savory, the rolls fresh-baked and buttery and the champagne a chill and bubbly delight.

Afterward, they sat beside each other on the sofa to enjoy their coffee and munched fresh strawberries from the bowl Pua had placed on the coffee table, along with Kirshwasser and confectioner's sugar in which to dip them.

"Lucky, I'm curious about something, but it's personal." Pua raised her sleek black eyebrows in mute question.

"Well, love, what is it? Something about my mysterious past?"

"Could be. How did you come to be called Lucky? Even your mother said, 'Good for Lucky!' the time you had me telephone her when you made Sergeant. I asked her then but she said, 'It's a long story, my dear. You ask him.'" Lucky laughed. "That's my Scottish mom all right!

It's no secret. She was only concerned about you running up a big long-distance bill.

"Okay, here goes, but I had to get the story second-hand, you know. I was born on the seventh day of the seventh month of 1957, a two-pound-seven-ounce 'preemie' weakling. How's that for starters?"

Pua's dark eyes went wide with disbelief. "Go on," she whispered.

"My father had come back from war pretty crippled up, but he was a stubborn man and insisted on taking a job at the huge truck farm near the Mojave Desert, where he'd worked before he enlisted. They lived in a small company house nearby. Just a month before I was born, he was killed in an industrial accident and between her grief and the blistering heat wave off the desert; my mother just couldn't carry me to term.

"Old Dr. Hailey, the company G.P. and a half-dozen wonderful women kept us both alive during the ten-day heat-wave, even without a proper incubator. They dared not move us. The doctor told me he put me in my mother's arms and prayed for a miracle. He felt nothing short of one could save us.

"Then Addie, his nurse, told him, 'It's an oven in here, Doc, 109 degrees. They'll both dehydrate. If only there was a little humidity, it would be a regular incubator.'

"Doc jumped out of the chair and hugged her and told her she was a miracle-maker. He asked her to run and get some neighbor women and tell them to bring all their bed sheets. While she was gone he filled the bathtub with water. He felt he had a chance to save at least one of us if his idea worked.

"When they came in, he grabbed the sheets from their arms and told them, 'We're going to turn this whole house into an incubator.' "He ordered the women to soak the sheets in the tub and wring them out and hang them over every door and window in that little house. As fast as they got them up, some were already dry and they kept repeating the operation. Working in shifts, for ten days and nights, they kept at it--and it was working. Both of us were still alive. Someone had an old-fashioned hand wringer and that made wringing out the sheets easier, but it was a monumental effort all the same.

"Then, as happens on the desert, the nights became cold while the days were torrid. Those nights, they took me from my mother and put me in a small basket on the oven door, with the heat turned low. They tell me I hated it and cried all night, but that was music to their ears. Pua, aren't you getting tired of all this?"

"No, no, I'm fascinated. Don't stop."

"The crisis over, the Doc came by one day and told my mother that we'd both be fine now and bragged us up as a couple of red-headed scrappers. Then he leaned over my crib and said, 'Tough it out, little Seven. I'll see you later.'

"My mother was puzzled and asked him why he called me seven. He said, 'Well, what's his name?'

"She looked blank for a moment and then began to laugh. 'You know,' she told him, 'with all the emergencies and everything, I forgot to name him! We kept calling him Baby. What on earth did you put on his birth certificate?'

"'Baby Seven Gregory.' He grinned like a leprechaun, according to mom. 'What else? Seven's got to be his lucky number--born 7-7-57, at 7 p.m., a seven-month baby. Of course it's time now he had a proper name.' And he told me my mother smiled tremulously and said, 'His name will be Blake Seven Gregory. His daddy, my Blake, never got the breaks, but he was a fine, fine man and this little boy should be lucky all his life, after the good start all of you people have given him. 'Pua's eyes were brimming with tears. "And she's always called you Lucky?"

"No, when she really wanted my attention she has always called me Blake Seven, but after the guys on my college basketball team started calling me Lucky, she started and that's what she usually calls me now. End of story."

"It's a wonderful story, Lucky. Thank you for sharing it with me. How about more coffee?"

"No more, thanks." He stood up, sighing with satisfaction. "It's been a wonderful evening, a super

29

dinner, honey; but I'd better go. It's going to be a day tomorrow. But first my sincere seal of approval of a job well done."

He bent over her and drew her to her feet and into his arms, tipped up her chin and kissed her gently. And quite without knowing how it happened, they were in each other's arms, their kisses tender, then passionate-- and somehow, filled with promise.

Chapter 4

Never one to waste time--he began to burn his bridges immediately. Dumping the four to midnight watches with Brayton, he had a good part of each day free. He put his apartment in the hands of a realtor to sell, knowing full well that with the scarcity of property in that area, it would be no problem to unload. He traded his convertible for a van, which he began loading with the possessions he wasn't prepared to part with and had his phone disconnected.

When this was accomplished, he was surprised and pleased--and a little shocked to note that the bitterness he had felt at being set up, had given way to anticipation of a clean, new start. Where, he wasn't sure. He had a few ideas to explore.

He ached to talk with Pualani; but she had called to tell him she had been assigned to attend a disaster relief forum for women officers, being held at Stanford University on Monday. She would be back sometime Tuesday. To his relief, Brayton had shown no signs of suspicion on the two days they rode together; and when they signed out the night before, he had said, "Oh, tomorrow is your day off, right? Guess I'll solo. I'm slated for a stakeout on a Korean bar which a snitch says is sweating out a drug delivery that's late."

"And you're going down there solo?"

"You still think like a rookie, Gregory," Brayton grated. "The snitch reported it late last night. If the snitch knows, the street knows; and that's all she wrote. Guaranteed, I'll have a quiet night."

Wednesday morning, he called the station and was mildly surprised to be put on hold. Then she said, "Yes?"

"Officer Kanai, dear," he said. "I think we'd better get together and talk about some things. Are you free for lunch?" When she failed to respond, he added, "Pualani, can't you talk now?"

"There's nothing for us to talk about," she answered, her voice chill and distant--absolutely nothing."

"Come on, Pua," he remonstrated. "I can tell by your voice you've already heard about my getting the shaft. Honey, believe me, things aren't what they seem. Pua, please believe in me. Nobody else, nothing else really matters."

There was a pause and then she said in that same icy voice, "I'm sorry--and pretty confused if you must know--but I think you were darned unprofessional in your behavior; and I don't go for that rough stuff, no matter what the provocation is."

"What rough stuff? What the hell are you talking about?"

"Walt. He's in the hospital. He reported this morning that you went berserk last night and beat him up right after your shift was over. It was such a bad beating they had to hospitalize him! My God, the man is nearly twice your age!"

"I did no such thing. Honey, the man is lying. I didn't even ride with him last night."

"Oh, come off it, Lucky. Your names on his

32

daily."

"Then he put it there. I swear to God I didn't."

"Oh? So he's the one that's lying? Yet you get a summary dismissal?"

"I get a what? I was set up for a fall, but it wasn't a summ--"

"Look," she interrupted. "I don't want to talk any more. You don't have to explain yourself to me. I think we'd better just leave it as it is--one of those things that could have been great, but isn't any longer. Please don't call me again," she said, her voice choking with tears and broke the connection.

He slammed the phone down. "Of all the pig-headed, self-righteous, narrow-minded--Oh Hell! I guess I blew it--Oh Hell!"

After a few minutes of despair, his mind began to function again. Something was going on down there that didn't make any sense. He searched his wallet for the direct line office number the captain had given him and was relieved to hear the gravel voice, "Captain Stone, here."

"Captain, what in name of all that's holy is going on?" His question was shrill with his anger.

"Calm down, Lucky, calm down. I tried to call you a while ago, but your phone's been disconnected. I gather you've heard the latest. Now listen, we know you weren't the one who beat up Brayton. Internal Affairs has had a man following him home ever since you talked with them. Last night, near the end of his shift, Walt was forced into the curb and a couple of the body guards of that pimp you told us about--the one called Foxy--worked him over, left him on the sidewalk by his car and took off.

"The IA man saw it happen and called for back-up and an ambulance. We know you weren't in on it. Hell, you weren't even riding with him. IA says he was soloing. You're in the clear.

"Brayton's in pretty bad shape--a concussion, multiple bruises, a broken ankle and collar bone and two of the worst shiners I ever saw. Frankly, I think the man's gone bananas. Maybe sensed we knew his dark secrets and his mind wouldn't take the pressure. But don't worry. The truth will come out and you don't even have to appear. Internal Affairs has seen to that, with a little prodding from me. It will all be over soon."

"Not soon enough for me, though. I've already lost my girl over it. I have to tell you, Sir, I'm getting tired of being the fall guy in this thing. Well, that's it then. I'll be in touch."

"Well, if it's any comfort, you have cleaned up an internal mess the department just couldn't afford. Without your input, we'd still be in Square One."

"Am I free to leave town?"

"You are, but as soon as you get settled, call me. I'll need your address so that those papers you want can be sent to you."

"I'll do that,"

"Within the hour, Lucky was on his way North.

Driving always seemed to blow away his blue moods. But it was a new experience for him to be rejected by someone he cared about. Actually, with the exception of his mother, he had few emotional attachments. There was old Lem Peabody, of course. He grinned at the thought of the man who had been such a good friend to him, as he was growing up, fatherless. He made a sudden decision. Lem lived out on his boat on the Monterey Peninsula. What was the name of the place? Lands End? No.

He pulled over and consulted his map. Here it was, Westland Cove. He drove back on the highway, cheered at the prospect of seeing Lem again.

It took some doing, but he finally found the little town, stopped for something to eat; then pulled into the marina parking area and strolled down the dock. There she was, the Anna B, the fishing boat Lem had bought after his wife Anna died. Predictably, there was no sign of life aboard at this hour, but he felt in his bones that Lem was there. He started to retrace his steps and as he did so, a light flickered below decks. He stopped.

"You lost, Sonny?" The old man held the beam of his flashlight on Lucky. "Great balls of fire! Is that you, Lucky Gregory?"

"Sure is, Lem. Did I wake you up?"

"Come aboard. Of course you woke me up. Anybody tippy toes down my dock and I wake up in a jiffy. How the hell are you and what are you doing down here?"

The two men embraced and Lucky said, "Just what I always used to do when I had a problem. Came to see

35

you."

"Well, come below. It's fierce chilly up here. I'll heat up the coffee. You're a treat for these old eyes, boy. What's it been, five or six years, anyway? Your mother was with you the last time. How is she?"

"Fine. She travels a lot and seems to enjoy life."

"Good. Now, let me just connect this shore power and we'll get some light on the subject."

The cabin was neat and clean, as Lucky had expected. The old man had always been fanatical about keeping a taut ship. "Now then, my young friend," Lem said, as they savored mugs of strong black coffee, "do you want to tell me about it now, or shall we get about five hours sleep in first? You look pretty rocky to me."

"I could use some sleep," Lucky admitted, "and you could too, I'll bet."

"Good. You don't plan to rush off again, then. Stay as long as you like. You sleep over there. That bunk's fresh made up."

Lucky slept till ten; then bleary-eyed and groggy, he made his way up on deck to find the old man painting his dinghy.

"Good morning," laughed Lem. "I'd begun to think you was going to sleep all day."

Lucky filled his lungs with fresh sea air and grinned back at him. "You must be starved by now," he said.

"Nope. I fixed and ate my breakfast down there

and you slept through the whole thing. Wait a minute and I'll fix yours."

Lucky shook his head. "I ate at that all-night place up on the highway just before I got here. I'll just get a cup of coffee." He disappeared below.

That was the beginning of four days of relaxation and conversation that restored him and made him ready for whatever was to come. Lem's talent for listening and advising gently was as healing as he remembered. Lem was quick-witted, wise and understanding--and just as Lucky had remembered from his early years, his advice was sound. The time flew by and the old man hated to see him go, but sped him on his way, knowing that the plans he and his young friend had discussed should be put into action as soon as possible.

When Lucky tried to thank him, he waved him off. "You're welcome here anytime, my boy. You remember that. Your job now is to follow your dream and make it reality."

As he drove north, he had to smile. Even on the subject of Pua, the old fellow had been wise. "Don't be stubborn, now," he had advised. "That girl got caught in the middle. Give her a chance to make amends. Women get so deeply hurt sometimes, that they don't make good sense. Even my Anna was that way. Call your Pua; give her the opportunity to change her mind about you, she'll come around. After all, what have you got to lose? A hell of a whole lot more if you don't try, than if you do and you can take that to the bank."

When he reached the City, Lucky checked into the

Mark, ordered a bottle of Scotch sent up, with a steak and salad to consider his situation coolly.

Money was no problem. His mother had started for him from the settlement she had received after his father's death. She made wise investments and kept the secret until he was ready for college. He remembered how dumfounded he was that all that money had been sitting there growing and growing all those years, while they lived a comfortable, but certainly not luxurious life on what she chose to call "my half."

She had laughed when he scolded her about that. "Look, son, there was more money to start with than I had ever heard of before and everything I touched seemed to make us more. The land back East, where I lived when I met Blake, brought in a whopping lot of money and there was life insurance and the Veteran's Insurance, as well as the accident and death settlement after poor Blake was killed. I just did with it what I knew would have made your dad happy. Besides, my tastes were simple and I didn't want to spoil you rotten, as I might have done if I hadn't salted it away for you."

Smiling reflectively, he reached for the phone and dialed swiftly.

"Hi, Mom, how's it going?"

"Oh, hi, Lucky darling," she cried. "How wonderful to hear your voice! Did you get my message? The desk sergeant said he'd try. How come your phone is cut off? Need money?" She laughed, wickedly.

"No, silly. I've left the L.A. area and I'm calling from San Francisco. I just got in."

38

"But your job? What's happened? You're not in trouble are you?"

"No, no, everything's fine. I'm making a career change, that's all. Things weren't that great down there.

I'll write you all about it one of these days. How about telling me what your message was?"

"Oh, yes, that's right. I just wanted you to know that I'm leaving Saturday on the QE2 for England and then on to Scotland again. Your Aunt Shelley is going with me this time."

"Mom! Scotland again? Don't you know there's a big world to see out there besides Scotland?"

"Now don't you scold me Son. I love it there and this time I want to show it to Shelley--where our forefathers grew up and all that."

"Okay, old girl, go for it," he chuckled. "I give up. You have a great time and take good care of yourself. You need anything?"

"Heavens no, do you? Want to come along with us? We plan to stay a month."

"No way, love," he groaned. "I've got to get a new career in gear. I'll tell you all about it when you get back. Give Aunt Shelley my love--and Mom, I love you!"

He was about to put the phone down when he heard her urgent "Wait, oh wait, I forgot to tell you something. Are you still on?"

"Just barely, Mom. What did you forget?"

"A girl called you--Pumani Kulani--something like

39

that. Said she got my number from your file and is trying to trace you. Are you listening? She said it was important. Lucky, is she the same girl that called me when you were promoted?"

A shock of excitement, as potent as electricity, shot through him. "You bet she is, Mom. What was the message?"

"She wants you to call her. She says you have her number. Now don't tell her I almost forgot--" and with that she hung up.

Never did they say goodbye. She was superstitious about that. Nice touch, really--kept them close, on-going.

He picked up the phone again, his fingers shaking as he dialed. He had to dial twice before he got it right and then listened to the familiar double-ring in her apartment. Once, twice--he'd let it ring seven times. On the ninth, she answered breathlessly.

"Hello--hang on a minute please," and she was gone. Back again, she said, "I'm sorry. I just got in and had to put my packages--"

"Pua," he interrupted her. "My mother told me--"

"Lucky!" It was a shout of pure joy. "Oh my dear, my dear, bless you for calling. Wherever are you?"

"I'm in San Francisco, Pua. Are you all right?"

"I am now. But what are you doing in San Francisco?

When will you be back?"

"Never would be soon enough for me. I'm up here

to make some career plans."

"I've been so angry with myself, Lucky and so ashamed. Those things I said. When I found out you had gone away, I couldn't bear it! And when I learned the truth about what had happened to you and realized how badly I had let you down, I--"

"Pua, don't. It's okay, baby. I understand. But I still want you to know what really happened."

"I do know, Lucky--at least most of it. The whole story broke two days ago. Brayton's been kicked out; as well as Dave Jones, one other detective and a couple of traffic patrolmen--and I'm out too."

"You! I can't believe that. How could they tie you--"

"You don't understand. When I found out the truth, what they'd done to you, I just waltzed into the Captain's office, explained in lurid detail what I thought of the whole self-serving outfit and quit on the spot."

"But you--" he began.

"No, Lucky let me finish. I've got to say this first. I'm so ashamed of my stupidity. I had no right not to let you talk to me. I know I should have believed in you. Can you ever forgive me? I love you, Lucky."

"God, Pua, you don't have to explain. I knew you all were getting brainwashed. Sometimes it takes a little experience to figure out who the good guys and who's the bad. Quit beating on yourself. We've better things to talk about. And in case you had any doubts, I love you, too, more than you can possibly imagine. What are your plans?"

"Nothing definite. My dad wants me to come home to Honolulu for a while. But I'm coming to San Francisco tomorrow!"

"You are? Wonderful! I'll meet you."

"No, my dear. My cousin Lili is expecting me and I will be staying with her a few days. If you are free for lunch, the day after tomorrow, I'll have her drop me off on her way to work. Where are you staying?"

"The Mark Hopkins."

"Perfect. That's reasonably near to her travel agency. Is eleven too early? Her shift starts at noon."

"I'll be waiting. And Pua, don't let's say goodbye, okay? I have a thing about that."

"I have a thing about that too. I'll just say Aloha!"

Chapter 5

Their reunion was as sweet and as natural as if their differences had never been. He met her as she came through the lobby door and their embrace, though brief, told each of them what they needed to know.

They lunched at an excellent French restaurant nearby. And afterward, hand in hand, they walked to Union Square and sat by the fountain. By tacit consent, conversation, up to this point, had been light and inconsequential, but now the mood changed.

"Pua, I'm upset about your walking out at South Hills P.D.," he acknowledged with a frown. "You were so dedicated and lust beginning to get the breaks. If my trouble caused it, it's a damned shame."

"That wasn't it at all! When Brayton came back in, complete with stitches and bruises, arm in a cast and I don't know what all, he repeated what we'd heard he said in the hospital, that you had jumped him and beaten him nearly to death. By then, even his cronies were looking at each other skeptically. I wasn't the only one who didn't believe him, not by any means. But by the time I got my head screwed on straight, it was too late to let you know how I felt. You had left.

"He was hustled into IA and within a few minutes, Captain Stone came out and announced that Brayton was going on 'enforced leave', which so obviously a euphemism for suspension that it was hard to keep a straight face. Then the captain ordered us all back to work."

43

Lucky smiled, ruefully. "So Walt and I both got axed. "

"Ironic, isn't it? Brayton did bring down Jones and the others with him, though. That's one plus for the good of the department.

"And then it finally got through to me that Old Stoney and IA had set you up to take the heat you took, basically to keep their damned brass shining! And that did it--all I wanted was out! So I marched right into Stone's office and gave him more than one piece of my mind. He kept trying to interrupt, but I was so hu-hu I kept on yelling at him. When I ran down, he told me you were in the clear and he was your friend.

"And I told him, if that was the case I was happy that he wasn't mine!" Lucky stifled a laugh.

"Pua, you didn't! What did he say then?"

"He had the grace to turn red; and then he told me someone had to get burnt in order to bring the thing down and that he had to do it to you without your knowing, or it wouldn't work. He also said you knew you could come back, when it was all over and keep your rank of Sergeant. And I said, 'Fat chance!'"

At this, Lucky burst out laughing. "Lord, but I would have loved to see the Captain's face. Seriously, though, honey, I think he was in a Catch-22 situation. You know, my darling Pua, you've made my day! Let's get on another subject. Have you any definite plans for the future?"

"Not really. Everything happened so fast that I'm

still confused. I want to do police work, but it bugs me that I might get into that kind of hassle again. What I really want is to get my teeth into detection and crime prevention--something where my work can make a real difference in the quality of people's lives. Does that sound too altruistic?"

"Not at all, Pua. It just blows my mind, how much our values mesh. Shall I lay out my own career idea for you?"

"Oh, please do."

"In every city of any size, there are business people who are constantly being harassed and victimized by everyone from cheap crooks to Syndicate heavies, including ex-cons, drunks and junkies, robbers and in my book, the worst of all--protection racketeers.

"These are modest shops, usually found on side streets, in clusters like small business neighborhoods; and they are absolutely defenseless against the creeps, because they are threatened and their families threatened, if they don't give in to the demands. Too many of them are shot and often killed, sometimes raped or beaten, their shops trashed, because they tried to defend themselves."

Pualani was staring, wide-eyed. "I know what you're talking about, Lucky. Those problems are rampant in Honolulu, too. My father has been battling them for years--but the trouble is that the damage is done by the time the police arrive, unless they happen to get lucky on patrol. And there are never enough policemen to cover every area--that's true everywhere, I imagine. Have you figured out a way to solve it? Is that what you mean?"

45

"I honestly believe so, Pua. Now then, these victims are people who are shy or downright afraid to go to the police because of threats and strong-arm tactics; they can't afford attorneys and Legal Aid is swamped. Some of these poor suckers can't afford to leave their shops to stand in line for hours in hopes of getting help from the few agencies that purport to assist them. They're in a no-win situation and I want to do something about it."

"You're talking about investigation in the private sector, aren't you? That's a super idea, but where is the income coming from? They can't afford detective service either, can they?" Pua asked.

"That's for sure--but that's where my idea comes in. Now just sit back and listen. Interrupt me whenever you have a question, or a contribution to make. Okay? I want you to play Devil's Advocate for me; help me get any bugs out of my plan."

"As we say in the Islands, 'Geevum!' Lucky." He grinned at her and stood up. "Let's walk some more, shall we? I think better on my feet." And as they strolled, he turned to her and said, "You know, I have a good feeling about this--see what you think.

"Now I don't have any locale in mind. But in any of these situations, nine times out of ten, a scam worked on one place successfully, triggers a regular plague of the same activity in the neighborhood. These leeches know that their victims can't protect themselves, so they keep at it until the area either runs dry or they kill or maim somebody, which automatically makes it a police department affair. And the vultures move on to another location.

"The way I figure it, we'd work an area we suspected was being victimized, talking to the businessmen and other potential victims in that area, proposing the organization of a mutual assistance program, in which they would all participate--the whole group rather than one individual. Maybe some of them wouldn't buy the idea at first, but if it works, count on it, they'd soon all come in. What's the problem, Pua? You look concerned."

"I don't mean to rain on your parade, but doesn't this smack of vigilante tactics?"

"No, ma'am, not the way I figure it. We would train them to help themselves, without any violence. We'd teach them to help themselves through a mutual protection system, an inter-shop alarm system; plus keeping personally involved on a daily basis. That's the backbone of it. I wrote pages and pages of ideas, while I was with my friend Lem. They have a similar system on a small scale for boat owners at the Marina. Works for them."

"From a practical angle--we are talking career here--I don't understand how you plan to make it financially feasible. Lucky, I think it's a marvelous idea, but you do have to make a living. That's one question. The other is, who is the 'we' you keep talking about?"

For a second, Lucky just looked at her searchingly. "Let me take the second question first. I am going to need a qualified associate; someone with a knowledge of criminal law; someone who is well-versed in police procedures; someone who is not afraid of tight corners; someone who wants to make a difference in the quality of other people's lives--and someone who is downright beautiful! Do you know anyone who fits that bill?"

She stared at him, wide-eyed. "You know I mean you, Pualani Kanai. Would you consider it, at least? It seems to fit in perfectly with your ambitions, don't you agree? I don't know yet just where it would take us, but we'd be together and that's important to me. What do you think?"

"I like it," she whispered, her face alights with anticipation--and something else; a secret idea of her own she was not ready to share with him yet.

"I like it, too," he said. "Now that that's settled, about your first question. You're right, of course, the income wouldn't be much to begin with; but think of it in the same light as group therapy. After one success, we could build it into a good profit-making business, by working the same type of set-up in another area having similar problems. If it works, the word will get around. "A comparatively low monthly fee, set by the mutual agreement of the group, would get us started. Our aim is to help them to help themselves and also to keep their business integrity and dignity in the process. They would expect to pay for our services."

"You're right, of course. It's an excellent idea." Pua said.

"And given a successful start to prove we are on the right track, better paying clients would seek us out from the referrals of the people we have already helped. We can afford to go slow, Pua. "Actually, money is no problem at this point. I'm no millionaire, but I have a good cushion, a sort of inheritance from my father. My mother set it up, proved to be a regular genius on investments; and it certainly gives me room to operate while the business builds. You'll have a good salary from the start. And I want no arguments about that. I need you, Pua. This thing won't work without you."

"You wouldn't leave me parked behind a desk?"

"There'll be that too, but we'll share in it. No, I may get scared for you at times, but I'll leave it to you to keep me in line. I know you can take care of yourself."

"Music to my ears," she said. "Now, let me ask you something else. Where do you plan to operate?"

"That, I don't know yet. I thought of staying here, but one look at the yellow pages and the list of established competition seemed overwhelming. We'd have to do some surveying. Any ideas?"

"Just one, but it might appeal to you. Have you ever been to Hawaii?"

"Once, when I graduated from college. It was gift from mom. "

"Well, I told you I talked with my dad, who's the Major of detectives in Honolulu. They have a shocking number of the very kind of problems you're talking about. And more often than not, a serious crime is committed before they have enough information to prevent it. Dad suggested that if I came home, I might tie in with one of the better investigators over there. The place is growing so rapidly that it could use a really dedicated pair like us. It's been on my mind ever since you said you were counting me in."

"Sounds good. What about the competition there?"

"There are a number of investigators, but most of the good ones are involved with big businesses, protective services, guard assignments, missing persons, straying wives or husbands, bad check artists and the like. Once my father understands what our main concern is, we'd have no trouble getting licensed, bonded and all the other details involved."

"Let's go over there and see what happens. It sounds ideal, including a good relationship with the police department and that's a basic necessity, if we're to function effectively. I don't know how they'll take to a tall, red-headed shamus over there though."

"Don't forget," she grinned, "we'll be associated with a 'local wahine' and that's a definite plus! You dig?"

"I dig. Let's go see how fast we can get our show on the road. Have you enough clothes with you? We can send for the rest of your stuff, right? All I have to do is sell the van I bought. No problem."

"Hey, slow down, Lucky; I gave up my apartment before I left L.A.; and all my stuff's already on the way to Hawaii, except for one suitcase. Look!" She burrowed in her purse and came up with an airline ticket. "I was planning to go home anyway--like Thursday. Let's get back to the hotel and see if we can make it two."

At the travel agency, Lili called the airline at once, and reported, "The Thursday flight is full but they have a couple of cancellations in First Class on Wednesday they can hold for you. Can you make it? That's day after tomorrow, you know."

"Can do?" Lucky asked.

"Can do!" Pua smiled.

Lili spoke briefly into the phone and hanging up, said, "It would be better if you go out to the airport and take care of it today, with the trade-in ticket and all. Might save confusion. American is holding those two tickets for you and we can handle it if you prefer; but with all the Hawaii flights so full, I wouldn't take chances on a foul up if I were you."

"That makes sense," Lucky said. "Thank you. Let's go, Pua."

"Lucky, it's after four and I have a little shopping I must do before I fly home. Do you mind going alone?" Her expression was so forlorn that he laughed out loud.

"Of course I mind! But I'll be back as soon as I can. Here's the key to my room. You can wait for me there. I should be back by seven or eight at the latest. Okay? We can eat later, right?"

When he returned, she was awaiting him with champagne and snacks.

"Guess I don't have to ask," She chortled, "you look as if you'd conquered the world. Everything went well, eh?"

"Better than you can imagine, Pua I've been a little concerned about the van, so on the way back I stopped in at a promising-looking used car lot and not only sold the van, but for more than I paid for it. The deal's all closed and the salesman is going to pick it up here tomorrow. Vans, apparently, are very big up this way."

"That's great! Load off your mind, right? Now take a load off your feet and let's have some champagne and pupus."

He looked startled. "Pupus? What the devil are pupus?"

"Better get used to that word, Lucky, that's Hawaiian for snack food. Here, have some. Oh and is it okay with you if we have dinner downstairs? I made reservations, in case you were late getting back."

"You're too much! That's great!" Much later, they sat at the window in the Top of the Mark, looking out over the sparkling city and Bay area and sipping after-dinner cognacs.

"Everything's falling into place so neatly, it's almost scary," she murmured. "I called my father and hinted about your idea. I told him he had to wait for details until you could get together with him. Let's see-- oh and Lilli's working tonight and she'll pick me up about Midnight. Oh, I hate for this day to end!"

"I suppose you have to go?" It was a query in a little boy tone that made her laugh.

She looked at him gravely. "I thought of it, Lucky, but you know, I believe we ought to take our time. Let's concentrate on getting the business in shape, boss man and employee for now. Keep our independence and see how everything goes; just one project at a time. I'd like you to agree with me on this--I'm tempted too--but when it's the right time, we'll know it. Do you know what I'm saying?"

He nodded. "You're probably right," he sighed. "You'll come in tomorrow?"

"I'll call you, but I doubt if I'll get in. Lilli is upset that I won't be here longer. She's taking the day off tomorrow, so we can talk story. We were as close as sisters when we were keikis and now we get together so rarely. We have a lot of catching up to do."

"I've plenty of business to take care of; and I want to talk to a few of my academy buddies down at headquarters.

Don't worry about me."

"Lili and I will pick you up at the hotel. She insisted; said the Airport Bus or a cab was not Hawaiian style for seeing people off--no Aloha! I'll let you know what time, when I call you."

"That's fine with me, but," he teased, "I can see already which member of this team is going to be boss."

As they waited for the elevator, he held her close and kissed her gently, tenderly. "I'll miss you," he whispered.

"Me too," she answered softly, "but it's not so hard to leave you, now that we have this big adventure coming so soon. We both have lots to think about."

Lucky Seven Goes Hawaiian by F. Kalaukoa & S. Cook

"Just don't change your mind, darling."

"Not to worry, I won't; and you'd better not either."

Chapter 6

As the plane began it's descent to Honolulu International Airport, the intercom advised, "A light rain is falling in Honolulu," and Pualani smiled with satisfaction.

"That's nice," she told Lucky. We call that the Hawaiian blessing. A good sign for our venture!"

"Hmmm, it seems that my little city girl has turned Polynesian in less than five hours," he mused. "You're excited, aren't you, Pualani. Well, I am too, if you want to know. Something tells me we're really on the right track now and I have had the strangest sense of homecoming ever since we broke through the clouds and had our first view of this incredibly beautiful island."

She squeezed his hand and kissed him lightly on the cheek. "Komo Mai, Ku'uipo," she murmured, welcoming him home.

Waiting just inside the vast airport complex were her parents, smiling, arms loaded with exquisite flower leis. While Pua tried to hug them both at once. Lucky stood back, feeling almost wistful at the uninhibited joy of their reunion.

As introductions in the same way, hugged and kissed, his hand shaken and leis placed around his neck as well as Pua's. At that moment and from then on, he knew, with a certainty that shook him emotionally, that he had found a new home. He was no stranger. He was surrounded by that strangely all-permeating love called Aloha.

In the car, as they sped down the Freeway toward the city, talking excitedly, he had time to admire the tall and gracious lady who was Pua's mother. She had an ethereal sort of beauty and quite fair skin, just sun-kissed enough to give it a healthy glow.

He thought that she looked fragile beside the good-looking, husky Hawaiian, who had been her husband for--what had Pua said? --28 years? He liked her father's broad, honest face, his eyes twinkling merrily, just as Pua's did.

He transferred his attention to the view of his new home, beautiful with its palms and umbrella-shaped trees; they are Monkey pods if he remembered correctly and the flowers blooming everywhere. On their right was the ocean, so blue, its white beaches dotted with sunbathers; and farther out, the darting figures of surfers, pure poetry of motion, as they worked their way in toward shore.

"Look up there, Lucky," Pua urged. "The rainbows." And he drew in his breath at the brilliant hues of two gorgeous arches seeming to rest on the silent mist that hovered above the rugged, soaring mountains. Right on cue, Keoki Kanai began to sing Hector Venegas' haunting song, "Where I Live, There Are Rainbows," and the women joined in, their voices harmonizing sweetly with his rich baritone.

"How beautiful!" Lucky's voice was choked with emotion.

"Music is just one of the ways we in Hawaii express our Aloha, Lucky. You're not feeling left out of things, are you?" Kanai asked. "When my wahine get to talking story, it's hard for anybody else to get a word in edgewise."

"No, no, Sir. I'm having a great time just drinking in all this beauty. How does anyone get any work done in such a place?"

"Like any place else, the work has to be done. The nice part is, the minute you leave the job each day, each week, and each month--its instant vacation. If you stay, you'll get to know what I mean. And say, Lucky, you don't have to 'Sir' me. Call me Keoki--or George--all same difference.

"And now, my friend, we are about to enter the wilds of Waikiki--land of the tourists, God bless them and presently a traffic nightmare. So hang on."

"Dad, you're horrid!" laughed Pua.

"I can see what he means, though." Lucky winced as a dozen or so Japanese tourists dashed across the broad one-way avenue, totally leaving it up to the drivers to miss them. Towering hotels on either side of Kalakaua, created a view-banishing tunnel and he breathed a sigh of relief as the concrete mammoths thinned out at Kuhio Beach and Kapiolani Park.

"We're almost home," Pua said softly. "We live just a little way beyond Diamond Head. You can see our most renowned landmark jutting out there now."

A few minutes later they turned through gates of a driveway that served several residences and pulled up at a rambling old home that had a wonderful aura of permanence and peace. Wide porches, shining windows, masses of brilliant-hued blossoms and exotic shrubs everywhere, gave it such a welcoming ambience that Lucky was awed into silence. Impulsively he squeezed Pua's hand. "How could you leave such a home?" he whispered. "When I'm away, I keep it in my heart. It's always here for me, just as it was for my forebears," she murmured, blinking back the tears that glistened in her eyes.

"Komo mai," Keoki said warmly and his wife echoed his welcome. "We'll get your luggage in later. Come in, now and relax awhile. We have plenty beer on ice and I'm ready for one--how about you, Lucky?"

"Sounds great! I'm going to take off my jacket, too, if that's all right with you. It's going to take me awhile to get used to this humid climate."

"By all means. In fact, let's get your things now, so you can cool off. Then we'll go out on the lanai, chug-a-lug a couple and escape the girl-talk that's sure to be going on. You can change in here," he added, pointing out a cottage under a banyan tree. And in just a few minutes, Lucky joined him, comfortably clad in shorts and a soft cotton pull-over."

On the wide veranda, the lanai, shaded by tall trees, he waited for his host, enjoying the cooling breeze sweeping up from the ocean, which shimmered like a blue-green carpet from the shoreline, some thirty yards below, to the distant horizon. And very soon, relaxing on colorful gliders, the two men were taking long satisfying pulls from the chilled bottles.

"God, Keoki, this is gorgeous! Have you lived

here long?"

"All my life, except for twelve years on Maui, where my career with the department began. I was born here; my father and grandfather were born here; and my great grandfather built the original structure for his bride. He was a scribe for the Monarchy at the time and got this land grant for his efforts. It's one of the few claims in this area that were never challenged and we own the land in fee simple.

"The old house has been added to and renovated from time to time over the years, but it's a tribute to those old-time builders. The little guest house out there, where you'll be staying, is relatively new--I helped my father-build it when I was 15."

"It's easy to see that the place has had excellent care all these years," Lucky marveled. "I was just noticing those beams. They're hand-hewn, aren't they?"

Keoki nodded, pleased. "Not many young folks notice things like that any more. My great-grandfather hewed those beams by hand, with help from some of his cronies."

"It's all magnificent; but look, Keoki, I didn't intend to impose on your hospitality. Thought I'd get a room somewhere, until I can find an apartment."

"We wouldn't hear of it. And my Mary would have a fit if I didn't persuade you to stay. You may have the use of that little house as long as you wish. Pualani tells me you have an interesting project to discuss with me later. We'll have some kau kau first."

"Kau kau?"

"That's dinner--food--Island style," Keoki chuckled. "You'll get onto our lingo after awhile. But right now, let's get your other bag and get you settled in. I brought Pua's in while you were changing."

The cottage was charming, with a bed and comfortable chairs covered in brilliant Hawaiian prints. There also was a roomy chest of drawers, a small bathroom and a kitchenette with a tiny refrigerator. Screened and louvered windows were open to the breeze.

"This is perfect," Lucky said. "I've heard about Hawaiian hospitality and here I am experiencing the best. Thank you. If it's okay, I'm going to unpack a few things and have a shower."

"You go right ahead. Come on over when you're ready. Wear what you have on. We don't stand on ceremony around here. Oh and get yourself another cold brew--there's plenty in the frig there." And off he went. While he stowed his gear, Lucky had another beer and then stood for a long time under a needle-brisk cold shower. Refreshed, he made short work of stowing his things. There was a pair of straw slippers in the closet and they fit reasonably well. Pua had said it's Hawaiian custom not to wear shoes indoors. He must remember that.

When he entered the house, he could hear muffled voices from a distant room and decided not to disturb his hosts. He looked around the large living room, admiring the comfortable sofas, with their Hawaiian print upholstery in a tasteful pattern of exotic leaves against a soft beige background. He examined a pair of antique chairs and guessed that they were family heirlooms, noting their similarity in style to the gleaming, old-fashioned dining table and chairs that occupied the far end of the room. Underfoot, thick, soft carpeting echoed the silvery gray-green of the far reaches of the ocean. Handsome glass-topped tables of gold-toned rattan and sturdy bookcases of teak wood, merged with the other things to give the room serenity and an informality that delighted him.

He was admiring the grouping of Polynesian flora, painted on natural linen, that decorated the inside wall, when he heard Pua's voice behind him. "Lucky!" She cried. "We thought you must have drowned in the shower at worst, or fallen asleep at best. How long have you been in here? Why didn't you sing out?"

"I didn't want to interrupt you, honey. You folks have a lot to say to each other. I've been enjoying getting acquainted with this room."

"You should have called out. When we get to talking story, time flies. We were in dad's study."

"Oh, there you are!" The Kanais were smiling as they came in, arms loaded with a tray of pupus and the makings for cocktails, plus a huge pitcher of iced tea. "Come on out on the lanai. Let's settle down and have a little refreshment," Keoki added. "Did you find everything you need in the cottage?"

"You bet I did! I feel great now. You people know how to make a man feel at home. You went to a lot of trouble to make me comfortable, Mrs.--" He hesitated as she held up her hand. "You call me Mary--or Malia-- whichever you prefer," she suggested. "And it was no trouble at all. We're delighted to have you."

"I'll call you Malia--it suits you perfectly."

She flushed with pleasure. "Help yourself to a drink and pupus and relax. Lucky. We're going to have an early dinner--then you and Keoki can talk. I'm an early to bed, early to rise type," she said, smiling. "It's so pleasant today, I think we'll eat out here. This big old table gets more use than the one in the dining room, when the Kona wind isn't blowing."

They sat there chatting until sunset, a magnificent display of color that moved and changed with the clouds until the great golden ball of the sun sank quickly beneath the horizon. Almost immediately, the banners of color changed to a darkening afterglow of rose and purple.

Dinner was a medley of delicious sweet and sour spare ribs, a heaping bowl of rice, fresh vegetables with a simple dressing and fruits with cheese. And there was a bowl of sour poi, which Lucky tasted cautiously at first-- and then asked for more.

"This is good!" he exclaimed. "When I was here on vacation, the poi was a tasteless and gluey."

"That's because it was fresh," Malia laughed. "We like it best fermented a few days. The texture is nicer and for it has a biter tang."

When they had finished, Malia rose and said, "Come, Pua, let's clear away these things and let the men talk. You can join them after you tuck me in." She bent to kiss her husband and said, "I'll say goodnight now. Sleep as late as you like, Lucky." And with a flutter of her hand she was gone.

"That's a very special lady, Lucky," Keoki said softly. "Best wife a man could have. I met her in England, nearly thirty years ago; her family had been killed in the blitz and she was an assistant in the crime lab at the CID. I was over there studying police science and when we met, we knew that, crazy as it might seem, we wanted to spend our lives together.

"It took the longest three months of my life, to get her to come here to marry me. It was such a different life from what she had known and I know there must have been times when she ached to be in England, but she would never leave me, not even for a day. She took to our ways so eagerly and she's always made me proud.

"Oh, there I go rambling on again--my favorite subjects, I guess, Malia and Pua. Now let's hear what you and my daughter are cooking up."

"I'm glad you told me about her--it's an honor. Well, this is what I have in mind.

"But before we get into the details, I want you to know that at the time this idea came to me, I thought that Pua and I were not going to be seeing each other again. We had--"

"She told us," Keoki said. "Those things happen, my friend."

"When we got things ironed out between us and I

told her my plans--gosh, I don't quite know how it happened, but she became a part of them. It's important for me to know that you understand there are dangers involved, --"

Keoki stopped him with a raised hand. "You don't need to go on," he said huskily. "Let me tell you, Pualani is our only child. We couldn't have another. But she has been, since she was tiny, both as daring and fearless as a son and as loving and lovely a daughter as any parents could wish.

We raised her to make her own decisions and we're not about to interfere now. So let's hear it.

"You know, of course, that I'm going to be strictly honest with you. If your plan is workable, you'll get my full support. The two of you can be of tremendous help to my department; so I've a selfish interest in this thing as well. We're so damned understaffed it's frustrating. On the other- hand, if it appears to me your project is impracticable, I'll tell you so. That's my way."

"I appreciate that, Keoki. It's the only way I would have it. If I'm on the wrong track, it's best I know now-- and take it back to the drawing board." They shook hands, solemnly, as if sealing a pact of mutual understanding and respect.

Chapter 7

"Before we get into this any further," Lucky said, "I want to clarify something else. I still feel responsible for Pua's decision to leave South Hills. I hope she'll never be sorry. She was just getting her breaks, when everything fell apart."

"We've talked it all out, my boy and I told her I was proud of her decision. I confess I don't understand how they could jeopardize your career that way--in cold blood--but I'm proud that she did the only thing she could do to express her own indignation.

"When it comes right down to it, every officer on their force was demeaned by their action. Even offering to reinstate you was an insult, in my opinion. No real man or woman would accept such a tacky offer. Police departments are composed of people--some good--some not. I'm glad you're both out of there. Now let's get on with a new career for both of you."

"Your efforts in behalf of these poor, bedeviled merchants can make a whale of a difference both to them and to us at headquarters."

"I'm sure you know the limitations of private sector operation, as well as the exceptional advantages you will enjoy, as private citizens working in that field. Let's talk about how that works."

They exchanged ideas, discussed guidelines, protocol, the do's and don'ts of their professional relationship.

As Lucky presented his plan, Keoki listened

attentively, asked penetrating questions and posed problems Lucky hadn't considered before--and nodded approvingly at the solutions he offered.

"It's an excellent plan," he said at last. "And you have presented it well. What a difference it could make to the little guys in the business world. Giving them an opportunity to work together to protect themselves— that's what impresses me most.

"I'm a little concerned about two points, however. One: I hope you understand that you will have to kiss goodbye to the 40-hour workweek concept.

"As P.I.s, you'll be on call all hours of the day and night. It means a lot of personal sacrifices for both you and Pua and a great deal of understanding between you. Are you on solid enough ground to survive those inconveniences?"

"I'm sure of it. And I believe Pua understands as well. We share the same eagerness. I'm sure she told you that, when you were talking in your study."

Keoki laughed. "You should have heard her giving me ground rules on this talk of ours. Without jumping the gun to reveal all of your ideas, she told me I must listen with an open mind; that she wants it to work as much as you do."

Lucky grinned. "We have talked it out together, Pua and l and we're deeply concerned about establishing a firm place in this business as quickly as we can. We're prepared to sacrifice whatever time it takes to that end. It's no news to you, I'm sure, that a personal relationship is developing strongly between us. But the social side can wait.

"We're agreed about that and we're both equally excited about what we may be able to accomplish together. The item: regular hours, isn't even listed among our priorities. We both see an opportunity to crusade actively against harassment and attacks upon the defenseless. Helping them and helping them to help themselves--that is our major project. Does that sound feasible?"

"Yes, it does, Lucky. I've spent a good many hours trying to come up with something effective to help those people, but I'm hamstrung by lack of personnel. Organizing the merchants and being on the spot when you're needed, makes your plan not only effective, but will take a lot of pressure off my guys. "It does bring up my second point. It's going to be hard to make a decent living, while you're developing the program. Have you thought about that?"

"I don't expect to make much at first. Any business takes a year or so before any real money starts coming in. I'm hoping that ultimately some of the people we help will refer others to us and that we'll get a reputation for successful operations that will sooner or later attract the interest of more affluent clients to our work. But there's no hurry about that.

"I can afford to carry us financially for at least a couple of years, maybe more; and that includes a reasonably good salary for Pua. I insist on that. I feel lucky about this, Keoki. I believe we're going to make it. But even if it doesn't work out too well pocket wise, I'm not going to be upset. I feel we all owe rent on the space we occupy on this earth and this is our chance to put back into circulation some of the fortunate things that have happened to us—the love, the understanding, the education and the opportunities we've been offered. I know that's an old-fashioned concept--maybe even corny--but I think it's a good way to live."

"I don't need to hear any more," Keoki said, smiling broadly. "I am convinced." And with an amused wink at Lucky, he called, "You can come out now, Pua."

She was laughing as she came out the screen door, carrying three frosty beers. Well, what do you think, Dad? Isn't it a great idea? Do you think we can make it work?" She turned an eager, expectant face toward him.

"Pualani, you are the limit!" he laughed. "After all these years, do you really think you can eavesdrop without my knowing? You just heard the bottom line. But yes, I like the whole plan, though I do have one major concern. It has to do with you, Pualani."

Both Lucky and Pua gave him a startled look. "You see," he continued soberly, "there's going to be a lot of groundwork to do; and plenty of desk-jockeying for awhile, typing case histories, keeping records and such. I had an idea that wasn't the kind of career you wanted. Could I have been wrong?" He eyed her with such an innocent smile that she was taken off guard for a second; then she laughed and began to pummel him.

"You're the one who's the limit! You better get serious Dad. You can bet your bottom dollar we are. Now quit baiting me, you big, bad kanaka." And then, in a more serious vein, she added, "Don't worry, with a project as rewarding as this, I'm in-for-a-pence, in-for-a-pound, as mom used to say."

"Glad to hear it," her father told her. "Now let's get down to business. We can sure use that beer. Talking dries a man's throat. Oh and honey, will you please bring out that note pad by the phone? I'd better write some things down as we go along."

By the time she returned, Keoki was already deep in the subject. "First off, we'll get the license taken care of. Both of you will need

"Right."

"There won't be any problem, I'm certain, but it takes a little time, with the red tape and all. Meanwhile, I'll see that you are issued temporaries and I'll vouch for you personally. The bonding is simple. You've never had any trouble with the law, I assume--no record, eh, Lucky?"

"Nothing but a couple of parking tickets and one campus party that ended in a brawl. No charges were pressed and no booking."

Keoki shook that off with a grin. "I want to meet that mother of yours one of these days. It's plain to see that she did a fine job bringing you up." He took a pull at his beer. "So the next step is to get an office set up.

I've been thinking. Not too far from headquarters is a nice condo with combination living quarters and offices. It's not fancy, but comfortable and reasonable-- plus it's in the heart of the area you'll be working in. We might check it out.

"Considering the people you want to deal with, it would be a mistake to overwhelm them with too much luxury. They're not used to it and it might just turn them off."

"My feeling exactly," Lucky said. "But I would like an office large enough to handle at least six or eight visitors comfortably. Pua and I will need a place where we can have meetings with these clients in a group, without their being afraid of being seen congregating together. 'Divide and conquer' seems to be the motto of this kind of criminal and our first major project is to organize these merchants, without the criminal element realizing what we're up to."

"That's the idea! Now let me make a call. See if that place has an opening. I know the manager--a retired cop. You kids ready for another cold one?" he asked over his shoulder as he vanished through the doorway.

"Sure hits the spot!" and Lucky grinned happily at Pua. "Your dad is amazing, girl! Once he makes up his mind, wheels start turning. He has me gasping for air-- such energy. Whoever said Hawaiians are lazy?"

Pua laughed with delight. "You've got it. That's my Pop. And I'll bet you a dollar he comes back with good news."

"Oh no you don't! Your salary is all the dough you're going to get from me! Tell me what you think of our progress. Are you as pleased--and as surprised--as I am? I thought it would take weeks to get the ball rolling and here we are getting organized our first night in

Hawaii."

"I'm pleased, that's for sure, but I can't honestly say I'm surprised. I know my father and the only question in my mind was whether it was practical enough to win his approval. Once he helps us get launched, though, don't worry about his trying to run things. It'll be our baby and it will be up to us to make it grow and flourish. That's his way. I know we can count on him for advice if we hit any bad snags--but it will be up to us to ask for it."

And just then Keoki reappeared, three more frosty bottles in hand. "Good news, people," were his first words and he stopped, puzzled, as the two of them burst into laughter. "What's up?"

"I tried to get a bet that's what you'd say and he wouldn't buy," Pua chuckled.

"Pua, shame on you! Well, Jake has a unit on the seventh floor, 22'x30' office space, a nice airy bed-sitting room, bath and kitchen, with decent carpeting throughout, except the kitchen, of course--and he'll hold it for us for a couple of days. There are others, higher up in the building, but he says this is the best one. How does that sound to you?"

"Sounds as if I lucked out again, thanks to you. What's great is that I can live right there--only one rent to pay--and talk about convenient to the office! Outstanding!"

"Well, don't get too excited yet. Wait till you look it over. If you don't like it, we'll find something else.

There's one catch. It comes unfurnished. Had you

71

anticipated that?"

"Oh, yes, I prefer it that way."

"And the rent is a bargain at $750; you pay electricity and phone. Water's included and that includes hot water--centrally heated."

"That's fine."

"While we're on the housing subject, Pua, your cousin Alika is on the mainland for six or eight months and you can use his apartment. He left the keys with me, told me to use it whenever I wanted. I don't want you driving out here alone every night. A place to stay in town will give you an option. Is that okay? No rent makes up for its bachelor pad decor, doesn't it? I've checked it out and it's a little strange, but lacks no comforts. Oh and you kids can use his car until you get your own transportation."

"That's great, Dad!" She beamed her appreciation. "But what's a good Hawaiian like Alika doing on the mainland?"

"He's in Portland, Oregon, taking special training at their Crime Lab. It's one of the finest in the country and we want to upgrade ours. Our family playboy is also a pretty akamai lad, Pua.

"Now let's work on a game plan for tomorrow. I'll have to be at headquarters fairly early in the morning, so we should leave here by 8:15. Then you can use the station wagon and give me a call tomorrow about 2 p.m. and we'll compare notes and work things out from there.

"Sometime in the next few days, I would like you

both to come in and meet some key people at headquarters- It's important to establish a good relationship with the detectives. And in the meantime, I'll do what I can to get the paper work started on you."

"Good Lord, Keoki, all I asked for was a little advice and here you are taking all this trouble-"

"Hey, hey, hey--I've a stake in this too. The more I think about it, the more I like the idea. You can do a lot that we at headquarters can't do and I'm anxious to see you get started."

Pua hugged him. "You're the best!" she said. "You forgot one important item though. Somewhere along the line I've got to give Lucky a crash course in the delights and horrors of getting around town and all the rest of Oahu. Fact is, I'll have a lesson or two to learn myself, with all these one-way street changes and the new sections of freeway that opened after I left here."

Lucky popped himself on the forehead with the heel of his hand. "That's going to be a bummer for me for awhile. I can remember streets and highways once I've been on them and easily. But directions over here seem all screwed up in my mind. "

Father and daughter laughed aloud. "Common complaint, son," Keoki said. "The best way is to just forget North, South, East and West and teach yourself Hawaiian directions. No matter what side of the Island you're on, Makai means toward the ocean and Mauka, toward the mountains. From your office, Diamond Head is this direction--Easterly; and Ewa is the Westerly direction, out towards the airport and beyond. Learn those four and it's pretty hard to get lost.

"We always tell tourists not to get concerned about finding their way back to Honolulu in their rental cars. Most highways and freeways have clearly marked Honolulu-bound signs. Except for the passes over the mountains, any error in judgment will take you either into the ocean, or bump you into a mountain. Avoid those snags and it's simple."

"I don't think it will take me long to get the hang of it with Pua to help me. I wouldn't mind getting lost with her, anyway, any time," Lucky teased.

"That's Hoomalimali, but I love it," Pua retorted.

"Ho-o-what?"

"Flattery, Lucky. That's Hawaiian for complimentary sweet talk," Keoki explained. "It comes in handy for keeping wahine gentled. Well, you two, I think that's about it for tonight--agreed? Okole Maluna!" He drained his bottle and Pua her glass and a puzzled Lucky followed their lead.

"That's Bottom's Up," Keoki said, grinning. "When you can see the moon through the bottom of the bottle. And now I'm off to bed. Get some sleep, kids. Breakfast's at 7:30."

"Mom will have a fit," Pua chuckled. "She wanted you to sleep late. Now dad has you getting up for breakfast. Things have a way of moving awfully fast, when dad's really interested in something. Come on, I'll walk you home."

On impulse, they strolled around the house,

enjoying the gardens bathed in moonlight and the heady perfume of the flowers. They held each other close and as they kissed goodnight, clung to each other even closer-- but it was gentle and undemanding--and as they parted, both knew that they were on the brink of a great adventure, one that was sure, when the time was right, to lead them inevitably into a wondrous intimacy.

He tipped her face up, memorizing each lovely feature aglow with tenderness, her dark eyes luminous with reflected light from the moon. Then he brushed her cheek with his lips as he whispered, "It was an incredible day, dear heart, one to remember. Thank you."

"For me too," she murmured. "Goodnight, sweet dreams." He watched her till she reached the door and turned to wave

Chapter 8

Lucky awoke, refreshed and eager to get started with this new day in Paradise. A glance at the bedside clock told him it was only 6 a.m. He was wide-awake, so he got up and hastily donned a pair of shorts. He toyed with the idea of putting on a tee shirt, but vetoed it and walked out into the yard.

Mornings such as this one have a unique charm in Hawaii. There's an almost opalescent glow as the sun, still unseen beyond the mountains, sends forth its promise of a fine day to come. A fresh coolness in the flower-scented air is stimulating, even though the temperature varies little from night to day.

Taking deep, appreciative breaths, he strolled out to the lawn and began to go through his whole regimen of exercises, finishing off with push-ups. He felt fit and confident--and altogether happy.

He strolled out to the edge of the property to watch a small fleet of fishing boats on their way to the fishing grounds, a dramatic picture against the wide reaches of the sea. As he watched them out of sight, other boats began to take out from the marinas--charter boats and private fishing boats fanning out to zero in on whatever area their skippers felt would assure them a good catch. Marlin, Mahimahi, huge Ahi tuna and Opakapaka were among their favorites. Lucky grinned to himself as he pronounced in his mind, the exotic names Pua had taught him.

The muffled sounds of traffic up on the highway, breaking the morning silence, told him it was time to shower and dress, if he was to be on time for breakfast. He returned to the cottage.

Breakfast at the Kanai's was a celebration of each new day, rather than just the refueling process it unfortunately becomes in so many busy households.

On this morning it had an especially festive air, for it was the beginning of the great adventures of Lucky Seven.

Malia brought to the lanai table slim glasses of chilled guava juice and halves of delicious red-meat Sunrise papayas picked in the cool of the morning from a tree beside the house. Then she disappeared into the kitchen and returned with a huge fluffy omelet liberally laced with melted cheeses, ham and bits of green pepper, fresh tomatoes and mushrooms, the whole surface sprinkled with finely chopped green onion tops. With this came flaky buttermilk biscuits, hot from the oven, with sweet butter to slather over them. Accompanied by the big pot of Kona coffee, it was a feast the four of them relished.

Lucky purred with satisfaction, as he finished the last bite. "Malia, you are spoiling me. I can't ever remember enjoying a breakfast so much."

"Thank you, Lucky. Sometimes this is the only meal we get to have together all day long. I love to make it special."

"And you do that, honey," Keoki said, tousling her soft blond hair.

As good as his word, Keoki took a last sip of

coffee at 8:15 sharp and announced, "I'll turn the car around. You kids meet me outside." Then he gave Malia a bear hug and a kiss and was on his way. Pua and Lucky followed and climbed into the station wagon with him.

"Have a nice day," Malia called after them. "You too!" they chorused.

"I didn't like to hurry you," Keoki apologized. "But with this early start, I have enough time to drop you off, introduce you to Jake and then I'll walk on over to headquarters. It's just a few blocks and I need the exercise. I won't be needing the wagon till late afternoon."

Twenty minutes later he pulled into the lower level-parking garage of an unassuming, well-kept building. A grizzled old man was checking licenses against a list in his hand. He waved and called, "Be with you in a minute."

"I have to get to my office, Jake. Take good care of these folks."

"I'll do my best, Keoki."

And he turned and said, "Okay, my young friends, let's go see if I have what you want. You fine these days. Miss Kanai?"

"I am, Jake. And this is Lucky Gregory.

"The Major sets a heap a' store by you two. Hope I can help you."

On the way up, Jake told them, "Had a young lawyer in here for a few months and he took good care of the unit. I don't think it's going to need much redecorating. That poor young fellow was trying to establish a law office on his own, but the competition is fierce for a new attorney. It was too much for him to handle financially, so he went with a firm over in Kailua. Here we are, Suite 711." Pua giggled. "Lucky number, eh Lucky? Bet you a dollar you take this." He laughed. "No bet. I'm going to have to do something about this gambling penchant of yours, my girl."

Jake unlocked the door and opened it to a spacious room, with cool beige walls, slightly-worn but good quality bronze carpeting and a huge picture window breath-taking view; and below it, louvered panels, open now to admit cool fresh air. Moving cross the room, Jake drew aside a bamboo screen to reveal the small kitchen and bar, complete with a pair of rattan bar stools.

"You can have those, or I'll take them out," Jake said. "There's not much in here, but anything you don't want, shove it in the hall and I'll get rid of it. I have a nice big bookcase you may use if you like."

The bed-sitting room was roomy and nicely proportioned, bright with sunlight and breezy from the louvers under the windows. The bathroom was off it, small but complete. The closet was a surprisingly generous and offered storage shelf as well.

"What do you think, Pua? Looks right to me, but from a woman's standpoint, what's your opinion?"

"I can't find a thing wrong with it. The basic colors are great for our purposes. The carpet could use a good steam-cleaning though."

"The cleaners are coming in this afternoon," Jake told them. "You won't have to worry about that."

"What about parking?" Lucky inquired.

"You have one residential stall and two guest stalls. And there are usually several others available. A few of our tenants don't have cars. I don't think that will give you any trouble."

"It's a deal then," Lucky said.

Jake was digging a card out of his pocket. "This is an old friend of mine who buys, reconditions and sells office furnishings- one hell of a good craftsman. You might want to take a look and see if he has what you want. Keoki told me you wanted to keep sort of a low profile. It's out toward the airport off Nimitz. You know the area, don't you, Pualani?"

She was examining the card. "Oh, easy," she said.

"Could I give you, say, $300 down to hold this unit for me?" Lucky asked. "I have to get to the bank, to have my accounts transferred here and establish credit. Will you accept my travelers checks?"

"Sure, but no need. I'll fix up your lease and when you come in you can take care of the whole shooting match at one time. I won't let anyone else have it."

"Then we have a deal," Lucky said, extending his hand.

As they reached the station wagon, Pua suggested, "If you haven't any particular bank in mind, let me take you to ours. Dad was going to call this morning to talk with his friend there about you. Thought it might speed up things for you. Did he mention it to you?"

"Yes. Said I was to see someone named Erick Madison."

"Right. He's the vice president in charge of new accounts. So, do you want me to drive, until you get used to our streets and traffic?"

"If you don't mind," Lucky agreed. "Let's go." The bank business took minimal time; and, carrying a letter of credit, he was soon ready to take off on the buying spree.

The office furniture outfit Jake had suggested turned out to be a gold mine. By the time they finished, he'd purchased a pair of files, two desks, a good-sized table and chairs, two desk chairs and a few other small items.

"That guy's amazing," Lucky said as they drove away. "I'm really pleased with the things I bought. It all has a nice 'lived-in' look, a bit old-fashioned maybe, but it's well-made and has dignity."

"Where to now, Lucky?"

"Weil, somewhere close here I noticed some automobile sales lots. Let's drop in on one and see what they have to offer."

"All right, if that's what you want, but I have an uncle who--"

"Pua, no. You have more angles than anyone I ever heard of."

"But he won't cheat you! You don't need a car

right away. We can both use Alika's. Wait until we go see Uncle Nornana--just to please me. His place is down Kailua side, over the Pali. We'll be going over there on one of our orientation drives anyway."

"I give up. What's next then?"

"Well, you'll need a sofa, a good chair to lounge in, a dresser or chest of drawers, a TV and I hope a new room-divider for in front of the kitchen. That bamboo thing is a disaster."

"Then we might as well get to it," he sighed. "Lead on."

"And then you'll need draperies and dishes and kitchen stuff--but why don't you let mom and I do that. She'll love it and it'll give us a chance to have girl talk without you men underfoot. And we're both frustrated interior decorators."

"If you'd really like to--that's a chore I could do without."

"You'll have to give us an idea how much you want us to spend, though. We'll pay by check and you can reimburse us.

Is that all right with you?"

"Sure. And don't worry about the expense. I saved a bundle on the office stuff and with my personal things, I prefer to go first cabin. You might want to pick out some lamps too, or am I piling too much on you?"

"Far from it," she cried. "Mom and I will have a ball! Tell you what, there's a really nice furniture store a block or so from here. Why don't we go check out what they have for furnishing your living quarters? We can call dad from there. What time is it anyway?"

"Quarter to two."

"Okay, let's make that call first. You can do it, Pua.

When Keoki came on the line, his first words were, "Things are lining up well for you two on this end; how are you doing?"

"Couldn't be better. There's too much to tell you now. Lucky took that place, Dad. We think it's a gem. Want to talk with him?"

"Not now, honey, I'm due at a meeting. Can you pick me up at five-thirty?"

"Will do. See you then."

"Pua, we forgot to stop for lunch. Don't know about you, but I'm hungry. Let's grab a bite before we do anything else. There's a little restaurant right across the parking lot there.

" After lunching on man-sized hamburgers and milkshakes, they both felt more like shopping and it was a breeze. They even found a handsome eight-foot sofa, perfect for the office area. In less than two hours, he had everything he needed, except the TV. Seems Pua had a cousin who would sell him a good one for "just a little over wholesale." He looked at her with a despairing grin.

"You and your bargains!" he sighed. It was nearly five-thirty when they turned into the police station parking area; and minutes later they were on their way home with Keoki at the wheel. Pua was bubbling over with excitement about their shopping adventures and they were nearly home before Keoki had a chance to answer the question uppermost in Lucky's mind.

"Things look really good for your project, Lucky. Your license is assured and I took the liberty of laying out your ideas at our island-wide Law and Order conference this afternoon. They asked a lot of questions, liked the answers and promised their cooperation. Several asked if you would be able to work in their particular areas on the island; and I told them I couldn't see why not, in due time, but they'd have to take that up with you."

"That's good news, but we're going to start out with this one hot spot of yours. It will be a learning experience and when we have solved the problems here, we can branch out. I don't want to spread us thin, Keoki. We have to prove ourselves first."

"I'm glad to hear it. That's the way I figured you'd feel about it."

"You've done so much to get this thing on the road, I don't know what to say. Thank you doesn't seem enough."

"Just see to it that you and this girl of mine do a damn good job. You haven't a clue yet of how much we need this service. I have a selfish motive for working fast. Oh, another thing, what are you going to call this operation? One of the guys asked me and I had to admit I didn't know."

"I'd like to call it just, plain 'Lucky Seven.'

Seven's my middle name, you see and I've been called Lucky most all my life. No Investigators or Protection Agency or anything like that. It's just Lucky Seven. The people that need to know what we do will find out when we make our presentation to them. No use advertising to the rest of the world. If we're good, the word will get around, don't you think? Right now, I want to keep low key."

"Good! Very good! Call Lucky Seven when you need help. I like it. Has good vibes. Your reasoning is sound, too.

By the way, what is your full name anyway?"

"Blake Seven Gregory, at your service, Sir."

"Thought I told you not to call me that!" Keoki growled--but he was smiling.

Chapter 9

Over the weekend, the Kanais took Lucky to some of the Island's most famous beaches--Hanauma Bay, Kahana, Sunset, Waimea and the renowned Banzai Pipeline, where their Malahini was treated to the sight of towering surf and the incredibly dexterous surfers who dare to ride those giant waves.

They drove through field upon field of pineapple and sugar cane, picturesque banana plantations and papaya groves. They explored the picturesque little towns, their art galleries and curio shops. All these and more provided Lucky with a new and fascinating concept of his new island home.

As they began the descent into Honolulu from the Pali, Lucky reflected, "You know it's a mystery to me why so many of my friends who come here on vacations, go back disappointed in Oahu. They say it is just another mass of concrete--same as any mainland city. But look at that!

Honolulu and Waikiki is just a tiny segment of the island. What we've seen today offers every imaginable variation in scenery, activities, cultural amenities and just plain natural beauty. Where do they go wrong?"

"What happens, Lucky, is that hordes of tourists-- young and old--who come here, go to their hotels, play out on the nearest beach, take a walk down Kalakaua Avenue to the International Market Place and maybe spend one evening at the Polynesian Cultural Center and perhaps an afternoon at Sealife Park--and that's it," Keoki said. "They never see what makes the island tick. Beach romancing and suck 'em up sessions at the bars take their time and their money. They honestly believe that's all we've got to offer."

"I can see how that could happen, but what a shame. The time I was here--just a week--we did a lot of the Waikiki Beach scene and had a great time, but I got a break. One of my college friends lived in Kaneohe at the time and he insisted on taking me around to see some of these other facets of island life, so I had a sampling of both."

"Including a romance?" Pua questioned slyly.

"Yep, a romance of sorts. She was tall and tan and young and lovely--an escapee from Ipunima, I think--but after a couple of days of too much sun, I was brick red and peeling and for some strange reason, I lost my appeal. She shook me off."

"Poor ting," Pua said in mock sympathy.

"Pua, be nice," Malia protested.

"That's okay. I was luckier this time. I brought my girl along with me," he laughed, hugging her close.

On Sunday, they traveled to the Leeward side, up the beautiful Waianae Coast to Pokai Bay, world-renowned Makaha and Yokohama Bay, picnicking in one of the many beach parks along the way.

By late afternoon, despite sunscreen and their prescribed short periods of sunning, Lucky's fair skin was brick red and sore.

Just as soon as they reached home, Malia hurried

into her garden for spikes of Aloe Vera; neatly slicing off the spines and peeling away one thin side of the stalk, so that the healing gel inside could be easily applied.

As she and Pua gently smoothed it over his skin, Lucky asked, "What is that stuff? It's instant relief."

"That's why we call it the Miracle Plant in Hawaii," Pua's mother smiled. "We'll cover all the burned areas and let it dry for about a half hour; then we'll put on another coat. And after an hour or so, you can take your shower and by tomorrow, you'll be turning tan."

"Without peeling, either," Pua added. "Tomorrow you'll still have all that macho appeal!"

"If you have any sore places tomorrow, we can catch them in the morning," Malia assured him. "This gel won't stain, once it is dry."

"Well if I get a tan, it'll be my first," Lucky said with enthusiasm. "It's a problem most red-heads share. But the soreness is gone already. That's fantastic!"

To his surprise, he slept soundly and if he had pain, was unaware of it. Sure enough, as he examined himself in the mirror the next morning, the beginnings of a healthy tan had already erased most of the ugly red. "Miracle is right!" he told his reflected image.

Monday, Lucky finished up his paper work at headquarters and met some of the key people there. Later, he signed the lease and arranged with Jake to accept delivery of his purchases the next day.

Meanwhile the women had been doing their part of the shopping and there was a lot of whispering and giggling going on. When he asked them about it, both refused to comment.

"You'd better finish what you have to do at the new place by Thursday morning," Pua directed, "because you're banished from the premises from noon Thursday until Saturday evening."

"Come on, Pua. I want to help. Tell her, Malia; she won't pay any attention to me."

"Sorry, Lucky, but I'm on her side. We want to surprise you. Now don't spoil our fun." Her eyes sparkled with mischief. "You gave us a free hand and we plan to make the most of it."

"Might as well give up," Keoki said philosophically.

"When these two speak, we listen! Don't worry; I've got plenty to keep you busy. There are some files I want you to study. Want you to meet a few more key people too."

"Okay, okay, I bow to the majority opinion," laughed Lucky.

On Saturday afternoon, Pua called home on the newly installed phone and, when her father answered, told him, "We'll be ready for company by six. What are you doing?"

"I'm beating the tar out of Lucky at gin. I don't think his mind is on the game. We'll see you in a little while. "

Even before the doorbell rang, they knew the men

had arrived. They heard a shout of pleasure as Keoki and Lucky caught sight of Pualani's gift--a discreet brass doorplate, simply engraved LUCKY SEVEN. Pua ran to open the door, singing out the classic Hawaiian greeting, "Ke Aloha no!" as she welcomed them in.

They stood just inside and stared in disbelief. The furniture was in place, just as Lucky had indicated and the room was transformed with gold-toned draperies, a handsome hanging lamp that bathed the large round table in a soft glow and shielding the kitchen from view, a beige retractable room-divider, with panels as soft as suede. On the walls were hung colorful Hawaiian flowers--Bird of Paradise, Orchids, Anthodium's, Plumeria and Hibiscus, each flaming out from the creamy white fabric on which it had been painted.

"What can I say?" Lucky gasped. "It's perfect and those floral designs are gorgeous. Wherever did you find them?"

"That's one question I'm proud to answer," Keoki spoke up. "Malia painted them, as well as those you admired on our hale walls. These are our gift of Aloha to you and your new enterprise."

As Lucky hugged Malia in speechless gratitude, Pua urged, "Come on, you guys, there's more."

At the entrance to the kitchen, she told Lucky, "Push this button.

And when he did, the divider drew swiftly back, disclosing the kitchen, now well stocked with everything he would need, right down to racks sporting bright new kitchen towels.

"Now, come on. Your pad!" she announced, swinging the door open. Beside his new lounge chair was a handsome new reading-lamp and a smaller matching one on the bed's headboard. They had chosen for the bedspread a puffy, quilted comforter in a small multi-colored design that featured the golden hue of the draperies and the deep forest green of his chair. The whole effect was pleasantly masculine--but not aggressively so.

"Now the bathroom--" and predictably, big thirsty towels and matching mat and shower curtain were neatly in place. "Is okay?"

"Wow! Is it ever! Right now, I'm speechless!"

"Good! Now we celebrate. Oh and about the bar stools. You'll have to do without them for a few days. I took them to be refinished and reupholstered. They were good quality; and I got a good deal. This fellow I went to school with--"

"Pua!" He roared with delight. "You and your good deals! What am I going to do with you?"

"Oh, I'll think of something," she teased. "This all cost you a big bundle and that's for sure!"

"I don't care what it cost. It's all perfect!" And he planted a quick kiss on the tip of her nose.

"We had a lot of fun, didn't we, Mom? Now open this champagne. It's time we did a bit of toasting around here." She went to the phone and made a brief call.

"Oh, Lord," Keoki said, suddenly. "That reminds me. I've got to call in. I forgot they didn't have the phone number here. When he came back, his face was wreathed in a sly smile. "That Pua!" he exclaimed. "Go look at your phone number, Lucky."

Mystified, Lucky obeyed. "I don't believe this! 555-7777? How did you manage that? It's super!"

"I'm afraid to tell you," she said, smugly. "You won't make me change it?"

"Of course not!"

"Well, you see, one of the supervisors is dad's cousin and she--" The rest was lost in general merriment.

While all this was going on, Malia had gone to the refrigerator for a platter of tempting pupus she'd made for the occasion and they gathered around the table to toast and munch and talk story in a light-hearted mood.

Well into the second bottle of champagne, Lucky said, "Now I don't want any arguments. Dinner's on me."

"Wanna bet?" Pua stood up, looking at her watch. "Just about now--" and the doorbell rang. "I ordered Chinese,'gooood kine'"; and opened the door to admit the delivery boy. When he had gone, she talked briefly on the phone.

"Jake's is going to join us for dinner. He doesn't drink, so I promised to call him when the food came." And she scurried off to get tablemats and napkins.

"We couldn't have done this without Jake," Malia said. "He put up the draperies and the new slides for the divider, wired it up to that button, hung the lamp and I don't know what all. We offered to pay him for his time, but he wouldn't take a cent. He was even shy about coming up for dinner."

"I can't understand all this," Lucky said, wonderingly. "It must be that Aloha Spirit we hear about, but don't really get through our heads- I've never experienced anything like it before. It's more than just kindness and hospitality.

There's a sort of glow about it that--I don't know how to put it--makes you feel that those who are doing so much for you are having a whale of a good time doing it. It's the kind of thing you want to pay back, but you wouldn't want to lessen the gift that way. I think the answer, for me at least, is to learn how to pass what I'm feeling on to someone else.

Does that make sense?"

"Perfect sense, Lucky," Malia said softly. "It took me awhile to figure it out when I came here as a young bride-to-be. It's a very special kind of love--Aloha." It was a feast of the tangy, spicy and altogether delightful specialties of North China and though new to Lucky's taste buds, he relished it thoroughly. For Jake it all had a special meaning as well. He had been a widower for several years and sometimes he felt lonely for the companionship of his old associates in law enforcement. He welcomed his new tenant as such a friend and it felt good.

Lucky would have stayed in his new place that night, but Keoki told him, "We'd like to have you stay with us at least another day or so. Come on, let's close things up and hit the road."

"Just let us straighten things up and dispose of this mess--give us five minutes and we'll be ready." Malia was busying herself in the kitchen as she spoke, while Pua cleared the table. They were nearly ready to leave when the phone rang.

Keoki looked concerned. "I'd better get that, Lucky. No one else has your number yet, right?"

"Not that I know of. Go ahead."

"Kanai," he said and as he listened his face-hardened. "Oh God, no! Is she alive? Has the ambulance arrived yet? What about Herb? Better send somebody over to get him. I'll be right there--what? Oh, fine. He can pick me up right across from Burns Drug--that's right."

He turned back to them, his face gray with anger. "A woman just found Joy Masters, very badly injured, at her flower shop. She was still alive when the ambulance picked her up, but Clark says she's in a bad way and the shop is all torn up, too."

"Oh, how dreadful!" Malia gasped. "Was Herb hurt too?"

"No, he was out at the Concert Hall tuning a piano. The boys have gone to pick him up."

"Can we do anything?"

"No, dear," he said, "but Lucky, I'd like to have you go along with me, if you don't mind. No, Pua," as she began to speak, "not tonight, honey. I want you to take mom home. We'll be there when we can. I'll get one of the patrols to give us a ride. Will you see the women to the car, Jake?"

He nodded, "Of course." Keoki and a grave-faced Lucky left at once. On the way down in the elevator, Keoki said, "I hadn't expected to break you in quite so soon, my boy, but you might as well find out now just what kind of skunks you'll be going after. This attack is one that hits me where I live. Joy and Herb are personal friends of ours."

"I'm sorry. Anything I can do to help, you have it."

As they reached the street, Keoki's car pulled up beside them. The patrolman driving it got out. "Here you are, Sir. Kea is picking me up here."

"All right. Tell him to take over at the hospital. You stick with him. I want a guard on Mrs. Masters' room all around the clock. I'll be over as soon as I finish at the shop."

"Yes, Sir."

A small crowd was gathering in the street and the major pulled up near them. "Go on home, people," he advised. "There's nothing you can do here, unless you witnessed something that will aid the investigation. In that case, speak to that officer over there." And with Lucky beside him, he moved into the shop.

Chapter 10

Inside, what had been a neat, colorful display of tropical plants, cut flowers and ceramic containers had been wantonly turned into a disaster area. Broken pottery, plants pulled from their pots--even some of the cut flowers from the cooler-display had been tossed everywhere, in a crazy, senseless destruction. The cash drawer was open--and empty--the register showing a somehow pathetic "No Sale."

Keoki turned a grim face to the sergeant in charge. "Where are the lab boys?" he asked. "Have they dusted for prints?"

"Just left, Sir. There were prints everywhere, but this is a busy shop. How they're going to narrow them down beats me."

"What about footprints?"

"They made quick-dry molds of two in those heaps of dirt over there by the counter, but things were pretty badly scuffed up. Looked like fairly new running shoes to me, but not much definition. There was another set, between the front door and the workroom, but they figure to be those of the woman who works for Mrs. Masters; a Mrs. Nogales, who found the victim and had us notified. Everything's pretty much as we found it. The boys took plenty of photos in both rooms. "

"Where exactly was Joy Masters found?"

"She was back in the work room, crumpled behind the table. We have chalked where she fell. God, Sir, I hope she makes it, but it looks bad. The woman who found her is waiting for you back there in the living quarters. You know where that is?"

"I know. Come with me, Lucky."

Strangely, the workroom showed little destruction, but blood was crusting on the floor where the woman had fallen. On the table lay an assortment of cut orchids, tuberoses, baby's breath and ferns; and a half-finished nosegay, obscenely bloodstained, lay near the spot where she had fallen. A pair of bloody pruning shears had been tossed into the corner.

"Sergeant," Keoki called. "You can send the shears over to the lab now. You got a shot of their location?"

"Yes, Sir. From every angle and the same goes for the shop."

"Good. Well Lucky, I think we'd better see what Mrs. Nogales has to tell us. Funny that she could get in. When Herb was out after dark, Joy customarily kept the door locked. She would put a sign on it, 'Ring for service,' in case one of her regulars wanted in. The shop stayed open until eight or nine at night."

He pulled aside a heavy curtain, revealing a doorway through which they entered a small living room. In a big chair, near the lamp, was huddled a woebegone, middle-aged woman, eyes swollen and red from tears of shock and grief.

Keoki identified himself to her and said, "I'm sorry to have kept you waiting so long. Are you all right? You've had a terrible experience."

She nodded and burst into tears again. "It's all my

97

fault," she sobbed. "I was supposed to help Miss Masters with those wedding bouquets tonight. We planned to work late, since the Mister had to work over at the Concert Hall, tuning the piano for tomorrow's concert. I was working on another job and was delayed, so I called her to explain. She told me not to worry. She was working on them and she'd leave the door unlocked, so I could just slip in. She sounded cheerful and kind, like always."

"What time did you call her?"

"Let's see. Must have been close to nine, before I got the chance-after eight-thirty, anyway. I took the bus from Kapahulu Avenue and I got here, what would you think, a little before ten?"

"That's close enough. Go on." When I got here, the lights were out and I figured that was to discourage late shoppers, so I just opened the door and called out to her. I could see a light in the work room, like always when we worked at night; but she didn't answer me." She rocked herself, as another paroxysm of grief shook her body.

"Ma'am," the major's voice was gentle. "You're not to blame for anything; but you can help us a lot if you can compose yourself. We need to ask you questions and you can't answer them properly if you keep crying."

She nodded, mopping her eyes with an already sodden handkerchief.

"Now then, what is your name?"

"Janna Nogales, Mrs. Pedro Nogales."

"And where do you live?"

"Over there, near the theater," she said, pointing, "624 Hale Kaikea."

"And you often work for Mrs. Masters?"

"Only when she has big orders, like weddings, graduation--that kind. Most of the time I work at a flower shop on Kapahulu."

"I see. All right. Now, can you tell us what you saw?"

Again she wiped her eyes. "I just hurried straight back to the work room, calling out and I saw the things laid out that she had been working on and then I heard a groan and there she was on the floor, halfway under the table and her head was bleeding bad." She stifled a sob. "I called to her and called to her, but she didn't answer and I thought she was dead. Then she opened her eyes and I don't think she even knew me; and I've worked for her on and off for seven years. Such a nice woman." Again emotion overcame her.

Lucky reached into his pocket for a clean handkerchief and offered it to her silently. Both men waited patiently, as she struggled to control herself.

"Then I ran to the phone, but it was pulled out of the wall; so I went to the door and screamed. A man was going by and he went to call the police; and I locked the door and kept it that way until they came."

"You admitted no one? And no one left the shop after you entered. You're sure?"

"Yes, Sir; excepting' for the police. I was so afraid! The Missus looked like she was dying--maybe dead even. I didn't know what to do. So I just waited there with her. But I know nobody else was there."

"Did you move anything, or notice anything odd about the shop when you came in?"

She looked puzzled for just a second. "It was dark in there and I had the feeling something was different, but I don't--oh, wait a minute--the floor, the floor was dirty; and Miss Masters couldn't stand any dirt spilled that way." At that point, from the doorway the sergeant spoke urgently.

"Major, we've had word from the hospital. The victim is alive and they want you over there. She comes to now and then and tries to talk. Her husband is over there now. They--they say you'd better hurry."

"We're on our way." Keoki patted the woman on the shoulder. "You can go on home, now. We'll send someone with you, to make sure you're safe. Leave your name, address and Phone number with the sergeant, so you can be contacted. Do you understand?"

She nodded. "Miss Masters--is she--?" She couldn't continue.

"We'll let you know, Mrs. Nogales and that's a promise. But it may take awhile. You call me at home tomorrow." And he gave her his card.

On the way out, Lucky, struck by an idea, stopped at the cash register and pressed a key. He copied something on a card and followed Keoki to the car.

Setting a blue light atop the car and pulling into traffic, Keoki asked, "Find something?"

"I think so, but I'm not sure. I worked an old register like that one once and it had a daily cash record, so we could check our cash against it. Took a chance and it paid off. This one had it too. If it's accurate, the take must have been no more than $88.52. It seems strange, but, according to the reading, there was less than $10 in change in that till when they opened this morning. There's nothing in it now."

"That is odd! It's small potatoes for a thief. We'll work on it, but it'll have to wait. Here we are."

A Security Guard was waiting with Sergeant Kea at the hospital's Emergency entrance. "Follow me, please," he said. Keoki stopped just long enough to give Kea instructions and hurried to the elevator. When it reached the third floor, the guard motioned them to the left. "Right down the hall. Mr. Masters is waiting for you."

They could see the hunched figure of an elderly man--and Lucky was shocked to see beside him, a white cane.

"My God, he's blind?"

Keoki frowned. "Sorry, so much has happened, I forgot you didn't know. Poor Herb has only seen shadows for the last ten years." He stepped up to him and put a sympathetic hand on the old man's shoulder. "Herb, I'm so sorry. Do you know how she's doing?"

Agony twisted his features as he answered brokenly, "I don't know, Keoki. She's in surgery. The doctor said there was subdural hemorrhaging and if they didn't go in immediately, she wouldn't live."

"Then they got you here in time to see her. Did she recognize you, do you think? Did she say anything?"

Masters shook his head. "She was unconscious most of the time, but when she came to, once, she said, 'Herbie, hand'--at least I think it was hand--she could hardly talk. Then a second time, she said, 'left, I saw'--of that I'm certain and she lapsed into unconsciousness again. She didn't even stir when I kissed her." He buried his face in his hands. "Who could do a thing like this to my little bird? She never hurt anybody ever."

Suddenly, his head came up. "Nobody has been able to tell me, was Janna hurt too?"

"No, Herb, she's the one who found Joy. She'd been delayed getting to work."

"I'm glad she wasn't attacked."

"So are we. But don't you fret, Herb. Whoever did this won't get away with it," Keoki vowed grimly. "You can be sure of that. We'll nail 'em."

During this exchange, Lucky had gone down the hall to the nurses' station. When he returned, he said quietly, "Keoki, it's going to be an hour or more. Why don't we go get coffee or something? If there's any change, they'll page us in the cafeteria."

"Come on, Herb, old friend," Keoki said gently, helping him to his feet. "Sitting here only makes the time drag more. This is an associate of mine, name of Lucky; he'll go with us."

The old man sighed. "Guess I might as well. I could use a little something to eat. Joy and I were going to have a late dinner when I got back." His voice broke, but then he straightened his shoulders, stood erect and tapping lightly with his cane, steered a true course down the hall.

A half hour later, they returned to their vigil; but then Herb said, "You know, Keoki, we're not church-goers, but there's a chapel around here somewhere and I'd like to go in to pray for her."

"We'll go with you, then. It's on the other side of the nurses' station." And the three men walked back, entered and knelt in silent prayer.

Returning to the waiting area, Herb seemed to walk more confidently. "You know, I think everything's going to be all right. I feel soothed and hopeful. I'd know if she wasn't going to make it."

And when the surgeon came through the door, pulling down his mask, he was smiling. "Mr. Masters, your wife is in the recovery room and she'll be transferred to ICU soon. We had a rough time, but I think she's going to recover completely, providing there are no complications. We have an empty room nearby, if you'd like to stay overnight."

Herb's face was alight with relief and hope and as they shook hands, he said, "Thank you more than I can say right now. I'd like to stay."

"Fine. Come on, we'll make the arrangements for your room." As they walked away, Herb turned and said, "You're a good friend, Keoki--you too, Lucky. Good luck to you both." Keoki sighed. "I'm afraid we're going to need it, Lucky. This whole thing doesn't make sense." A few minutes later they intercepted the doctor. "I know you're tired, but could we ask you just a couple questions?" Keoki asked.

"Sure. Come on into the doctors' lounge. I need a cup of coffee. How about you?"

"Thank you, but we just had some. We'll only take a little of your time."

As they settled down, he inquired, "Now then, Major, what can I do for you?"

"First, when will it be safe to talk with Mrs. Masters?"

"If all goes well, she should be alert enough in three or four days. I expect her to be in intensive care for that long, at least. She's a tough little customer though. Why don't I call you? It was touch and go for a while there, but I'd say she's over the worst. How long it will take her to get re-oriented mentally is a moot question. It usually takes older people longer to make it back, after such a close call, you know."

"We certainly don't want to jeopardize her recovery, so we'll wait for your call. You can get a patch through to me any time on this number," and Keoki handed him his card. "Now then," he continued, "did your patient say anything in your hearing?"

"No, not a word. But the head nurse told me she had mumbled something about a hand and something about leaving, as I recall. Nurse Davis--that's her name-- went off duty after the surgery, but you can call her tomorrow afternoon here, if you like."

"Thank you. We'd better go now. Appreciate your cooperation."

Back in the car, Keoki exclaimed, "Auwe! It's nearly two a.m.--call in and tell them to have Kea wait for us. He lives out in Niu Valley way and won't mind dropping us off."

As Lucky complied, Keoki added, "We're having a temporary car shortage and I like to leave this one at headquarters in case it's needed."

They had Kea drop them at the gate, in the hopes their arrival wouldn't disturb the women, but as they walked down the drive, they could see they need not have bothered. Every light in the house seemed to be on.

Keoki chuckled, "Never fails. When I'm going to be late, Malia always figures I mustn't go to bed hungry. Or pretends there's a TV show she just couldn't miss. Or whatever excuse comes to her devious mind. What she really does though, is fret--but she doesn't know I know that.

Thinks she has me fooled. She's a good cop's wife. I'm fortunate. Come on let's go in. You can count on it; both of them are waiting up. They're both worried about poor Joy."

Chapter 11

Keoki stirred restlessly, as an angry buzzing interrupted his sleep. He groaned and batted at the air as the sound persisted.

Malia shook him gently. "It's the phone, darling. Pick up your phone."

Groaning again, he fumbled for it. "Kanai."

"Sorry to disturb you, Sir, but we have a problem." It was the desk Sergeant. "Mrs. Nogales just called; says she has to get into the flower shop to finish the bouquets for the wedding--it's today. I have her on hold."

"I'll talk to her. Is there any word from the hospital?"

"Yes, Sir. Mrs. Masters is holding her own."

"Thank God," Keoki said. "Okay, let me talk to Mrs. Nogales; then come back on the line for instructions."

"Yes, Major."

"Good morning, Ma'am. What's the problem?"

"Oh, Sir, I got to finish the nosegays before ten-thirty this morning. Island Deliveries will pick them up then. Can I please go in the shop and do it? I not touch anything. I not take anything. I not afraid to go in."

"I understand, Mrs. Nogales. I'll have an officer there to let you in at seven and she'll stay with you. She can help you with the flowers, if you like."

"Oh yes, Sir; and thank you. Miss Joy would be

106

upset, I no finish. Is she still okay? Officer called me last night like you said. I am praying for her."

"We all are, Ma'am. Officer Janet Allen will meet you at the shop."

"Thank you. I feel more better, if someone with me."

"I know. You had a rough time last night. I neglected to ask you how it was that you failed to notice all the broken crockery and plants all over the place, when you went in?"

"Like I said, no lights were on in the shop, except small one in cut flower case. I just went straight in and took flowers I needed from there, calling out that I'd be coming in. Now I think of it, some vase was broke. I forgot that."

"There's no problem, Mrs. Nogales. Naturally, you'd be pretty upset. And after you screamed for the police, you shot the bolt on the front door?"

"Yes, Sir. When they came, I went back and open door for them. "

"The lights were still off?"

"Yes. I just run back to Miss Joy. The switch 'way over on other wall by the counter--I just didn't think about anything like that--so scared for Miss Masters."

"I can understand that. And then the police asked you to wait in the Masters apartment until we could get there."

"Yes. I was crying so hard and I felt sick, like I

might faint."

"That's understandable. Are you sure you feel well enough to do the work today?"

"Yes, Sir. I'm all right now."

"Very well, Mrs. Nogales."

"Thank you for let me finish job."

"Sergeant," Keoki said, "you still on? Good. The boys finished at the shop last night, including sifting all that soil, right?" He listened intently then asked, "Things pretty quiet this morning? That's good. Now, Jane Allan has the duty this morning, right? Send her over at seven to let Mrs. Nogales into the shop; and have her stay there with her. They're to lock themselves in and admit nobody until the delivery truck arrives. Got it? I'll call in later. I'm beat. "

"I'll bet you are, Sir. Try and get some rest. We'll call you if anything breaks."

"Oh boy," Keoki moaned as he put the phone down. "My head's full of cobwebs." He struggled to sit up.

Malia put out a restraining hand. "Keoki, go back to sleep, dear. You can't function on just three hours sleep. Please, honey."

He lay back against his pillow, grinned at her groggily and fell asleep instantly.

Much later, as they sat at brunch, a second call came in from the hospital. "This is Dr. Siddon. Mrs. Masters is stabilized, but she's conscious only minutes at a time. She wants to say something, but it's difficult to understand her and she seems worried. I wonder if you'd stop by this morning. She keeps muttering your name.

Perhaps you could ease her mind. It might make all the difference. She's too tormented to get the rest she needs so desperately, if she is to recover. Will you come?"

"I'll be right there," Keoki said and putting down the phone, he turned to Lucky and Pua. "Come with me. Maybe we can get the key to this thing."

Malia reached out to touch his arm. "Darling, I know our rule, but maybe this is the time to break it. Perhaps I could help. I'd like to try."

Keoki shook his head, sympathy evident in his eyes. "You have never asked before, sweetheart--not once since we agreed to keep that part of our lives separate; and I can't, I just can't--"

"I know, dear. I can help by praying for her."

Smiling, she kissed him tenderly and said, "Now run along, you guys."

On the way in, they were unusually quiet. Finally, Keoki broke the silence. "When we were first married, Malia and I made a pact that she would not become active in any of my police work, wouldn't even ask. In return, we devised what we call our Cerebral Sanction. I would talk out my difficult cases with her and she would give me her in-put. She's a very smart lady and I can't begin to tell you how much she has contributed in that way, cutting through to the salient facts that had become lost in the confusion of events. That's our brand of comradeship.

"Well, before we get to the hospital, we'd better do a little planning. You probably will not be admitted into ICU, but you'll be able to hear what she says. I want each of you to write down what you hear and then we'll compare notes afterward. By comparing notes, we should get the message. God, I'd like to crack this thing fast!"

At the hospital the doctor, who urged them to hurry, met them. "She's showing signs of waking up again," he told them. "She's very restless and that concerns me. I can only admit one of you. I suggest you be that one. Major. She keeps asking for you. You young people can listen on the inter-com, right outside ICU."

Opening a small box just outside the glass partition, he handed earpieces to Lucky and Pua.

"You'll be able to hear what is said with these. There's a sensitive mike at the head of her bed." And with that, he led Keoki into the room.

Joy looked very tiny in the bed, her head swathed in bandages and purple bruises on her left arm a shocking contrast to the white sheets.

A nurse was bending over her, adjusting the IV and urging, "Mrs. Masters, wake up now. You have company. Come on, wake up and see who is here." She turned, shaking her head. "Maybe you can rouse her," she told Keoki.

"Joy," he said softly, "Joy; its Keoki. Did you want to tell me something?"

Her eyelids quivered and then opened, slowly. A

110

barely discernible smile appeared on her pale lips, to be replaced with a worried grimace.

"Man, han, leff," she mumbled and the blue eyes closed again. A long minute passed; then she said with pathetic agitation, "Flo'rs, wedding," and looked at him pleadingly, "delivery boy."

"It's all right, Joy," Keoki smiled, "Janna is at the shop fixing the flowers right now. You don't need to worry about that. They'll get to the church in plenty of time. Just try and tell me about the man who hurt you."

"Black cap, holes, see man," she said, her voice stronger. "I--can--hear--throw pots, pull out, hand, only one, right--" and her words faded away, the eyes closing again.

Keoki looked at the doctor with concern, then bent and told her, "Okay, Joy. I understand. Now you sleep for a while. We'll get him." And the doctor motioned him from the room.

"Don't know about you, but I didn't get much from that," Keoki said as they walked down the hall. "Let's go down to the cafeteria and compare notes. I could use another cup of coffee. I'd better check with Herb first, though."

"Oh, the nurse said he had gone out for awhile, now that Joy is stable. Took a cab." Pua was watching her father anxiously. "Take it easy, Dad. You know what mom says--that you never do your best work when you're uptight."

"I know, I know. We can see him later, then."

As she sipped her coffee, Pua's face was a study in concentration. "You know," she said, "I have an awful feeling that poor Joy regained consciousness for a time there on the floor. Enough so she could hear what was going on in the shop, anyway. He must have broken those pots after he'd hit her, or she'd never have been sitting at the worktable when he got to her. She'd have come out as soon as she realized it wasn't Janna who'd come in."

"That's true, Pua. It may just have saved her life that she didn't get back into the shop. That mess he made in there smacks of a mind out of control with anger, or frustration, or perhaps fear. The way it happened, at least she has a chance to survive."

"Now let's compare notes and see if we can make sense from what we heard." Keoki quickly jotted down the words as he had heard them. Then he said, "Okay, Pua, what do you have?"

"Man, hand, left flowers, wedding, delivery boy, black cat, clothes, seaman, throw pots, pull out, only one, right. Your turn, Lucky."

"Mine's the same, except I heard cap instead of cat, holes instead of clothes and I thought she said 'see a man.'"

"I did too," Keoki studied the three lists. "Let's try to solve the discrepancies first. She was trying to describe the guy I think. Now he was either wearing black clothes, or a black cap with holes in it."

"Like a mask has, perhaps?" Pua offered.

"Could be. There would be no percentage in

112

wearing black clothes as a disguise--he'd stick out like a sore thumb here in Hawaii. Look here, supposing it was one of those black knitted caps merchant marine seaman sometimes wear--that would fit in with Pua's reading of 'seaman.' What do you think, Lucky?"

"Those caps are rolled up, you know. If eyeholes were disguise and roiled back up, the guy would be ready for the street with nothing unusual about his appearance-- and nothing to get rid of. I do believe the lady's right, Keoki."

"What do you say we buy that for now, anyway. What's next? Let's see, from the first, Joy was trying to say something like man, hand and left; could be he was left-handed."

Lucky frowned. "I rather doubt that. She was lying on her floor on her right side, judging by the chalk marks they made. The shears were beyond her in the corner; and her injuries were on the left side of her head. That would be one hell of an awkward angle for a southpaw, seems to me."

"Why would she say 'left flowers' do you suppose?" Pua asked. "Could it have been a delivery boy?"

"I can't figure it out. Wait a minute. I want to check something." And Keoki went to the phone. They watched him curiously, as he talked and listened and finally hung up and walked back to them with a grim smile creasing his face.

"Get this, there were two prints on the broken vase and one on the shears--man-sized thumb prints, apparently. The problem is, those two are mucked up with something, like glue or plastic. They couldn't get them clear enough for a make on points. There's something odd about them that might prove significant, though. Either of you have a guess?"

Pua, who was studying the list, gasped, "There both from the right hand?"

"You got it, honey," her father beamed approvingly. "We've got us a suspect who is a probably a merchant sailor, past or present, who has a missing left hand."

"Probably past rather than present," Lucky put in. "A one-handed seaman wouldn't be much good on a freighter, I shouldn't think. Unless he'd been injured and it was in a cast."

Keoki was thumbing back through his notebook. "Got it. Remember, Lucky, the nurse told us that when they first brought her in she kept moaning something about a hand and--get this, 'something about leaving.' Not 'leaving'--it was 'left,' I'll bet. Everything's beginning to fit. Let's go. I want a make on this creep, wiki wiki!"

"Wiki wiki?" Lucky asked Pua as they hurried off to the car.

She smiled grimly. "To my dad right now that means 'Damned fast!' "

"Now, you two, while I'm getting things moving, do you want to do a little street work?" Keoki asked.

"Sure! Anything to help!"

114

"Now, what I want is for you to walk down Hotel, King, any of the Honolulu streets in that area where there are bars open. Stay together, but do it hit-or-miss, no set pattern. Just keep your eyes open on the chance this guy is spending the day sucking up beers to calm his nerves. He can't feel all that cool after his crime. It wasn't the neat kind of operation a real pro would commit. You can't be obvious about this. We can't afford to spook him.

"If you get a clear chance, inquire of the bartenders. Most of those guys like to keep on the good side of the police. If they ask you for ID's, give them the number on this card. I'll leave word with the operator. She'll confirm you. You don't need to press. Just keep track of anyone who refuses to talk, if you suspect information is being held back. We'll give them an official visit later. Got it?"

They nodded.

"Then get along with you. Come back in a couple hours, or call me if you happen to get lucky before that."

As Lucky and Pua walked away, she chortled softly. "The good news is that we're getting a start together, Lucky. The bad news is that dad still can't get it in his head that we're trained for this kind of thing. Think he'll ever get over it?"

"Not really," he answered. "Letting you walk into potentially dangerous situations is tough and I respect him for spelling out how we're to handle ourselves. He'll get over telling us how to operate-- as soon as we're officially in business, that is--but he'll always have that concern for his only daughter. For that matter, so will I.

That loving kind of chauvinism goes with the territory, gal."

"I suppose."

"Patience is the key word. I'll tell you one thing; a of a lot of cases and too many police officers are just because they don't realize the value of teamwork."

"I know, but tell me, Lucky, isn't it just as important for team members to have equal responsibility and equal respect for each other, regardless of sex?"

"You bet it is."

"And would you and my father have more faith in me if I were a man?"

Lucky considered; then with a sigh, said slowly, "To be honest with you, I expect we would. I think we must be born with that sense of supremacy. I also must admit that we're wrong. I'd rather have you as a partner than anyone in the world--not just because you're my girl, but also because you're good! You are perceptive, fearless without being foolhardy--and you deserve the same degree of faith and trust that you place in me."

"That's all I wanted to hear, my love," she said, smiling contentedly.

He grinned at her, a trifle anxiously. "Friends?"

"You better believe it," said Pua. "The best!"

Chapter 12

Hotel Street and its environs seem to change very little from day to day or year to year. This Sunday was no different—its oddly appealing, tawdry shabbiness, its garish atmosphere, a sort of stubborn bravado against the fate which has branded so many of its denizens as failures or losers.

On this Sunday afternoon, it had all the charm of an old hag with a hangover. The neon signs that came to life after dark appeared as jaded and sleazy as the "topless waitresses" and "adult movies" they advertised. Even the street people were missing from the scene and the few prostitutes looking for an early trick, all had an air of hopelessness and boredom. A gypsy fortuneteller dozed in her doorway and a handful of winos slept in the stairwells of the old buildings.

The smattering of tourists, obviously feeling more comfortable to explore the dark side of Paradise by day, rather than face its real or imagined perils by night, strolled along its littered sidewalks. They peered in the windows of its cheap stores; stared askance at the porno movie theatres, 'adult' bookstores, massage parlors and pawnshops.

They seemed to puzzle over the occasional quality shop, sandwiched among its unseemly neighbors and the handful of what was, apparently, nice restaurants cheek-by-cheek with much less appealing bar and grill establishments.

Lucky and Pua assumed that same tourist image as they walked along. From time to time they would duck into a bar, look around, speak to the bartender and move on. Time after time, their inquiries evoked no more than the shake of a head, or at best a "Naw, most of our people are regulars;" or "Hey, I keep out of trouble by keeping my mouth shut." Even the judicious dropping of the Major's name failed to illicit any helpful information.

Finally, when both were getting footsore and weary of the whole thing, Lucky suggested, "Let's drop in at that bar on the corner. It looks fairly good and we can have a beer or something. Maybe we can come up with an idea of where to go from here." Pua agreed.

They took seats at the bar and looked around. Most of the tables and booths were deserted. The few customers drank in moody silence. At one table a foursome of men were arguing boisterously about a poker game they'd apparently spent the night playing- In a narrow booth, an old man slept, his head cradled in his arms on the table, a half full mug of beer perilously near one tattered elbow.

At the end of the bar, two weary-faced elderly women chatted quietly over their beers. There was a curious somnolence about the whole scene, which the bartender seemed to share.

"Where is everybody?" Lucky asked, as they were served. Swiping at the bar surface with a damp cloth, the man grimaced and said, "Sleeping off Saturday night hangovers, I guess. Old Jesse back there was burned out of his apartment the other night; has no home any more. I let him get a little rest here, when we're not busy.

"It's often like this on Sundays. If I had my way,

118

we'd close Sunday afternoons, but my boss doesn't agree. I could sure use the sleep. I was here until two this morning. I'm out on my feet. Guy supposed to work this shift didn't show up, so I got called back." He eyed them cannily. "What's up? You folks didn't join us for the fun of it. What I've got here is the deadest place in town, right now."

Lucky commiserated with him and then said, "We need some information. You didn't happen to notice a fellow with one hand in here last night, by any chance?"

"You the heat?" he asked, squinting suspiciously. "What do you want to know for?"

"No, not the heat. We're just helping Major Kanai find a guy that either has only one hand, or has a crippled one. He's wanted for questioning."

"Kanai, eh. He's a right sort of guy. Well, I might be able to help you. There was a guy in here that kept one hand in his pocket the whole time. For all I know he didn't have one. Reason I remember is that he wanted to pay me with a Century bill and need I say I don't see many of those down here. Anyway, he used that one hand—let's see, his right, I think it was--to take that bill out of his pocket and I could see more of 'em in there. I thought he was pretty damned stupid to carry that kind of money down here. He was buying beers for the chicks and actin' real macho--noisy S.O.B. too. I figured we were gonna have trouble sooner or later, but he finally left with one of the hookers."

Lucky and Pua looked at each other, startled. "How much money would you say he was carrying?" she asked.

"Close to a thousand--maybe more. Looked like one hell of a wad. Can you beat that? What the hell was he doin' down here with that kinda dough? And lettin' everybody see it--that was just askin' for trouble. Did something happen to him?"

"Not that we know of. What time did he come in?"

"Jeez, man, I dunno--ten, eleven, maybe later. He went in the lua, to clean himself up, for one thing, or I'd a kicked him out. I think he'd been in a fight--had blood on his jacket. Wha'd he do, cream somebody?"

"We don't know if he's our man, or what the charges are. We're just trying to do a little footwork for Kanai," Lucky said, shamming boredom. "You know the major. Doesn't like to bug you folks down here with uniforms, unless he has to. "

The bartender grinned. "Good thing, too. It sure doesn't do business any good when HPD shows up. I remember one time when Charlie Dangue's wife had a baby boy and Charlie had a party in here--everybody invited. His brother-in-law is a cop and he just dropped in for a second to congratulate Charlie--still in uniform--and just like that the party was over. Folks streamed out of here like the place was on fire or something. Guess lots of folks have something to hide." He shook his head, grimacing.

Pua spoke up. "What was this man wearing, do you recall?"

"I'll tell you, little lady, he didn't get it at Liberty

120

House. One of those gray-blue cotton jackets, kinda cruddy jeans and one of those stocking caps, black or dark blue it was--all rolled up tight and sittin' cocky-like on the back of his head. Oh and he had a pair of those outsize shades on all night--and how he could see through them in this dark hole, I don't know. Looked silly, but it was none of my business. I don't think he ever did take 'em off."

Lucky looked thoughtful. "This fellow, can you tell us what he looked like--build, age, hair color, that sort of thing?"

"I'd say he was in his thirties, medium height, dark hair, sort of broad face, what you could see of it. Kind of a husky guy."

"Local?" Pua asked.

"I don't think so. It's hard to tell in here. Sounded mainland kine'."

"Well, thanks. He could be our man. Tell you what, if he comes in again, or if you think of any other details, call this number, okay?" Lucky suggested, passing Keoki's card across the bar.

"Sure--can I pour you folks one on the house?"

"No, thanks. We'll be getting on."

"Well, good luck."

Back on the street, they looked at each other in a kind of daze. "It sure sounds like our man. Do you think we could be so lucky?"

Pua laughed. "Lucky, with you on it, what

121

else?" Then, sobering, "I can't figure all that money, though. Why would a guy with that much money beat up a little old lady to steal less than a hundred?"

"I haven't a clue, Pua. It doesn't make much sense. Hey, we'd better get back and see what your dad has to say about all this. We've been gone nearly three hours. We'd better get down to the corner and catch a cab. Think he'll still be at the station?"

"Either there or at the hospital. He won't rest until he gets some kind of angle on all this."

Sure enough, they found him at his desk, hard at work. He waved them to chairs. "We've got three possible," he announced, turning a trio of mug shots so they could see them. But we can't get a match on the fingerprints yet. The lab says his hand was so dirty, or covered with that clay or whatever, that they still can't get a reading. They're still working at it. Haven't got much hope, though. They say it coated the whorls like sealing wax. Did you get anything?"

"Could be." Lucky was staring at the three photos. "If we did, you can throw out this one," tossing aside the one described as one-armed. Wrong arm. And with plenty of assistance from Pua, he laid out the information they had come up with.

Keoki listened attentively and with growing excitement, until they told him about the money. "I don't get it," he said slowly. "I even asked Herb if they had any money stashed away some place. He didn't know of any. Why would a guy commit a crime for peanuts, when he had that much cash on hand? Doesn't make sense. Wait a minute."

He spoke briefly into the phone; then returned it to its cradle. "There was a liquor store heist last night, but that was just before midnight; and another shopping bag robbery at a little grocery store up toward Kaimuki, but the boys nailed that guy in a stolen car.

"Our man's still on Oahu, though. We've had an all-night check on all flight departures, inter-island, mainland and foreign."

"Ships?" queried Lucky.

"Nope. Only ships to sail last night were the Constitution and the Independence on their island cruises and they were buttoning up to go to sea before he could possibly get there. Their security is tops, too."

Pua was studying the remaining mug shots. "This couldn't be the one, either," she said. "Remember, Lucky, that bartender said he had a broad face? Look."

"You're right. And look here, this last one is over six feet tall--that's not 'medium height' by any means."

Keoki puffed his lips in a discouraged sigh. "Pua, what bar was your information source, the Pa'ani?" She nodded. "Bartender a big Portagee with a small mustache and beard?" She nodded again.

"That's Benjy. I'm going to get him in here tomorrow with our artist; see if we can get a reasonable likeness.

I'll give him a call now. While I do that, look over these shots of Joy's shop; see if anything occurs to you."

As he talked, the two examined the photographs. Suddenly Pua pointed to the piles of broken crockery and uprooted plants. "Look, Lucky, how could he do it with only one good hand? See, some are pulled out, soil and all. Some pots are broken, but in big pieces, not shattered like they would if they were thrown down or just brushed off the shelves. It's like he went after each one separately. Don't you think that's strange?"

"Sure as hell is."

Keoki turned back from the phone just then. "Benjy's coming by in the morning. What's up, you got something?" Pua explained. Keoki examined the photo carefully.

"Well, it could be, honey, but it looks to me like just plain malicious destruction. Let's keep that theory in mind, though. I'm going to call the hospital and then we'll go home to Malia. Some kind of Sunday we're having, eh?"

As he listened to the information, his jaw tightened; and when he turned back to them, he said, "Joy's having a rough time. They had to take her back to surgery to relieve more pressure that was building. She's in Recovery, now. Her condition is improved; but Doc Siddons says the she's got something worrying her so bad that it's dangerous. Herb is with her trying to understand anything she says. She keeps trying to talk about pots and orchids. Worrying about her stock, I imagine."

He picked up the car phone and made a brief call to headquarters. "I want a guard on Mrs. Masters' room day and night. I have a hunch that so far; this creep thinks

124

he killed her. But if he finds out she's alive, I don't want him anywhere near her."

They were silent the rest of the way home; each one wrapped in thought about some phase of the puzzle. As they turned in the drive, they saw Malia in the potting shed, trying to shake loose a large orchid plant from its ornamental container.

"Ooh, am I glad to see you!" she exclaimed. "You're just in time to rescue a lady in distress. I can't get this darned thing out and it has to be divided or it's done for.

The roots seem to have grown right into the clay."

"I'll do it, honey, here." And taking it, Keoki struggled to dislodge the plant. Then, scowling, he said, "No way we're going to get it out this way. You're going to have to get a new pot, love," and grabbing the stalks of the plant firmly, he struck it against the side of the work table; then stooped to pick up the broken pieces of crockery. "There, how is that?"

"Keoki Kanai, that was the cachepot your mother gave us! Oh dear, I guess it served its time though. What is the matter with you three?"

They were staring at each other in a comic blend of consternation and dawning understanding. "He had to be searching them, that's what and couldn't get the plants out without banging them against the counter or something. He was after money, or maybe a locker key-- God, I can't believe she'd hide money that way though." And Keoki turned, caught Malia up in his arms and whirled her around, while she laughingly protested.

"Sweetheart," he shouted. "You just gave us the best clue of the day! Come on, let's go in and talk about it."

"I can't, right this minute," she said. "You go on in, I've got to wax out these broken roots first."

They had started toward the house, when Lucky stopped short. "You what?" he asked.

"I don't want the tips of these broken roots to bleed, so I put this soft wax on them to heal them. It only takes a minute. It stays soft in its closed can, but once it's in the air it hardens almost instantly."

"Keoki!" he called. "That's it--the fingerprints! He put that stuff on his fingers! He did it to make sure he didn't leave prints. Malia, any time you want to join Lucky Seven, you're hired." And he ran into the house, leaving her bewildered, as she pressed the wax firmly around the root tips of her prized orchid.

Chapter 13

Sitting comfortably on the spacious lanai, cool breezes sweeping over them, tall icy drinks in hand and a platter of Malia's tempting pupus nearby, they outlined for her the progress they had made--and toasted her for her part in it.

"But I didn't know I was helping," she protested. "I was just doing my gardening, for Pete's sake. It was Lucky who picked up on it. I don't deserve any credit. So knock it off, now and tell me what else is going on."

Keoki gave her that special smile that was hers exclusively. "Will you take credit for saving three people from starvation? These are great," he said, munching happily.

"With pleasure," she smiled. "But don't eat too much. I'm fixing Ahi the way you like it with the fresh tomatoes and green peppers and all my secret herbs plus a whisper of white wine."

Sounds of anticipatory approval escaped simultaneously from Keoki and Pua. Lucky was mystified. "Sounds terrific, but what is ahi? I remember Keoki said it was a great fish, but what kind?"

"Ahi is Hawaii's yellow-fin tuna. If you like fish, you'll be sure to enjoy it. I'm fixing a whole one in the oven."

"Super. I love fish--never had fresh tuna before, but just the description has me salivating."

Keoki stretched and rumpling his own shock of curly hair, admitted, "Sorry, gang, but I can't get off the subject of the day. If you don't mind, let's just toss it around among us for a while.

"It's another 'why'. Why was Joy so impatient because we couldn't get her drift about the delivery boy? There's something there, but I can't see what."

"Keoki, you're scowling, dear. Relax and just let your thoughts flow and you may get your answer."

"I'll try, love. I just can't get my mind off the little mysteries in his case," he admitted. "You know, when she said 'only one'--could it be she meant one hand instead of one flower pot, as we assumed? We had reassured her about the delivery of the flowers to the church. But that seemed to make her even more frustrated. It was as if she knew she wasn't getting her message through to me. The whole thing is nagging at me."

Lucky looked up. "I have something bugging me too. This thing had to be done by somebody who knew the Masters, knew how they operated and what their habits were. I think she knew him, or recognized him because of that missing hand.

"Nobody in the neighborhood heard a sound from the shop that night. She must have been sitting at the work table; and you'd think a barrier like that would give her plenty of time to cry out. Whoever it was had to come in the front door. Then they went through the shop into the workroom. Yet she just sat there waiting. She was expecting Janna. I wonder if she heard someone out in the shop, thought it was Janna and what? Maybe told her to bring in some more flowers or boxes or ribbon or whatever? Does that make sense?"

"Sure does, but I don't think the man had a clue that anyone was there. He expected he'd have plenty of time to do what he had to do. Herb said they usually left a workroom light on at night to discourage break-ins and the like--so that wouldn't bother him--not if he knew that it was customary."

"But the door was not locked. Shouldn't that have tipped him off?"

"Not necessarily." Lucky paused, thinking out the possible action. "He might have assumed it was locked and just shoved a plastic card in the crack and opened it. Or, wait a minute; what if he had a key? Oh, I don't know. He'd still have to believe Joy hadn't bolted it, when they went out.

That's a distinct possibility," Malia said. "Herb was always after Joy to remember to bolt the door. She had a habit of leaving it on the latch, until she was sure no one else was going to be coming in--and then forgetting to throw the bolt later on. And he wasn't there that night to remind her."

Pua looked up, startled. "I bet the man was around somewhere, when the cab came and figured both of them were going out. Probably hid, till the cab pulled out of sight."

Keoki nodded. "It was common knowledge that she worried about him going out at night, alone."

"That's right," Malia said. "When I went to string leis with her one night and he had a call; she wanted him to put it off until she could go with him and he asked her, 'What's the difference? Night and day are all one to me.'"

"So one way or another, this person gets in and she calls out, thinking its Janna. That had to be one hell of a shock. He decides he has no option but to take her out, knock her out; and that's when he cuts the eyeholes in his cap and covers his face--probably used those little ribbon scissors she kept on the lei counter."

"I don't believe it was in his plan to kill her," Malia said. "I think he had no intention of doing anything but buy time to get what he came for."

Lucky nodded slowly. "So he pretends to get flowers out of the case, breaking the vase in his awkward haste and walks in on her. "

"She might not have even looked up from her work. Simply assumed it was Janna, called out to her and went on with what she was doing. We knew she was hurrying to get the order ready for the morning pick-up," Pua remarked. "Knowing Janna would be late, she was probably working at top speed."

"Hold it," Keoki interrupted. "Who did pick up the flower order? I'm going to give Janna a call."

When he returned, he slumped into the chair. "Should 'a caught that before. The truck didn't show up, so Janna got a friend to make that delivery. Malia, have you any idea how long this so-called delivery boy worked for the Makua's Island Deliveries?"

"Let's see. Joy called me on the phone when old man Makua had his stroke about three months ago. Later, she called back to tell me Mrs. Makua had hired a young man to drive for them. So he's delivered for them for more than two months now. She told me he kept getting

130

lost at first, but was gradually finding his way around and was quite dependable."

"Makua owns the delivery service?" asked Lucky.

"That's right. He started Island Deliveries years ago, a sort of one-truck operation for small stores around town that needed delivery service, but couldn't afford the big outfits. Joy doesn't drive any more, you see and Makua was both dependable and reasonable." Lucky's eyes narrowed. "Must have been a--a Malahini, if he didn't know his way around at first. Hmm?" Keoki frowned. "Could it be that he was hurt while on his way to Hawaii? He could have recuperated here and then decided to stay. That would account for his lack of experience on our streets. Because we have the reputation of being a resort area, plenty of unsavory characters come here to prey on our people. When it comes right down to it, this driver would sure have inside knowledge of the flower shop, if he was making their deliveries."

"Joy's shop is very popular--her things are predictably fresh, beautifully arranged and the prices attractive. Local people, visitors, hotels and travel agencies are regular customers. He'd keep busy--that's certain."

"Did you ever see him, Malia?" Keoki asked. "No, dear. He usually came in the morning and was through by early afternoon. I never get in to see Joy until three or so. I can't remember ever seeing him, actually."

"I see. Okay, I'll ask one more question. Do I have time to make a call before dinner?"

"Of course, but keep it short, okay? Come on, Pua;

131

let's get things on. Let's eat out again. It's so pleasant tonight." Keoki came back glowering. "Great balls of fire! Their delivery boy quit without notice. Didn't work at all yesterday. Took the truck early in the morning and didn't come back. Mrs. Makua was frantic. He'd had several deliveries to make and when complaints began coming in yesterday afternoon, she called HPD.

"And here's the pay-off: Mrs. Makua was afraid he'd had a wreck. She'd tried to check with Joy on the phone, but, of course, the phone had been pulled out of the wall. Would anyone care to hazard a guess why Mrs. Makua was worried about his having a wreck?"

"He was minus one hand."

"You've got it, honey. When I asked her how she happened to hire him, she told me that he was the only one to answer her ad; and since he had a commercial driver's license from California, she gave him the chance. Could be a phony license, though—more than likely stolen. The name on it was Charles Smith. Mrs. Makua said he liked to be called Smitty."

"But Joy called him Andy," Keoki said and threw his hands up, defeated. "Let's drop this subject for awhile. My mind's going round in circles."

He glanced up at Malia, who was standing patiently by the table. "Is dinner on? Come on, Lucky, the pieces are beginning to fit together. Let's forget it for now and enjoy our dinner."

And enjoy it they did. The fish was firm as chicken breast and lusciously juicy, its sauce delectable. They ate their fill of it, along with poi, an excellent slaw and fresh fruits and cheeses for dessert.

Afterward, Malia brought out Keoki's ukulele and he played, at times singing the melodic music of Hawaii in his native language. The women sang along with him occasionally and Pua performed graceful hulas with some of his selections. When he laid the instrument aside, he stretched and said, "It's been a long day. I think I could do with some sleep."

Lucky, who had listened and watched in rapt fascination, said simply, "Thank you. That was wonderful.

It made me feel as if I were looking right into the heart of Hawaii."

Impulsively, Keoki threw an arm around his shoulders. "Music is a magic healer of confusion," he said with a warm smile. "I feel a lot better now, myself. I have a morning assignment for you. Will you and Pua go in with me? I'd like to have you." Both eagerly accepted the invitation. "Don't stay up late, then. We'll talk about it on the way into town. Breakfast's at 7:30, remember. Coming, Malia?" And together they said their goodnights and went into the house. Minutes later. Lucky and Pua followed their example.

"Think you can find your way to the cottage tonight?" Pua whispered, as they kissed and held each other very close.

"If I don't, I'll sing out. Now off with you." Strolling back to the cottage, Lucky knew that he wasn't going to get to sleep quickly. His mind was teeming with facts, conjectures and that teasing awareness that they were making great progress toward the solution of the mystery.

He decided to sit down on the stone bench and let his thoughts flow, before he sought sleep.

Why was Joy Masters so upset, that her very life was at risk? Could it be that she had hidden a large sum of money for reasons of her own and was worried that it was gone? Was the strange man in the bar the "delivery boy" she had trusted? Had he seen her do something that gave away her cache? It had to be that--had to be. She'd been saving money in one of the pots and he'd wised up to it and he'd uprooted those plants and broken the containers as he searched them all. Wow! "Only one." That's what Joy was trying to say. Her money, or key, or whatever she'd hidden, was in only one of the pots. It all made a crazy kind of sense, sure as God made little green apples.

Where had that driver come from anyway? What was his name? Andy? Smitty? Lucky had the feeling that it was Andy. On the face of it, the driver's license was more likely to be the alias. If so Andy what? When and how had he lost a hand? Joy's neat account books stated only that name Andy/Delivery and the amount she paid him each week--each entry in the outlay column allotted to cash expenditures.

Lucky sighed, aware that, like Keoki, he was dizzy with teasing questions that needed answers. "Who" seemed to fairly clear, but "when, where, how and why" still needed to be examined more thoroughly. And those five questions were just as indispensable to case solving, as they were to every news-hungry reporter. He stiffened. Wait a minute!

If the accident happened on shipboard and he was hospitalized after reaching Hawaii, surely the papers would pick it up. And the hospital would have a record. He could zero in on the date by getting that information. He could check the microfilms of the newspapers around that date.

Suddenly his feeling of frustration evaporated and hope and purpose surfaced--and he felt very sleepy. Yawning, he went in to bed.

Chapter 14

"What do you have in mind to do today?" Keoki asked, as they approached headquarters the next morning. "I have a batch of work on my desk that must be dealt with, so I'm going to be tied up for awhile."

"Well," Lucky said, "I did some thinking last night, after we broke up. See what you think." And briefly he summarized his late night conclusions.

"If you haven't any particular job for us today, Keoki, I'd like to take Pua with me and follow up on the identification angle. If we can nail down who he is and what he is, we should be well on our way to his motivation."

"Precisely what I had in mind for you. But first, let's see if we have a response to our inquiries to the Coast Guard--should be in by now. How come that big smile, this morning, Pua?" her father asked.

"It's just that I'm so relieved by the fact that Joy is making progress at last. Doesn't it make you feel like wading in and getting this case solved quickly, so they will be able to have a good, normal life when she gets home?

"Herb was so cute on the phone this morning," she went on. "He told me, 'My little toughie is going to make it!' And he was half- laughing, half-crying. I hope we'll have some good news for them soon."

"I think we just might, too, if what I'm thinking pans out," Lucky said.

Predictably, Keoki's desk was stacked with papers.

136

"Auwe!" he groaned, shuffling through them quickly; and grunted in satisfaction. "Here we go," The Coast Guard, reports that an ordinary seaman, Jason Enders, sustained serious injuries, aboard the Coral Belle, en route to Hawaii. USCG responded, with Medevac helicopter. Patient off-loaded at helipad Kaiser Hospital. Injuries unspecified."

Lucky spoke up. "Shall I call the hospital for details?"

Keoki shook his head. "Waste of time at this point," he said. "All kinds of red tape to cut. Patient-doctor confidentiality, for one."

"Tell you what," Lucky suggested, "Why don't Pua and I go down to the News Building and do a little reading. With that date and name, we have a starting place now."

"Fine! You can--" The phone rang and the Major answered, then gestured to Lucky to get on the extension. "Go ahead, Sergeant."

"We've got that delivery truck, I believe, Major. I was Field Training Officer for Rookie Ellen Frakes on her first run and when we were checking out the parking lot down by the Ilikai, she spotted it. We checked it out-- nothing in it but a lot of withered flowers in back. Looks to be wiped clean, but we're taking the usual precautions. What are your orders?"

"Have it towed up here, Kea, so the lab can give it a going over."

"On our way. Oh, wait— Officer Frakes is a real

go-getter. She just pulled a plastic contact sign out of a garbage pail. "It reads 'Makua for Flowers.' Easy to see it had been pulled off the side of the truck."

"Great! Good works."

With the help of a clerk and a quick locate button, the pages of October, 1988 were soon rolling up the monitor. The first find was a report of the storm, a hurricane of incredible magnitude, reported to be battering ships at sea and threatening the Big Island of Hawaii, unless its course veered.

Continuing their search, their eyes were caught by a headline beginning "Pacific Storm Veers." They read that the storm had changed course; that the Big Island would experience gale force winds, but would escape the full onslaught of the hurricane, providing it kept on its present course.

And three days later: "Seaman Jason Anders, aboard the freighter Coral Belle, en route to Hawaii, was a victim of shifting deck cargo, which severely injured his left arm and hand. Anders was air-lifted to Honolulu by Coast Guard helicopter and is reported to be undergoing surgery on a badly mangled arm and hand, at Kaiser Hospital." Lucky caught his breath. "Pua, look, it says Anders! The Coast Guard report said Enders."

"Typo?" Pua suggested.

"Could be, I suppose; but twice in one article? Not likely. Let's look further."

The monitoring went on and Pua cried, "Hold it. Here's something. 'Jason Anders, the merchant seaman injured aboard the Coral Belle during last month's hurricane, was released from Kaiser Hospital today. Anders, 35, underwent surgery for the amputation of his left hand, as a result of injuries sustained when he was pinned against a bulkhead by shifting deck cargo during the storm.

'Anders informed this reporter that he plans to sue PacCom, Inc., owners of the shipping line, for damages. He is claiming criminal negligence in the stowing of cargo.'"

"Holy Moses!" and Lucky whistled. "There may be more on this; Key in PacCom. As she complied, the computer brought up what they were seeking. "Jason Anders has withdrawn his $1,000,000 suit for damages against PacCom on advice of his attorney. Anders admitted that he had gone on the cargo deck of the Coral Belle in direct violation of Captain Rick Nordt's orders to remain at his assigned post below decks."

There was more, but it added nothing to the sum total of information. "There's the makings of an angry man," Lucky said slowly. "On the face of it, going on deck was a dumb thing to do, particularly against orders. Either he was nuts about storms, or had a buddy up there, or craved excitement and danger. Just plain stupid!" And then his jaw sagged. "Oh, my God! Anders--Andy's a perfect nickname for a man named Anders. How could I have missed that? Well, now we call your dad."

"You call, Lucky. I want to thank the clerk who set up the files for us."

After he made his call, Lucky told her, "That

father of yours--he's absolutely unflappable. When I 'fessed up about Anders' name, he just said, 'I don't recall you telling me you were infallible. If you had, I'd wonder about you. Can't stand people that don't goof once in awhile. It's catching the goof and doing something about it, that's what's important.' And then he added, "We're closing in on him. Now take that daughter of mine to lunch."

"That's my dad," Pua beamed. "And lunch is overdue. Let's go."

Pulling out onto Kapiolani, he asked her, "What and where is the Chart House? Do they serve lunch near there?"

"Oh, yes; right there, as a matter of fact. The Chart House is a great restaurant. It's down by the Ala Wai Boat Harbor and we can sit by an open window and enjoy the view while we eat. What made you think of it? Turn here onto Cooke Street, Lucky--then left on Ala Moana and it's almost a straight shot from there."

"What made me think of it? I want to see where Andy left the truck; and maybe figure out why he chose that spot."

"Could be he arranged for someone to pick him up there. But, gee, leaving it in that area was asking for attention—a parking ticket--it's patrolled so frequently. Of course he may not have realized that. Take a right here, Lucky and another down at the corner and we're there."

With the station wagon safely parked and metered, they took the stairs to the balcony area of the restaurant.

140

Pua scrutinized the menu. "Oh, good! They have scampi as the special--and it really is special here."

As they waited to be served, Lucky looked out at the broad parking area and the picturesque waterway beyond. "I suppose on a busy night, it would seem to be a pretty safe place to lose a truck," he mused. "That must have been where he put it."

"It must have--Oh, Lucky, look!" Moving smoothly through the water glided a large pleasure boat, making its way out of the waterway to the channel, its deck colorfully crowded with boisterous, scantily clad young people.

Lucky was amused. "That strikes me as daring--all those kids in shorts and bikinis. I would burn lobster red, if I did that."

"They'd better have a darned good tan to start with, or they're going to be in real trouble. Any time between eleven and three, the sun is dynamite! Tourists frequently end up in the hospital because they aren't used to the direct sun rays we have here--particularly at this time of day."

"Let's hope they find a guardian angel like Malia to slather on aloe. Your mom literally saved my skin."

After they'd downed the last morsel of succulent scampi, Lucky suggested that they take a walk and get a closer look at the boats that occupied nearly every slip.

"Tell me," he asked, thoughtfully, "does any one live on any of these boats?"

"Gosh, I don't know. When I left the Islands, there

141

was a big brouhaha going on about hippy types buying or renting old junk boats and living in them down here. The powers that be were gradually thinning them out. Whether there are any left, I don't know."

"He might leave the truck here, because he needed a place to hide out; and he's a seaman. Supposing he has a friend on one of these boats and is lying low there? I can't see him registering at any of Waikiki's beach hotels."

She nodded, a touch reluctantly. "It could be the answer, I guess. Providing his boat-owner friend was willing to harbor a fugitive. That could get him into bad trouble. For that matter, I wouldn't put it past Anders to break into one of the boats and hole up. But still, I doubt it. Boaters usually know their neighbors pretty well and keep watch on each other's property.

"But some owners don't come down here very often, either. I don't know, Lucky; your original idea makes the most sense. The friend wouldn't necessarily have to be living aboard to have a guest there temporarily."

"It's a cinch he would be more likely to persuade his friend, if he didn't admit he was a wanted man," Lucky said. "Tell you what, let's play tourist and take a casual walk along the docks, keeping our eyes and ears open for something off-key. You're not tired, are you?"

"Heavens, no. I'm enjoying this. And who knows? We might get a break. Timing might be very important. I doubt if Anders plans a long stay, if he's down here."

They walked what seemed miles, passing every kind of boat from small sampans to elegant yachts, launches to Boston Whalers, motor boats to sleek sail boats.

One grizzled old man was fishing, sitting alone on the very end of a slip. They strolled out to watch and began to talk with him.

"Catch anything?" Pua asked.

"Naw, just some live bait," he answered, gesturing toward a big plastic bucket beside him, teeming with tiny silvery fish. "Going out after sunset."

"Do you come here often?"

"Darned near ever' day, Ma'am. That there's my boat," he said, indicating with his head, a sturdy, older craft across the dock. "She don't look like much, but she's seaworthy--more'n some of those new ones." He spat in the water.

Lucky spoke up. "You haven't happened to see a fellow down here, a man with only one hand--might be wearing one of those knitted heavy-weather caps?"

"Naw, never see'd any one like that He owns a boat?"

"I doubt it. He might have been looking for a friend that owns one."

"Naw. Did see something funny, though, come to think of it. Yesterday, it was. See those sailboats anchored out there? See that smaller one? She's been there fer a long time, just settin' at anchor. Yesterday, it was, I seen a man on her, spreadin' somethin' on the deck--dryin' clothes out, I figgered. Looked to be near nekked, 'cept for a towel or somethin' tied around him. Crazy landlubber!"

"I don't get it. What was crazy about it?"

"Why, Hell, Son, we don't spread wet stuff on the deck. Make them fast to the boom or the rail and they're dry in no time, a flapping in the breeze that way. Takes longer lying flat and they dry all stiff-like. The breeze leaves 'em nice and soft and smooth--no need to iron 'em even if you was a mind to."

"That's logical."

"Other thing seemed strange to me--feller wot owns that boat died about three weeks ago. Dunno what's gonna happen to her. She's a trim craft, too. Maybe she got sold. I couldn't figger out who'd go aboard her like that. Ain't seen hide or hair of him today. Well, I gotta go, now. Got plenty a bait." Gathering his gear together, he picked up his bucket and without further ado, trudged away to board his boat.

They watched him for a minute and then Lucky said, "I have a weird feeling that we've stumbled onto something. If that's our man out there, he won't be leaving until dark, unless he's spooked, that's for sure. Come on, Pua. Let's go lay this on the Major."

"I could stay and watch, if you want me to."

"No, let's just keep strolling until we get to the end of the dock; then get to the station. If we've been noticed, we don't want to seem like anything but gawking tourists."

"I get you."

144

By the time they reached the station, they were filled with misgivings. Away from the harbor, it all seemed far-fetched; but they agreed they should go ahead and get Keoki's reaction. They gave him a detailed report of their activities.

Then, slapping his hand firmly on the desk, he exclaimed, "Good work! Right or wrong, your thinking was orderly and it's the first decent possibility of a break that we've had all day--that and locating the truck. Damned if I don't think you've found him, and about those wet clothes. He wouldn't be about to hang stuff up in plain sight, if he had no business being there in the first place. Could be he paddled out there on a surfboard or something and got wet. I doubt if he was doing laundry. Ah, there's the man I want. Come in here, Kea."

"What's up, Sir?"

"Do you have an Aloha shirt here?"

"Yes, Sir, in my locker."

"Get it on," Keoki ordered and grabbed one of his own that hung from a hook on the coat rack. "I think we have a break in the Masters' case. You and I are going fishing."

"Fishing! You feeling well, Major?"

"I sure am. And you know what? I think we might just catch ourselves a biggie!"

Chapter 15

As the two men prepared to depart, Keoki reached into his desk drawer and tossed a set of keys to Pua. "I want to take the station wagon, so I think it's time for you to pick up Alika's car. You remember the place? The manager will be expecting you. So will Security. I'll see you at home later."

Pua's face fell. "But, Dad, the case. Can't we--don't we--help?"

"No, Baby. What you and Lucky have dug up gives us a tremendous advantage. But you must realize that the department has to take charge at the enforcement stage."

She pursed her lips and nodded. "I understand, but it's sort of like leaving a movie before the climax."

"I know, but remember, crime prevention and investigation is your kuleana. Enforcement is ours. Tell you what, though. If you get the car in time and want to watch from the Chart House, it's all right with me."

She was somewhat mollified. "Guess I'm not being very professional, eh? Okay, we'll watch."

With an approving smile, he turned back to the sergeant. "Kea, have an unmarked car or two meet us down there, but tell the men to keep out of sight until they see us on our way back from that boat, with or without the suspect. Once he's in our boat, they can move in. Got it?"

"Yes, Sir. I'll do that right now." And when he returned, he gave the shaka sign.

"Good. Now then, you still have your Boston Whaler down at the marina, don't you, Kea? If we can use it, we'll have a surprise advantage we wouldn't have if we took the Harbor Police launch. If our man is on that boat, he's probably pretty nervous and may be skittish. I'd sure like to keep it simple, if possible."

"No problem, Sir. Matter of fact it's all primed and ready to go. Momi and I were planning to take it out for a little fishing tonight."

"Hopefully, we'll be back in time for you to keep your date." Keoki checked his side arm and grinned. "Sure hope I don't need to draw this in a hurry--I'd hate to get it all tangled up in this Aloha shirt-tail. Let's go. We'll drop you and Pua off at Alika's, Lucky; it's on our way."

Although neither one of them would have admitted it, Pua and Lucky were feeling a little wistful, a little let down, as they watched the car moving away from them a few minutes later. Not to be in on the action wasn't easy to take, but they both knew that they must expect this in their Lucky Seven careers.

In one way, the private investigators had it all over the police force. In the private sector they were not sworn to enforce the law and had no authority to do so. They had the same rights as any citizen to make an arrest, but no more than that. As long as they obeyed the law, stayed within the bounds of the law, they had a freedom of action not enjoyed by enforcement officers. As trained police officers, it would take them a little while to make that adjustment in their thinking. But in the long run, the special freedoms of their work would make it both

147

productive and satisfying.

Approaching the Security kiosk, Pua identified herself to the guard.

"Oh, yes, Miss Kanai, you're here to pick up the car?" And at her nod, he said, "Welcome. Your father dropped by here a day or so ago. Filled her up for you. It's right over there, stall 619. Are you moving in today?"

"No, but I expect to soon."

"Well, Miss, let us know if we can be of any help to you."

"Mahalo," she smiled and they walked on to the car.

"Mmm," Lucky murmured as they approached the smart little Fiat, "Cousin Alika has a nice taste in cars. Do you think my long legs will fit into it?" Pua chuckled. "Don't worry. It's got more legroom and head room than the wagon. Alika adores it and he's as big or bigger than my father. You drive, Lucky; you know the way now."

"I'm learning anyway. Well, let's hit the road then. We don't want to miss the show."

By the time they reached the Chart House, they could see the Boston Whaler already making its way out toward the sailboat anchorage, aiming for one of the larger sloops at the Diamond Head end of the row.

Seated at the same table they had occupied at lunch, they watched as the two men in the boat gesticulated as if they were discussing the various good or bad points of each sailboat they passed; moving ever closer to the less impressive ketch, where they hoped to take a prisoner.

The detectives were looking around casually, attempting to observe their target without being obvious about it. They maneuvered in and out among the anchored vessels at a leisurely pace, discussing the lines of this one, the need for a paint job on another, making no attempt to get too close to their ultimate goal.

"Hell, I don't see any signs of life, do you?" Keoki asked in low tones.

"No, it looks abandoned to me--but wait a minute, Sir. What's that hanging there, just over the side, on the rail? See it? Isn't that a cap?"

"By God, I think it is. Let's ease in a little closer.

That's the way. Now move out toward the breakwater. Yep, that sure looks like da kine cap we're looking for. Tell you what, can you rev up a little, then choke down; make the engine miss or cough? That's it. Get us between him and the breakwater. Now, if he's there and comes up from below to see what's going on, we'll have the advantage. He'll have glare problems. Try that engine noise again. If he's there, that should make him curious. Wait a bit and follow my lead."

In a disgusted voice, he said, "Well, for Pete's sake, Joe, is she going to conk out on us? You got plenty gas in her?"

"Will you just knock it off, Ed? It's okay now, isn't it? I know what I'm doing. Thought we were out for a good time and what do I get but bitch, bitch, bitch." Kea's smothered grin showed that he was having a ball, telling off his major.

"And there, my lad, he is, taking a quick look at us from the hatch." Keoki's hushed words radiated satisfaction, not surprise. "Let's move in across the stern.

"Ahoy, the Pace-Maker! Anders, you are under felony arrest. This is Major Keoki Kanai of the Honolulu Police Department. Come up on deck with your hands on your head. Do it!" he roared.

As Kea expertly glided his boat abaft the ketch, Keoki stood up, holding his revolver at the ready, arms extended full length. "Are you alone?"

It was a high, frightened voice that answered. "I'm alone. I'm alone. Don't shoot! I'm coming out. Don't shoot me. I ain't got a gun. An' I ain't done nuthin'." And as he came up into full view, both men could plainly see that one hand was on his head. The other was missing, the leather-cuffed stub canting awkwardly toward the sky.

As the Sergeant tied up his boat with a few quick hitches of line, Major Kanai stepped board.

Ander's face was gray and splotchy with fear.

"Why d'you wanna bother me for. Can't a man have an afternoon on his boat without gettin'hassled?" he blustered; beads of sweat bursting forth on his forehead.

"You know why Anders. And this isn't your boat."

All the starch seemed to go out of the man. "I didn't mean to kill the old dame," he cried hysterically. "She just came up at me with them damned shears and I

150

took 'em away from her and hit her with 'em--only once--and she just fell down dead. I only wanted to knock her out for a while. I ain't a killer. I didn't want--"

"All right, all right. Hold everything. Now listen to me. I show you my credentials. You can read?" Anders nodded. "Now then. You are Jason Anders?"

"Yeah, but I dunno how come you found me here. Did that stupid, son of a--somebody ratted, huh? Can't even trust a shipmate any more."

Keoki ignored the question. "I am taking you into custody to answer charges of breaking and entering, felony theft and attempted murder, for starters." He snapped a cuff around the prisoner's right wrist and then stood, nonplussed for a moment, staring at the leather-covered stub that was extended to him. Then he shook his head and locked the other handcuff to the rail.

"Did I hear you right? Attempted murder?" Anders gasped. "The old dame ain't dead? Oh, I'm glad. I'm glad," and he held his maimed arm across his eyes, choking back wrenching sobs.

"It's still touch and go with her. We're very worried. Now I want you to read this card and follow along as I give you your rights." Holding it up so Anders could read it, he began, "You have the right to remain silent--" and continued on to the end of the familiar and necessary formality.

"Do you fully understand these rights, or do you have any questions about them? If so, I'm prepared to answer them now."

Anders shook his head. "Naw, no questions. I've heard all that before. You aren't lying to me? That old gal is still alive?"

"No thanks to you Anders. But she's still critical. You better pray that she doesn't die. The doctors are still fighting to keep her alive."

"Oh, my God!"

"He's the one to talk to--that's for sure. Now get into the boat." Keoki was unlocking the cuff from the rail. "And sit down. I warn you, don't try anything stupid. It'll only make more trouble for you."

"I ain't goin' nowhere." Keoki left him in Kea's custody and went below to the cabin. It was apparently undisturbed except for one bunk, spread with a piece of crumpled, soiled tarp. Quickly he checked the mattresses and storage lockers beneath the bunks, glanced into empty clothes lockers, the head and the tiny galley, where a half-eaten Big Mac and a couple of milkshake cartons cluttered the small table. In the locker under the sink, in an empty coffee can, he found what he was searching for; a thick plastic folder crammed with $100 and $50 bills. This he sealed into an evidence bag and went back up on deck, carrying it with him.

Closing the hatch doors, he found the lock broken and hanging loose. He'd have to send someone out to tend to that. Then he reached over the side and rescued the cap, still slightly damp. In the process, he caught his finger in one of two horizontal holes, which had been cut into it. Holes still sticky from the tape with which Anders had attempted to close them.

152

"Damn fool," he muttered to himself. "He should have deep-sixed this, first thing." With a final look around, he stepped into the Whaler and cuffed himself to the prisoner.

Ashore, Pua was tugging at Lucky's arm. "What's happening now?" she asked nervously. "Can you make out what's going on? What's taking so long?"

"He's probably searching the cabin. It's hard to tell from here, the bow is so high. Oh-oh, the Whaler just pulled away. It looks as if they're coming in now--and yes, see? A third man is sitting by Keoki in the tern."

"And there go the patrolmen out to the dock.

Everything's under control, don't you think?"

"It certainly appears so. Of course, you must realize it might just be a trespasser on that boat--like the old man assumed. We'll have to wait for the rest of the story. I think we might as well leave, Pua. Your dad is going to be busy for quite awhile. No time for us to be underfoot."

"I know. This is sure one hurry-up-and-wait business we're in. Let's go see mom--maybe take a little drive first. We can put the top down and let the breeze clear our heads.

I feel sort of strange and shaky all of a sudden. Do you?"

"Goes with the territory, honey. You have to get used to that letdown sensation, that comes when the tension's off. We'll go relax awhile with your mom and when Keoki gets home, he'll bring us up to date."

They enjoyed a leisurely drive up toward Koko Head, letting the breeze whisk away the letdown mood, gradually achieving that good feeling of wellbeing and accomplishment their work had earned them. Then they turned back and when at last they turned in between the stone pillars, they could see Malia sitting on the lanai steps. She hurried out to meet them.

"Good news," she called out, as the car came to a halt. "Keoki just called, said to tell you everything went down smoothly and he'll fill you in later. They even recovered a lot of Joy's money. That's what it was, a cache of money. It has to go through some formalities, of course, but she'll get it back in due course. And the other good news is that Joy is much more alert and is definitely on the road to full recovery. Isn't that marvelous? Now come on in and let's have something cool to drink and a bite to eat."

As they relaxed, Pua said, a questioning look on her face, "Seems to me we still have a big mystery to solve. What on earth was the deal about all that money? Did dad give you any inkling?"

"Only that this Anders person admitted he stole it from her. I agree with you. I can't imagine where she'd get that kind of money--Keoki said there was at least $4000 in the folder, or whatever it was they recovered. We'll just have to wait it out, kids."

She looked at their anxious faces. "You know what? I could use a swim. How about you?"

"Good idea," Lucky said, "but we'll have to take your car, Malia. Three of us will never fit in the Fiat,

154

roomy as it is."

"We don't need a car. There's a lovely little cove just down the hill and a nice path to get to it. Come on, get into your swim togs." Malia hurried inside, followed by Pua, while Lucky went to the cottage to change.

The narrow path was soft underfoot and as they followed its serpentine course down to the beach, Lucky marveled again at the lush beauty around him. Flowering trees, tall and graceful palm trees leaning precariously toward the sea, hibiscus, anthurium and bougainvillea abloom with rich, vibrant colors. Did ever anyone take it all for granted, he wondered? And as if she had heard his thoughts, Malia smiled back at him and said, "Isn't it gorgeous? I just never get enough of it."

Reaching the shore, they turned to the left and there it was, a pocket-handkerchief of white sandy beach and a sheltered cove, the shimmering surface of limpid water rising and falling with the pulse of the tide.

"See that big brain coral head rearing out of the water there? That's my diving board." And swimming swiftly out to it, Malia executed a trio of graceful dives and swam back to them.

"Your turn, Lucky," she cried. "Go off on the ocean side. It's about twenty feet deep here."

They all dived and swam and cavorted in the pleasantly cool water for nearly an hour; then fell on beach towels spread over the sand, to let the afternoon sun dry them and restore them.

"One good thing," Malia murmured drowsily, "this

time of day you don't have to worry about burning. During the next three months at least, after about three in the afternoon, the sting goes out of the sunshine and haoles like you and me, Lucky, can relax completely in its warmth without fear of an uncomfortable aftermath. Am I correct, Pua?"

There was no answer. Pua had fallen sound asleep.

The climb back up to the house was leisurely; and as they parted to take their showers, Lucky realized that this pleasant adventure had refreshed them and relieved their tensions as nothing else could. He must remember that when the going got tough--as he was sure it would at times, when Lucky Seven was in full swing.

Chapter 16

Malia was busying herself in the kitchen, when the phone finally rang. She spoke briefly and then hurried to the lanai, her eyes sparkling with joy.

"Martinis!" she cried and Pua leaped up and the two of them hugged each other and did an impromptu dance, as Lucky stared at them, amused but puzzled.

"What the devil--" he began and instantly they sobered.

"Oh, I'm sorry, Lucky dear," Malia, said contritely. "That's our signal. That's Keoki's code word when a tough case is wrapped up. That's the only time we have martinis is why. "

"Super!" he said. "I thought you were going berserk for a moment there. What did he have to say?"

"'Martinis!' Just that. And that means that everything is okay; he'll be home within the hour; and there's nothing to worry about. Neat, eh? And now I'd better go get them made. He likes his martinis very, very cold."

"May I help?"

"Not with the martinis, my dear. Keoki says I make the best in the world," she laughed, coloring. "I use only good old English Tanqueray Gin, with just a whisper of dry Vermouth and a wee tot of olive brine and serve them with three huge stuffed olives on picks. He swears that what makes them special is the way I stir them. Tell you what, though. Pua, you get the olives ready on their picks and you, Lucky, how would you like to be my

157

baker?"

"I'd probably do better with the olives," he laughed.

"No, I made the pupus this afternoon and they're chilling in the frig. All you have to do is brush each little half-moon pastry with the egg and sour cream glaze I made, then bake them quickly in the convection oven, a few at a time, until they come all golden brown and crispy. After that, you just slip them in the warmer to keep them that way. Are you game?"

"Lead the way. Sounds as if I could handle that assignment without goofing it up."

As he worked, he asked, "What are in these, anyway? They smell wonderful!"

"They're a family favorite. I call them surprise pies. Those little half-moons of pastry are stuffed with good things, like ground meat with bean sprouts and mushrooms, cheese and crunchy bits of celery and seal lions, shrimp with water chestnuts and crabmeat with a delicate mustard-caper sauce--it's always a surprise, 'cause they all look alike, so you never know what you're getting."

"You ought to write a book, 'Pupus that are Lulus', or something like that, Malia," he said, teasingly."

"Write a book and give away all my secrets? No, thank you. Besides, I sort of dream them up as I go along--and then forget exactly how I did them. Keoki gets huhu at me sometimes for that--when I can't remember how I made a favorite of his. But he forgives me when I make something he likes even better. I wouldn't dare forget how to make these, though. They're our official celebration pupus."

"Huhu means, provoked?"

"That's right--angry, annoyed, whatever. Provoked--I like that."

"This about right?" He asked, taking a pan full from the oven.

"Perfect, love. Just keep them coming."

Everything was ready when they heard the station wagon coming down the drive. Everyone was in a fine mood--and so was Keoki, as he walked toward them, a big smile replacing the concern he'd shown through the last few troubling days.

Seated on the lanai, sipping Malia's ono martinis, oohing and aahing over the fresh-baked pupus and admiring still another of the Island's spectacular sunsets, they waited for Keoki to begin his story. Pua couldn't stand the suspense and turned to him.

"Dad," she began--her voice trailing off, as her mother silenced her with a gentle shake of her head.

"Never mind. I'm ready now, Mother," he said. "Just getting my thoughts together. The best news yet is from the hospital. That's where I was when I called you. Joy is so much better; she was able to talk with me. She solved what was left of our mystery. "Guess I'll tell you about that first--the money thing.

She had been saving up money, unbeknownst to

Herb--even sold most of the jewelry her grandmother had left her--to make the $4500 difference that their insurance and Medicare wouldn't pay on a relatively new breakthrough in eye surgery. Hopefully, it will restore at least some of Herb's sight.

"She didn't want to bank the money, because Herb takes in the receipts nearly every day and they always explain the balance to him, because he can't read them for himself. She said he would never have permitted her to save up for it, had he known.

"So she'd sock away $50 or $100; and then slip out and change it into a bill. She kept the bills that waterproof vinyl wallet thing, which she concealed inside one of the orchid pots under that Hapuu mixture she uses as her planting medium, put a 'Sold' tag on the pot and move them around occasionally. She felt it was as safe as in a bank, since she was the only one who did any selling.

"When the packet finally got too thick, she hid it by the roots of that huge orchid that blooms all the time-- you know the one, Malia, that six-footer, which has been marked 'not for sale' for as long as I can remember. How Anders got onto it, comes later. My God, it took her nearly three years, to get enough money together. Told me the jewelry brought over $2000, though. No wonder she was so troubled when she was unable to make us understand about it.

"She's happy that she'll be getting back the $4050, I think it was, that Anders hadn't had the time to spend."

"Oh, that poor foolish woman," Malia cried. "With that pride, I guess she just couldn't bring herself to ask

160

one of us to help her or advise her."

"Now then," Keoki continued, "I want to go back and fill you in on what we found out about Anders. He had a record out of San Francisco under the name Landers--two convictions; one for petty theft of a liquor store; the other for stealing money from his mates aboard a ship he was working on-- Served six months in jail on the first; and a year in 'Q' on the second.

"Somehow he got the job on the Coral Belle, after he got out of prison and it was on the Hawaii leg of his first trip on her that he had his accident. You know most of the rest, up until he went to work for the Makuas. "It was during one of his delivery calls to the flower shop that he first saw Joy, as he put it, 'messing around with the potted orchids and looking scared as Hell' when he arrived early. He inferred that he had seen her at those pots more than once and it was her anxiety that tipped him off that she was stashing something pretty valuable there."

"Good Lord," expostulated Lucky, "he spilled all this under preliminary questioning?"

"We couldn't have shut him up in any case. He refused an attorney; said he was so glad 'the old dame didn't die,' that he wanted to get the whole thing off his chest and pay his dues.

"He thought sure she was dead, after he attacked her. He'd come in the shop very quietly and was exploring the pot he thought she'd hid something in, when he accidentally knocked one over. At once, she called out, 'Hi, Janna, bring in more silver ribbon and the rest of the cut flowers, as soon as you can, or words to that effect.

Joy told me it didn't even dawn on her that it might not be Janna."

"Anders said he froze for a minute, because he had thought no one was there--he'd seen the cab arrive to pick up Herb and figured they'd both gone out--just as we suspected. Then he caught up those ribbon scissors she keeps on the lei counter and cut the eyeholes in his cap-- no easy trick, with only one good hand, but he's pretty clever at getting traction with that leather thing he wears over his stub.

Anyway, he pulled the cap down over his face, dug his fingers into a jar of stem wax in the cut flower case--accidentally breaking a vase in the process— grabbed some flowers and walked in on her.

"He said she didn't even look up at first, but when she did, she knew she was in big trouble and she picked up those shears and tried to defend herself. He told me he didn't think she recognized him, but he wasn't sure because of that missing hand, which he was trying to conceal. He decided he couldn't take chances. He figured to knock her out long enough to find the loot and make his escape."

Taking a folded paper from his pocket, Keoki told them, "I ordered a copy of his description of the attack. This is word-for-word. 'I just grabbed them shears, held them tight in my hand and hit her hard once and she fell down. She laid there so still, I thought she was dead. I went around there and reached over to touch her and see if she was alive or not and got some of her blood on my sleeve. She wasn't breathing, best I could tell. So I just left her there and went back in the shop and kept looking until I came up with that wallet thing. I was so damn mad! I thought it was going to be so easy!'

"And then he had the nerve to complain that it was really her own fault that she got hurt, because she tried to stab him. Self-defense, he called it. Can you beat that?"

"That's dreadful," Malia gasped.

"I know, sweetheart. I think he didn't know how to deal with the fact that she was there, in the first place; and panicked when she dared to defend herself. It was as simple and as sad as that."

Keoki shook his head, as if to clear it of that mental picture and turned to Pua.

"Honey, how about another of mom's martinis--the best in the world, as usual." Malia flushed with pleasure.

As she poured, Pua asked, "But Dad, did he explain why he trashed the whole shop that way?"

"He just completely lost his temper when he couldn't find anything in the smaller pots, where he'd seen her put something and just systematically banged every one against the counter to get the plants out--just as I did with mom's pet orchid and cachepot. The more he broke, finding nothing, the madder he got and when he got to the big one, he just picked it up with his one good hand, steadied it with the maimed one and banged it down hard on the floor until it broke--and the wallet thing fell out at his feet. Then he took it and what was in the till and ran back to the truck, which he had hidden in that old abandoned garage shed in the alley."

"Did he tell you how he planned to get in the shop in the first place? That's a bit of a mystery to me," Lucky said.

"Oh, Joy had an extra key, hanging in the workroom. He simply took it one day, replacing it with an old key of his own. He'd planned ahead. He never did realize the door was already unlocked. Just stuck the key in and turned it and pushed on the door and it opened. "Just as you deduced, Lucky, he assumed they both went out in the cab together, as they usually did.

"You were right in your surmise that he had a marina friend, too. He told us he had an old buddy, staying on a boat down there, but when the guy found out he was running from the law, he told him to get lost. But he also told him about the abandoned sailboat as a possible temporary refuge.

"That's when Anders took a bus to Hotel Street and decided to live it up a little--get himself together, as he put it. He thought he was home free at this point and the more he drank, the safer he felt. He spent a couple hours that night with the hooker in some cheap hotel room; but booted her out about 2 a.m., when he caught her trying to lift his stash. Then he took a bus back to the corner by the Ilikai and saw a police car cruising the area, so he walked over to MacDonald's and had breakfast.

"It was still dark when he finished, so he swam, clothes and all, out to the sailboat his friend had told him about and somehow managed to pull himself aboard over

164

the transom. It was the only one he could hope to board from the water, anyway. It had a fixed step on the stern. He decided to lie low a couple of days, till the heat was off and then hop a flight to Kona, where another friend of his has a fishing boat.

"That old man you talked to down at the dock. What he saw was Anders trying to get his clothes dry, all right.   He told me he tied a towel around him while he spread them. Everything else was soaked. The cap he left hanging out, because it was so heavy it didn't dry fast. Lucky thing for us, Kea spotted it and we were pretty sure we had him. He was so damned glad Joy wasn't dead that he gave us no trouble at all."

"The poor dumb sucker. If he'd just played it straight, he'd have come out with more than he stole. He has company insurance coming to him--about $10,000 worth, according to the shipping office in California. Looks like it'll be a long while before he can collect it."

"Well, he has only himself to blame for that," Lucky commented. "But Keoki, how did he expect to survive out there. What about food?"

"That's one thing I had been wondering about. But when I arrested him, I found the remains of Big Macs and two milkshake cartons in the galley.

"He told me he bought them to-go there at MacDonald's before he took his swim and asked the counter man to put them in a plastic bag. He put the money in with them, closed it up good and swam out with the darned thing held between his teeth. Can you beat that?"

"So what happens now?" Lucky looked wistfully at the last of the pupus and at Malia's gesture, winked at her and took it.

"It's a wrap as far as we are concerned. Anders signed his confession; is in jail and has a meeting with the prosecutor tomorrow morning. Says he's going to plead guilty in court and take his medicine. That's three counts—aggravated felony assault, breaking and entering and felony theft. Gives the D.A. lots of leverage. Anyway, it's their baby now.

" Keoki stretched and reached for his martini. "I want to tell you two that your work made a great impression on everyone concerned. I think Lucky Seven is going to have little if any trouble with HPD and I have high hopes of it giving people like Joy and Herb and the other small merchants, a chance to make a decent living in peace."

"And that reminds me," Lucky said. "I think its time I move into my new place, buy that car and some other stuff I need and get started. How do you feel about it, Pua?"

"I'm 'way ahead of you. I packed the things I'll need right away, when we got home from our swim."

"Well," Malia sighed. "I won't hear of your going before morning. I have a cold supper ready. Come help me put it on, Pua and get your father's ukulele. I think we all feel like some music tonight." Much later, as they sat in contented quiet, star-gazing and wrapped in their own thoughts, Lucky said, "You know, you've taught me a lot in these few days. Your hospitality is so special that I

166

don't like the thought of leaving. Thank you, my good friends--you make me feel like family."

"And that's what you are, my boy," Keoki said gently. "Family--we call it Ohana. And, hey bruddah, you aren't moving to the moon, you know. Whenever you want to use the cottage, you're welcome and we expect to see a lot of you and," grinning slyly at his daughter, "you too, Pua. "

Malia, with that sweet smile that reminded Lucky so much of his own mother, said, "My feelings exactly."

Chapter 17

Never to be forgotten was Pualani's moving day. Alika's apartment was much lovelier than she had expected. It was only after Lucky had stowed her things in the large dressing room; and the two of them began to explore, that her father's comments became evident.

Two white leather easy chairs flanked a handsome bed-sofa, which was backed by a stereo sound system, and the big, quite-dramatic lamps were on a rheostat, all operative from a king-sized remote control system that lay on the adjacent coffee table.

"Wow!" Pua laughed. "Instant seduction!" She pushed buttons to get a variety of effects in lighting and music and then added, "Here's another button. What's it for?" As she pushed it, there was a soft purring sound and they both watched in amazement as the sofa transformed itself into an amply proportioned bed and the table rolled to the head of the bed. They howled with unrestrained glee. When he was able to speak. Lucky gasped, "What's a nice girl like you going to be doing in a place like this?"

"I'll never tell!" she giggled. "Looks to me as if this wasn't designed for the girl-next-door type. I was only here once before and it's certainly changed since then. And Lucky, here's another button. Do I dare press it?"

"Sure." And when she did, a huge television screen rose from a cabinet on the opposite side of the room, which further contained a VCR and library of tapes.

While Lucky tinkered with Alika's electronic

168

wonders, she looked through cupboards and drawers, working her way to a dinette and on to the refrigerator-freezer and opening its door, made a discovery that prompted her to call Lucky to her side.

"Will you get a load of this? My dad did more than fill the Fiat's tank. Look, a ham, fresh eggs, bread, cinnamon twists, a 12-pack of beer and I don't know what all." She opened the freezer section to find a stack of Stauffer's and Le Gourmet frozen specialties and a note from her dad. She read it to Lucky. "Just a little housewarming gift, honey. Mom says you should make yourself a good breakfast every day.   Love, Dad. P.S. There's some liquid refreshment in the cooler beside the bed."

"Beside the bed? Pua, that little cabinet on the other side of the bed is a refrigerator!"

"I'll be there in a minute. I want to put my cosmetics in the--"

There was a long pause.

"Pua?"

She didn't answer.

"Pua? Are you all right?"

She walked in, looking stunned. "There's no tub, Lucky--just a good-sized whirlpool bath, complete with shower. Can you believe all this?"

"What a guy!" Lucky said. "Come on, I'll show you how to get your sofa back again. Watch. He touched another button and it reversed itself--coffee table and all."

169

"You're sure? I don't want to get trapped in this thing."

"Positive!" And he demonstrated.

On the way to their office, Lucky began to chuckle. "I can't wait to meet Alika," he said. "His place shows a zest for the good bachelor life that is downright enviable."

"Your style?" she grinned. "Alika never seems to settle down to one girl. A wide variety of slim wahine is his bag."

"No, not my style, but he's got to be an interesting man." He reached over and squeezed her knee. "I'm a one-woman man, myself."

"He's fun--and he's smart--but he's also a nut," said Pua. "Has a heart as big as this whole island though and a list of interesting friends that won't quit!"

Jake saw them coming and waved them down. The bar stools came. I took the liberty of putting them ins ide--okay?"

"Great! Thanks, Jake." And they found them in place, looking like new, to Pua's delight. And in the living quarters, a fine new color television was in its place opposite Lucky's chair. On it was a hand-printed sign, "Mahalo nui loa ka ko'u--Keoki."

"That means 'My very great thanks,'" Pua murmured. "Dad must have brought it up early this morning."

"Pua, I can't accept this--I didn't do--"

170

"Let him have his pleasure, Lucky," Pua interrupted. That's what we call Hawaiian-style. It's Aloha. Your response is 'Aloha nui loa ka ko'u.' Do you understand?"

Lucky smiled and hugged her close. "I'm beginning to," he said.

"Then let's go over the Pali and shop for your car. That's all you need now to get Lucky Seven into business. Right?"

"Right."

Uncle Nomana proved to be a wiry little man, full of nervous energy, his face creased with lines from a lifetime of smiling and emotional reaction to whatever came his way.

"Be right with you, folks! Just give me a couple of minutes."

"Is he your father's brother?" Lucky asked. "They certainly don't resemble each other."

"They're brothers, but not by birth, Lucky. He's hanai. You see, when Hawaiian children are born to families which for some reason or other can't keep them, they are taken in by a family member or close friend and become their hanai child--sort of like adoption, except that the natural parents get to see the child whenever they want to and there's no heartbreak involved. Hanai children never feel unwanted or unloved. That's why there are no orphanages for Hawaiian children in Hawaii."

"That's amazing! What a pity more of the world

171

hasn't adopted the idea."

"Uncle's natural father was a treasured friend of Tutu Kane--Grandfather--Kanai. Sadly, the father was killed just before Nomana's birth. His mother couldn't support the baby and asked Grandpa and Grandma to take him in as their hanai child. She saw him frequently, before her death. Oh, here's Uncle now."

"Sorry to keep you waiting. What can I do for you folks?" He shook hands with Lucky.

"Don't you remember me, Uncle?" Pua kissed him soundly on one wrinkled cheek.

"Pualani, is it really you?" And he threw his arms around her. "Hey! You turned into one wahine u'i! How are Keoki and Malia? Haven't seen 'em for months."

"Busy and happy. Uncle, this is Lucky Gregory and he needs a car. I told him you would have a good deal for him."

As they walked to the showroom, Lucky briefly outlined the new enterprise and then told him, "I love good cars and I want a good one, but it can't be too flashy. I'll need plenty of power on occasion, I expect and I've got to have dependability."

Nomana, with a sly grin, suggested, "Would you consider a used car?"

"Oh golly, I don't think so. I've had some bad experiences."

"I understand. But let me tell you a little story. There's a young fellow in this town just made a killing selling off a piece of land he owned. First thing he did was go out and buy himself a Porsche, a beauty, I'll admit. But since I'd always taken care of his automotive needs before, he felt guilty and brought in his other car for me to sell for him. It's back here, a real Chev BelAir Classic." And with dramatic flair, he swept the dust cover off it.

Lucky sucked in his breath. This car was a gleaming golden tan beauty--as Nomana had said, a true classic, beautifully restored.

"It converts into a soft top convertible, you know. We just redid that top last year. Has super-charger, plenty of power and the rubber all 'round is in great shape. No gas eater, either. Now it's expensive, but I can give you a real good deal. How does it strike you?"

"Strikes me speechless!"

"Rev her up. She's ready to go."

As the motor came to smooth-humming life, he suggested, "Take her out for a spin. Pua, you stay with me. I want to catch up on family news."

And so it was that for the second time in as many months, Lucky fell in love. It was a dream to drive and as he turned back into the sales lot, he knew he had to have that car.

"Let's talk business," he said.

Silently, Nomana took a dollar bill from his pocket and handed it to Pua. "Ought to have known better'n bet with her. She's chewing up my profit," he grumbled.

"I knew you'd take it," she exulted. "It's a '57, the year of your birth--how could it miss, Lucky?"

"Now listen, Nomana, don't let this girl beat you down in price. I want this car and I know you'll be fair. I'm not about to take any of your commission."

"No problem. My take is already set. Let me give him a call--see what he'll take. Can you pay cash?" Lucky nodded.

They could see him through the glass panes of his office, sawing the air with one hand, as he cajoled and argued. Then he nodded and came back to them, eyes almost lost in the folds of a giant grin.

"I got him to let it go for eleven thou," he trumpeted. "Convinced him he'd make a hell of a lot more by having the money in the bank earning interest than he'd get letting this beauty sit around. He don' need money, anyhow. Well, is it a deal?"

"It's a deal." While Pua leafed through an old copy of Wheels, they finalized the paper work and Lucky made out the check.

All the way back to Honolulu, he was aching to see what she could do, but with Pua following close behind, he stuck to the speed limit and admired the shining dashboard, the soft leather of the upholstery and the awesome perfection that was now his.

He led her to her apartment house to drop off the Fiat and while he waited for her, enjoyed the unstinting approval of the guard. Handing Pua into the car, he said with exaggerated gallantry, "Princess, your coach awaits you."

Impulsively, he suggested, "Why don't we go back to the Chart House for lunch. It's been lucky for us so far."

"Fine. But afterward, we'd better go grocery shopping. I'll need a few perishables, like sour cream, fresh vegetables and milk; and we'll have to stock up for Lucky Seven, as well. Tell you what. I'll cook you a steak dinner tonight. Sound good?"

He leered at her, twirling an imaginary mustache. "Your place or mine, me proud beauty?"

"Yours, most definitely yours, you lecher."

While Pua stowed their purchase away, Lucky began to study the list of businesses Keoki had already provided.

"Great guns, Pua! This one should be a natural. Can you believe this? This man, Garcia, owns a little Mexican store and cafe--he's been hit six times in the past year and he was pretty badly beaten on one occasion. Do you know the place?"

She came to look over his shoulder. "No, but I see here that the Kimura's Japanese restaurant has had trouble; and twice, the frame shop owned by an acquaintance of mine, Albie Keach, has been vandalized. See? Right here. I knew both families pretty well. Went to school with Reach's daughter. His wife Waiola was my first hula teacher."

"We'll use those three for a nucleus, then. Undoubtedly, we'll get more leads from them."

"Would you like to walk down to see Keach now? He's open till eight, it says here and I doubt if he's very busy this time of the afternoon."

"Let's do that."

The little shop was less than a block away and when they reached it, they could see Keach working on a large picture frame. No one else seemed to be there. They walked in and Pua introduced herself.

"I don't know if you remember me. When I was a keiki I took hula lessons from Auntie Waiola."

"Of course I remember you," he said. "Pualani Kanai, right? You went to school with Leinaala too, didn't you?"

"Indeed I did. I hope they're both well."

His jaw tightened. "They're well, but they're on Kauai right now. Sure do miss them. Lei's doing graduate work at UH and had to take a little time off for this trip. It's a shame she has to miss her seminars, but it can't be helped."

"Oh, that is too bad. I'll look forward to seeing them when they return. May I introduce Lucky Gregory? He'd like to talk with you. Lucky, Mr. Keach."

"Albie. Nice to meet you," he said, as they shook hands.

"My pleasure, Sir. Can you give us a few minutes of your time?"

"Sure. Come back here and have a chair. What's up?"

176

"Pua and I are private investigators and we have an idea you might be interested in. Pua's father told us about your problems with vandals and we would like to help you solve those problems."

The man shook his head and a kind of terror seemed to reflect in his eyes. "You came to the wrong man, Lucky. I have no trouble right now," he said, "and I can't, I won't go back to the police. I'll put my family in more danger if I do. God, man, I've had to send my women away for their own protection. I'm a stubborn old Aussie, but when I tried to defend myself, fight these bloodsuckers, telephone calls began coming in threatening my wife and my girl. That was the only thing that made me knuckle under. I don't know which way to turn."

"That's a rough situation. Now, we're just starting up, Albie and all we'd like to have you do, at this point, is come to a meeting with some of your neighboring merchants and let us outline a plan that may help all of you. Neither Pua nor I are officially connected with the police department. We are simply interested in starting a system by which you people can protect yourselves and your families."

The man thought a minute. "Where are you located?"

"Here, let me write the address for you. It's on the seventh floor, just left of the elevator. Name's on the door: Lucky Seven."

"Guess it wouldn't hurt to come and listen to your plan anyway. Is it okay if I bring the Kimuras with me?

They're having a hard time too."

"I know. We were going to contact them. We'd appreciate your letting them know about it and bringing them along with you."

"We all get rapped down here. Damn it, all we want to do is make a decent living. There's the butcher, Palani, too and the Garcias' and more."

"Ask whomever you wish, but I'd suggest that you don't come all together. If anyone's casing you people, we don't want to be too obvious about this session. We're planning to low-key our operation as long as possible."

"I'm glad about that. We never know what's going to happen next, or where. I just can't stand these vultures pecking away at all of us, as if we were the targets in a turkey shoot."

"One thing's a cinch, Albie. If you folks band together against a common enemy, you are more formidable than if you try to fight back individually."

"That's true. There's got to be an answer--maybe you're it. What time?"

"Any time after eight. We'll see you then?"

"I'll be there and I'll see that some of the others come too. I like the way you present yourself, young man. For the first time in a long while, I have a ray of hope in my heart. I can't tell you how much it would mean to me to be able to bring my womenfolk home. But you have to understand, if I hear your plan and it doesn't sound to me as if it will work, I'll have to pass."

"We wouldn't have it any other way. It's purely voluntary."

"All right, then, I'll get busy rounding up my neighbors."

"Good. See you Monday evening."

As they walked back, Lucky told her, "You certainly picked the right man to start with. And knowing you, Albie is willing to give us his trust. That's a big plus.

"Lucky, I had that figured out from the first time we talked about all this. If you hadn't asked me to work with you, I'd have pointed out the advantages myself. You just beat me to the punch is all. You do recall, don't you, that I was the one who suggested Hawaii?"

"Touché," he said, echoing her laughter. "And you know what? You really are a conniving little wench."

Chapter 18

On Monday morning, they drove out to see Malia and show her the new company car. After a short ride, she remarked simply, "It has style and dignity, like a perfectly kept old home, impressive, but not pushy. I think you did exceedingly well."

"Uncle Nomana said to give you his Aloha. Wants to know when you and dad are coming over. Oh and he's planning a luau a couple of months from now and he wants the four of us to come. It'll be Lucky's first real Hawaiian luau. Uncle said he'd call as soon as the date is set."

"Oh, how nice," her mother said, "We'll have a great time. Nomana's luaus are classics. And speaking of dates, can you come for dinner Sunday night? It's awfully quiet around here, since you left."

"We'll plan for it," Lucky told her. "But you know, of course, Malia dear, if we have a job to do that night, we'll have to cancel."

"That I understand, Lucky. I haven't been a cop's wife for nearly thirty years without learning those priorities. Run along now and come back whenever you can."

Jake intercepted them down as they drove into their parking area. "Sergeant Kea brought this by; said I should give it to you," he said, handing them a large chart and waving them on to their parking space.

"This is great. Lucky! It's like a map of the area where most of our clients have their stores complete with addresses, owners and telephone numbers--the works. What a help it will be!" Lucky examined it in the elevator and agreed. When they entered the office, she slipped it under the glass top of her desk.

Proudly, she displayed it for Lucky's approval. "Instant reference," she said. He was properly impressed. "Your dad's work?"

"Right. I sort of hinted."

"Good. I've just noticed something else, Pua." He was leafing once more through the reports. "The silent alarms to headquarters aren't working out at all. See, here and here and here, where threats were made if they attempted to use them. And two poor fellows who did were beaten severely when they defied them and stepped on the button. These are mostly old buildings, according to your dad and those antiquated buttons on a squeaky wooden floor are going to give them away every time. "The police work isn't at fault. It's just that the hit is made before they know anything about it. They are afraid of those squeaky buttons. Plus, most of these people are so intimidated, they are afraid to involve the police anyway."

"Oh-oh, in this one a patrolman observed suspicious activity and walked in with his gun at the ready. The suspect at the register put his hands up. A second man who was hiding behind the door shot the officer. Both fled the scene. The officer was shot in the shoulder and is now back at work, according to this note Keoki attached. But his Injury wouldn't heal properly, so he's riding a desk job. "

"Here are copies of arrest reports, Lucky. It's pretty grim reading, believe me. Only three convictions out of a dozen arrests and they were out of Halawa jail in six months or less with insufficient evidence and failure to press charges. You're right. They're all scared to death. I think there's more to all this than meets the eye."

"I agree. I'm more and more convinced that preventive medicine is the key, Pua. And I don't know about you, but I'm beginning to get a picture of a gang effort. The MO's are similar, but nearly every storeowner that has been hit, describes a different person. The merchants aren't much help. They're too frightened to give any useful ID information. And, damn it, in a way you can't blame them."

"It looks like a machine operation to me too, Lucky. Terrorist tactics. Well, we may get a different angle, if this meeting tonight works out."

By eight thirty, only three people had shown up: Keach and the Kimuras. Lucky was about to start the meeting, when there was a tap on the door and the Garcias came in, looking insecure and nervous. Pua filled mugs with coffee and the group gathered around the round table. And then a huge Hawaiian came, introducing himself as Palani Alena, the butcher.

Lucky and Pua opened the meeting. "We appreciate your coming tonight," he began. "And at the outset, I want you to understand that whatever is said in this room is confidential and will be revealed only if you authorize its use, personally. My associate and I are private investigators and unless any of you are criminals--

182

" He paused, as the first uncertain smiles were exchanged. "--Lucky Seven is obligated to work only for you and in your best interest. "

Mrs. Kimura spoke up, shyly, "But what about Pua? She's Major Kanai's daughter. Isn't that almost like police? Those men say they'll hurt or kill our family if we talk to the police."

Pua held up her hand. "You know my father, Keiko-chan. You know he is honorable. Do you really think that he would put any of you, or the two of us, in a position of danger? He understands your problem and he believes that our plan will allow us to help you and you to help each other, without endangering your lives, or those of your families, or ours. And that's where we come in-- preventive measures and a self-help program involving all of you."

"I'm sorry, Pua. It's just that we're so afraid. Some man tried to pick up our little girl at school one day, but she ran back to the teacher and he left. I just so scared."

Lucky said gently. "Listen to what we have to say, Mrs. Kimura and if at any time you feel our plan won't work, or will endanger you and your family, please don't feel that you need to stay. What we propose is a volunteer group action of self-protection for you folks. You already know you haven't been able to do this alone."

"We would like to propose that you join forces with us and help yourselves, with our assistance."

"Sounds good to me," said Keach.

"Then let's hear from you, Mr. Keach."

"Name's Albie--call me that. My frame shop was broken into about a month ago, in the middle of the night it was and nothing was taken; but the whole place was a wreck when I came in the next morning. Expensive frames were broken and tossed every which way. A stack of frame material, already beautifully beveled--monkey pod, oak and teak--was sprayed with red paint and hammered. My tools had been covered with my own glue."

"You say nothing was taken?"

"Not then. But a few nights later a guy came in just before I closed. He had a gun in one hand and was covering his face with a--what do you call it--bandanna-- he just held it across his face; and he told me, 'Mr. Keach, you had a little trouble in here. It could get worse. This stuff would burn pretty good. You need us. We'll see it doesn't happen again, if you give us $100 every week for our service. That's not much to pay for security, is it?' That's about it. I couldn't forget his words. He was so damn sure of himself."

"I told him I didn't keep money in the shop and he said, 'That's okay --just bring some on Friday."

"Now I make a pretty good living; have Bishop Museum, Honolulu Art Center, retail art galleries and stores that buy my frames regularly, besides the private owners--but $100 a week for protection? --I only pay a little more than that for rent!"

Shaking with remembered anger, he continued, "I called the police the next day and told them about it and an officer was hiding in the shop when Friday evening rolled around. The guy never showed up. But before I was out of bed next morning, my phone rang--at home, mind you--and a woman's raspy voice said, 'Mr. Keach, you don't listen very good. You were told not to call the police. Now it's going to cost you $200 a week, unless, of course, that daughter of yours needs a loan for her hospital bills.'

"I yelled at her, 'what bills? There's nothing wrong with my daughter!'"

"And she said, 'Not yet, but the University Campus is not very safe sometimes. And then there's your wife. What a pity if she couldn't go on teaching hula because of an accident to her legs. Think about that, Mr. Keach.' And she hung up.

"I don't scare easy, but that plain terrified me. That afternoon I put Mama and Lei on a plane for Kauai. They've been at my sister-in-law's place ever since.

"And," he sighed, shame-faced, "so far I've paid a total of $600. The first time I planned to hand over an envelope with paper in it and take him on when he reached for it. But before I could, he said to me, 'How are things on the neighbor islands?' Need I say I shelled out?"

"So you've been paying ever since?"

"Right. I can't afford not to. But it'll break me sooner or later. As it is, I can't even afford to hire a helper, let alone keep giving them money. Thanks to a scholarship my daughter won, we were assured with what we could contribute, she'd be able to go to UH and get her Masters, but with this--" He buried his face in his hands. And there was a long silence.

"That's almost like happen' to us," Mrs. Garcia said. "Tell them, Jose."

"Maria! You say too much. I'm not talking."

"You do, or I do!" she answered firmly. And when he didn't speak, she went on, "The first time, a man came in to eat my enchiladas. I pay no attention to him and he pays his bill and left. When I clear up table I see a note. It say 'Nice place. It's too bad if it gets trashed. My people protect you for $50 a week. Put in mailbox on Tuesday. Use the mailbox where you live. And he signed it, Jose? Nice Heart Protection Agency?"

"Good Heart, Maria, Good Heart! You get all mix up. You forgot he said in note, 'don't get funny and call police. They can be hazardous to your health, 'or something' like that.'"

"We pay one time in our mailbox and next time Jose say 'To hell with them guys.' That's when they came in kitchen door after we close up and beat up Jose and tomorrow me in corner and take our moneybag all ready for night deposit. I try chase him, but he disappear; and then police came. We didn't call them, they just came."

"Could you identify the man?"

"No. First time he was jus' customer. I don't pay attention. Next time he had blue rag thing over part face. All I know, he smelled bad, like stale beer and he had on dirty plaid shirt."

"Were either of you hurt badly?" Lucky's face was a study of concern and anger. "Ambulance took Jose to Emergency and they sewed up cut, there on his cheek still scar, but they hit him on head. Mexicans have hard heads. I hit my head, got dizzy a minute, that's all."

"You didn't pay them any more?"

"No, but some woman call, say our bill now $150 past due and we better save up for when they come collect."

The butcher had been listening attentively. "Okay, count me in," he said. "When they came after me, I picked the guy up by the seat of his pants and threw him out the door. Puny fellow, he was. Oriental. Know what they did then?

"Shoved a demand through the mail slot. I ignored it. And on Saturday night after I left, they cut my electricity. Dummies didn't know I had a back-up generator system; so the cold room was okay on Monday, but the stuff I had left in the display case was pau, spoiled.

"It is like an ice chest, with trays for pre-cut meat, but I didn't usually leave anything in it. That night, I was so damned mad, I wanted to get to the police station, so I plain forgot about the steaks and stuff in there.

"While I was gone, they slashed the tires on my delivery van. But the worst was," pain crossed the big, florid face, "the bastards killed my dog--I'd had old Job since he was a pup. Poi dog he was, with the saddest looking eyes you ever saw--that's why I called him Job. They didn't get a dime out of me, but I'm beginning to wonder what the next pilikea will be. I know damn well I haven't heard the last of it. I could sure use some help."

"The police?" Pua said. "You went to them. What happened?"

"Oh, they took my report and came out to the shop, but there were no fingerprints. Did I mention he was wearing cotton work gloves? They want to help, but there's no handle on this thing to get ahold of. I don't blame the police. Like the cop told me, 'It's like walking through a roomful of feathers!'"

"Why didn't you use the silent alarm, when the little man came in that first time?"

"Hell, it was clear in the other room; and after I tossed him out, it was too late. I just went down there."

"You've never paid their demands?"

"Hell, no! But it's cost me plenty, just the same as if I had."

Lucky took a deep breath. "All right, now, unless someone else wants to talk, let's put what we have together and see what we have."

Mrs. Kimura's pale face reddened. "If you no mind," she said, "I like make report private. I had some-- some shame."

"Perfectly all right," Lucky said and both of the Kimuras bowed and thanked him in their native tongue.

"Now, then," Lucky told the group grimly, "What we have here so far is clear evidence that you people are being methodically victimized by an organization, not individuals working independently. The woman on the phone made the reference to 'we' when Albie was confronted. The fact is that they have obviously scouted out information about your families, even the note signed; Good Heart Protection; all definitely pointing to a gang-type operation. Is that a fair statement?"

Eyes met eyes, as they murmured agreement.

Palani raised his hand. "I forgot to mention that when that guy came in my butcher shop, first thing he said was don't try anything. You don't have a chance with us.' Then he told me he was black-belt karate and had friends outside. I'm quicker than I look and I came roaring around the counter and when he kicked at me, I grabbed his leg and the back of his pants and slung him out the open door. He took off. I didn't see anybody else, but I was so mad I couldn't see much of anything--the idea of a wiry little squirt like that challenging me!"

"But your family wasn't threatened?"

"I don't have a family on this island. Just old Job-- and he's gone now."

Pua looked up from her notes. "It seems that most of the attacks happen during afternoon or evening hours. Some of the other complaints indicate that, as well; and threats to family and property seem to be general. Also, it seems that all the culprits fled on foot. Somebody must be hanging around to pick them up, unless they have a hang-out around here."

"We'll have to look into that. It's a cinch they don't just melt away."

Albie Keach was stirring impatiently. "We need some more storekeepers in on this. Can we have another meeting soon?"

"Absolutely. Can each of you do some recruiting?" Again there was general agreement and Albie added, "We need a little more information on this. First, you two are in business to make a living. How do you figure to handle that? We don't expect a free ride, but neither can we afford the kind of money you can haul down."

"That's the beauty of our plan," Lucky smiled. "If we can get at least ten of you merchants to participate, we can get by for as little as $25 a week from each business. We're not in this for the big bucks. We're eager to establish ourselves as a viable agency to solve such problems as you people are caught up in. We want to stop this systematic draining of your resources, the threats and the destruction, without it costing you a bundle."

"Sounds more than fair to me," Albie said and the others echoed his sentiments. "It's a hell of a lot better than shelling out $100 or $200 a week to these creeps who are wrecking our lives. Can we call you, if we need you?"

"Absolutely. We expect you to. And we won't go into it tonight, but you must realize that the basis of our defense of you lies in your willingness to organize to help yourselves. Pua and I have been working out a plan in which all of you can participate, safely, though unarmed. This is not a vigilante operation. We'll go into details at our next meeting. Let's try for Thursday. Okay? We'll let you know."

And as he closed this initial session, spontaneous applause broke out in the room.

190

Chapter 19

After the rest had gone, carefully spacing their leaving time as Lucky had suggested, he turned to Mrs. Kimura. "You had a special problem?" he asked gently.

She looked beseechingly at her husband, then said, "I so 'shame, I not tell before. But I know it too important. If I tell someone else the same man might hurt us. Then it would be my fault. And I'm afraid for my little girl, too. You say you no tell others bad part my story?"

Lucky smiled, reassuringly. "We won't tell anyone anything you want to keep personal."

Glancing nervously at Pua, she said, "You such nice young woman--maybe you shouldn't hear. It isn't nice what I tell."

"If you really want me to leave, I will. But I have been trained in all kinds of police work just like Lucky and I'd like to help."

"I like you stay, then. I tell both." She took a deep breath and once more sought the eyes of her husband for strength. He smiled encouragement. "One night haole man came to door just after we close. Say wife left gold lighter in restaurant, when they had early dinner. I look, but no find and he look angry like maybe I steal, so I say "come look for self"--and let him in. Papa went out back for put out trash and burn papers in inclinator.

"This man, he push me to cash drawer, where I been count money and grab all bills; then say, "You got more?" I told him no more and he makes mean face.

191

"He say, 'Okay, pretty Japan lady, I take out in trade" and start push me into tatami room." She blushed painfully and lowered her eyes. "Then he try take off my kimono--tug at obi till it tear--then throw me down on tatami mat and hunch down over me, an' tug top part kimono 'way down--and try put mouth over my--" Mr. Kimura reached over and patted her hand. "Is okay you tell," he whispered.

She took a deep breath. "Then he pulled at his pants. I so scared.

"I hear Papa drop can outside and I hope come back in: and man look up, like scared. Then he came at me again.

"I start scream, but he put hand over my face hard and say he kill me and Papa if I don't shut up. Then he reach and pull down his zipper in pants and--and pulled my hand down--there. I yell. And then I--I--"

"Go on, Keikochan," her husband said, as she hesitated.

Blushing furiously now, she said, "I didn't care he kill me or not. I push him back and hit him hard as can down there--in the--tender, man place--and he double up, swear, making moan sound; and let my hand go. When he look up, he say, 'Now I kill you.'

"I grab Shabu Shabu pot off end of table, where broth boiling and throw it over him. He yells and made scream sound and hit me with fist; and then try run away. Papa hear man and me yell all the way back yard, come rush in and man knock him down too and then run out."

192

"How brave you were!" Pua exclaimed. "What a dreadful experience! But how did the boiling soup happen to be cooking there so late?"

"Oh, Papa and me, we eat after clean up place and that night he want Shabu Shabu. Vegetables and meat already cut and in frig. No foods in pot yet, you see, just water, seaweed, shoyu, spices from Japan. Simmer long time make better. Shabu Shabu cook fast when broth boil good. If we not have it that night, I don' know what happen." She shuddered.

"Well, I still say you were very brave, to hit him like that. You used a lot of common sense for one so frightened. And Keikochan, you shouldn't feel embarrassed. You didn't do anything wrong. You were wonderful!"

For the first time, the woman's face reflected satisfaction. "I very' mad, so I did it. I stiff-arm him good. No big thing," she said. "They taught us best defense in karate class Papa made me take when we open our place.

"They tell me, if bad thing happen, jus' jab hard that soft part. Kick, yell, do what must to save self." She shuddered again. "I never have to use what I learn, before. I hope never again."

"You didn't see him or the woman after that night?" asked Lucky.

"No, but big reason I tell story now is that two days after, some man try to pick up our daughter Emi, like I said. We tell her never talk to stranger or ride with stranger and she 'member that and run back in school. Her aunt pick her up ever' day since then. Her auntie always keep her till we get home. That's why I tell you whole story. I scared for Emi. And that man might rape some lady who don' know karate. "

Lucky and Pua were staring at her with a mixture of admiration and sick dismay. "Weren't you burned when you threw the broth?" Pua's voice was ragged with concern.

"She burned all right," Mr. Kimura said angrily. "Show, Keiko." And he helped her push back her long sleeves to reveal ugly red scars. "Hands too." As she opened them, they saw the deep scars the hot pot had left.

"When did this happen?" Pua asked.

"Two week, yesterday. No hurt much now. Papa keep put special Japan tea poultice on--ver' good for burn."

Lucky was looking through the reports, again. "I can't find anything here about that incident, even about the robbery," he said.

The woman looked up, horrified. "We no tell nothing to police. Only you. I no want lose face. If I tell about robbery, I 'fraid they ask more. So I no tell any of it."

Her husband looked away and said, his voice shaking, "I cannot go against her in this. I love her. I could not bear for her hang her head in shame. It's Japanese way."

"I see. Mrs. Kimura, may I ask you a few additional questions?" Lucky spoke gently, but with urgency. "It's very important."

194

"Yes, Sir, if help. I trust you."

"Can you describe the man?"

"He some tall, with light hair, light blue eyes, hard and, how you say? too shiny. He had on gray coat at dinnertime, but not later. He sweat a lot. I remember wife. That help?"

"Yes, it would."

"She look older, have red hair, dyed kind and sour face. She no like Japanese food and complain. She smoke all time, drinks sake, not eat much. They no talk, no laugh--just stare 'round and whisper some. I try please them. She tell me, 'Get lost--we call if we want you,' and she talk rough, like have sore throat."

"Which one paid the bill?"

"She did, said 'awful lot to ask for that garbage.' I say nothing, but hope she don' come back."

"Those descriptions may help a lot. You'll probably never recover the money, though, you understand."

" Mr. Kimura spoke up. "We don't worry about money, just our daughter and other women.

" Lucky cleared his throat. "Now I need your permission to discuss your problems with Major Kanai-- not the intimate details--just enough so he knows what the attacker looks like and how dangerous he is. Do you trust me to do that?"

She looked first at her husband and then back at Lucky. "I no have to say nothing or go to police station?"

"I don't believe so. I have to ask you to trust us. We won't do anything to endanger you, or embarrass you.

" She looked into his face searchingly. "I trust you to do what's right. I no worry."

"Thank you. You won't have cause to regret your trust."

"We let you know if we see those people again," Mr. Kimura said. "I feel good now, Mama-Chan, don't you?"

She reassured him with a little smile and together, the couple bowed deeply in the polite fashion of their race, murmured "Arigato" and departed.

As she closed the door, Pua said sadly, "That poor woman. With her background, it must have been terribly difficult to tell us her story. I can't help but feel admiration for her. She looks so fragile, yet she's as spunky as she can be."

Lucky grinned. "I think she's pretty good at handling herself in tight situations. That chop she gave her assailant must have shocked the hell out of him and hurt like the devil. And that boiling soup! Wow! But good Lord, Pua, this attempted rape presents a whole new pattern, doesn't it? I have a strong feeling, though, that it was his own idea, prompted by his disappointment in the amount of money he got and the fact that Keiko is such an attractive little thing.

"Frankly, I don't believe his bosses, whoever they are, would go for that kind of action. They're in business to intimidate, terrify and take money; but rape is a crime that carries a lot of heat. I doubt that they even know they have such a deviant in their employ. The last thing they want is that kind of publicity."

"There's nothing in the reports to indicate such a crime has been attempted before."

"Not a thing of that nature has come up, anyway, although that business of someone trying to pick up the little girl has me concerned. We'll talk it over with Keoki."

"The meeting tonight was productive, don't you think so, Lucky?"

"Indeed I do. I could sense new purpose and comradeship--along with good, healthy anger--and they don't even know the details of our program yet. They've had their fill of trying to fight their battles alone, or just knuckle under; and they're talking cooperation instead of any sort of independent action. Thank God for that."

Lucky picked up one of the reports. "Listen to this, from the pawn shop robbery three weeks ago: 'Perpetrator described as medium-tall, 185-190 pounds, blond medium-long hair, glassy, light-blue eyes, clean-shaven, age mid-thirties. Victim said he was 'on something, probably dope.' I knew that Keiko's description of her assailant rang a bell. This guy must be a regular on the crew."

"All the more reason to alert dad, huh?"

"Right. Yep, I think we made a lot of progress tonight, but I was sorry Albie brought up the fee thing before they even know what we're all about. They did seem eager to get it on a business basis, though. I guess it's like my mom taught me long ago--paying one's fair share is a sign of dignity and integrity. They have a right to that."

"And they have a choice, which they certainly haven't been getting from these toughs," Pua added.

He shuffled the reports together. "Hey, you must be hungry, Pua darling. You've had a big day."

"I could eat," she admitted. "What will you have? I'll cook."

"No, honey. I'm hungry for a great big pizza with everything on it. I'll have one sent in."

"Great! But have 'em hold the anchovies, huh?" He was already at the phone. "And hold the anchovies," she heard him say and smiled approval.

"So what's up for tomorrow?" she asked as he returned to the table.

"Well, first thing I want to do is report our progress to your dad; and then go talk with that electronics wizard he recommended and see what he can provide in the way of inter-store communication. Remember those pressure-sensitive deals they demonstrated at the Police Academy-sponsored Citizens' Self Help Conference? Activated a bell or light in a separate location as a warning signal? That's the kind of plan I want to explore."

Pua nodded agreement and then jumped, as the doorbell rang.

Lucky started for the door. "There's our pizza; they made good time. Why don't you pour us some milk, while I take care of it."

"Ooh, it smells heavenly," Pua crooned, as they began their feast. "Now go on. This is a fascinating concept."

"Hard to talk and eat this," he grinned, munching contentedly. "Anyway, that's what I have on my mind for the morning. I'll lay the idea on electronics professional and we'll see what he comes up with. I'll meet you here after I get the answer and by then we'll know how to go on with it. Your dad gave me a business card, ElektroShak; I think it's called. Says a Mr. Henley is the man to see. He's done work for the police department."

"So, given the signaling devices, what comes next?" Pua asked, between bites.

"Getting the merchants' personal involvement worked out; and that is a whole different subject. We can work on that tomorrow, too. Realistically, I don't know how much significance their participation will have-- maybe a lot, maybe little--but the big thing is to make them feel that they have an opportunity to help each other any time one of them is in trouble."

"Have you a definite plan in mind?"

"I guess it could be called definite. The way I see it, these crimes are usually happening when there are few if any people in the place of business. I've been over and over those reports and most of the problems have occurred late in the afternoon or early evening, or around the noon hour, depending apparently on the type of business.

"Somebody's got to be casing each place to find out when each merchant is most vulnerable. They expose too much knowledge of the area and the people, for it to be coincidence. It may be that they have some kind of a back-up plan of their own.

"What I'd like to have happen, is for everyone who can possibly get away, when alerted by the signal, to get out on the street and move toward the spot under attack, as quickly, but as casually as possible; and keep an eye out for anything suspicious--like a car in an unlikely spot, or someone running from the premises, --or even running from the vicinity. We've got to find out where these miscreants get to and how. They don't sink into the earth. Every single report in which the victim tried to run after a culprit states that they just seem to disappear. We've got to solve that. Is all this making any sense?"

"Sure is. And wouldn't the merchants have a good chance to identify someone they'd already seen--or even been victimized by-- for example?"

"That just might be a good thing to emphasize. I want to compare identifications on a few of these complaint reports, also; and give all our people a chance to see them. Some people notice one thing; some another and we might get a make by putting some of their descriptions together. Won't hurt to try."

Pua was frowning. "What if they pull a robbery on another store, while our people are out on the street?"

"Well, we'll have to address that problem early on. But in the reports, not once has there been two crimes at the same time; which further suggests that it's an organized crime operation, well choreographed to avoid complications.

God knows it's been working for them."

"Wow! That pizza really hit the spot, but I've had it." Lucky stretched and patted his stomach.

"I'm pau too and I hate to admit it, but I'm exhausted," Pua said, sipping the last of her milk. "Think I'll go over to my pad, have a hot shower and go to bed. It looked comfortable, if a bit overwhelming. Have to face it sometime. I just hope I don't push that button in my sleep and get buried alive! Oh, I just remembered. I don't have the car, you know. How about a lift in the Golden Monster?"

"Easy," he said. "I wish you would stay here, though." He took her into his arms and kissed her with a special tenderness. "We're a good team, Pua. We belong together you know, my darling," he whispered.

"I know," and her smile was radiant. "But be patient, love, okay?"

"Okay, me proud beauty," he said severely, twirling a non-existent mustache; "but I'll have me way with you yet. Wait and see."

"You nut!" she laughed and made her escape, Lucky close behind.

Chapter 20

The coffee had been brewed and Lucky had already gone by the time she got in the next morning. She felt restless, without him there; so she poured a cup of coffee and let her thoughts ramble.

To her own amazement, she had slept very well in Alika's strange, but comfortable bed. Her cousin had come a long way from the Kauai sugar cane fields, where he worked as a teenager. In those days he had slept and quite soundly, in one of the narrow, hard bunks the company provided. Now, he showed a healthy taste for the good life.

"Chuckling to herself, she began to sort the case histories, checking names against the locations on the chart.

It was going well and the hours sped by. She checked her watch. Then she heard steps in the hall and ran to open the door.

"Hi, honey, you're--oh, I'm sorry Jake. I was expecting Lucky."

"So I gathered," he said, with an amused leer. "Come on in. He should be here around noon, I think.

Can I help you?"

"Well, yes, I guess that would be all right, you being a partner and all. You can pass it on. An odd thing happened this morning before you came in and the more I thought about it, the more I felt you should know." He scowled and scratched his head.

202

"Is something wrong? You look worried. Here, have a cup of coffee and we'll talk."

"Thanks--just black, please. Well, I don't know if it means anything or not. A rough looking character came by while I was checking licenses and asked me if I was the manager--and then went on to ask about rentals. Said he needed an office. I didn't like the looks of him and told him we didn't have any available.

"'You do have offices in the building, don't you?' he asked me; and before I could speak, he told me he was a private investigator and was trying to locate some colleagues who had moved into the area."

"Oh, Lord," Pua breathed.

"Now don't get excited. I told him we specialized in mail order firms and had a couple of public relations offices--which we have--and suggested he tell me the names of his colleagues."

"He said, 'No need, I'll keep looking,' and left. I got a strong impression he plain didn't know the names. Now it could be nothing at all, but I thought you and Lucky ought to know about it. He seemed so damned sneaky. But he did appear satisfied that this wasn't the right place."

"You'd never seen him around here before?"

"I don't believe so--and yet, somehow he looked familiar. Like maybe I saw his picture in the paper or something."

Lucky stuck his head in the door. "Mind if I come in? --Oh, Jake, I didn't see you. What's up? You look like a man with a problem."

"I don't know. I just may be reaching for trouble, Lucky, but you be the judge." He proceeded to repeat his story.

"Oh, boy," Lucky sighed. "It sounds as if someone in the gang has some suspicions about us, doesn't it."

"That's what I figured, but it may have been a fishing expedition only. He seemed to accept what I told him; and I watched where he went. He high-tailed it for the Clybern Building up on the next corner. They rent to a couple of shoddy Pi's there. The way I get it, those guys just chase down cheating husbands and wives for divorce lawyers--that sort of stuff."

"Well," said Lucky, "thanks for alerting us. Sooner or later somebody's going to get wise to us. I was hoping for later. But you handled it just right and I'm grateful. How about more coffee?"

"Thanks, but I haven't time. Plumber's coming. It beats all how folks will stuff the damndest things down the luas. Take care, now."

"Hey, give me a smile," Lucky coaxed; "and don't be upset about this Nosey Parker. It may be a coincidence. If it isn't, we can deal with it. It's no big thing, anyway. We knew we couldn't keep it secret indefinitely."

She smiled up at him. "Okay, Mr. Right, I'll take your word for it."

"Better had," he growled. "I stopped by to thank your dad for the TV and fill him in on our progress; and darned if a report didn't come in that seems to be right up our alley.

"You know that little place next door to the frame shop, where they have fabrics and all that sewing stuff, the shop where women can get sewing lessons?"

"Yes, I've noticed it, but I've never been in there."

"Well, when the owner--Stella Conley I think her name is--opened up this morning, her yardage was unrolled and scattered all over the place, spools of thread slung everywhere, tables turned over--a general mess. Police answered her call; and it's the same old story. No prints, nothing taken, a hole cut in the glass front door, so it could be unlocked from the inside."

"How awful! Had she had any trouble before?"

"No. And she swears she claimed she hasn't had any warning or threats. But somehow, neither Keoki nor I buy that. She was more frightened than angry. We talked with her, when they brought her in to file a complaint and there was something about her behavior that didn't ring quite true. I have a strong hunch that she's afraid to spill all she knows.

"Keach stayed in her shop doing his best to get it back in some kind of order. They're good friends and I have a feeling that he may persuade her to tell the whole story. I wouldn't be surprised if she shows up with him at our next meeting. I hope so. These people have got to fight back, or go down for the count."

"I know. Did you eat, Lucky?"

"I had breakfast. What do you say we walk down

to Kimura's place--what is it called--Keikoya, named after her, I presume. Don't Japanese noodles with a side of tempura sound good for lunch?"

"You're making my mouth water. Let's go." On the way, they passed Palani's butcher shop and decided to stop in on their way back. They were surprised at how busy the small store was. He was cutting a steak to order as they passed, holding it out to his customer for approval.

"I'm surprised," Pua admitted. "It looks to me as if he is a real old-fashioned-type butcher. No pre-packed 'you takes what you gets' meats in there."

They were equally surprised at the small, but delightful restaurant the Kimura's owned. The dining room held only a few booths and tables, but on the far side they could see past the sliding shoji doors into a tatami room with its pale tatami mat, low table and floor cushions. Everything was neat and clean and Keiko herself was charming in her colorful kimono and obi. She welcomed them warmly.

"I hope we're not too early," Pua said. "We're hungry for noodles and tempura."

"I bring soon," and Keiko hurried away. When she returned, she brought two bowls of steaming noodles with bits of fishcake, green onion tops and thin bamboo shoots, topped with a shredded seaweed garnish. And then a plate heaping with golden, deep-fried shrimp and fresh vegetables, luscious in their fragile, crisp coating. She added a pot of tea and little bowls of the crunchy vegetable pickles called namasu. They found it an

206

altogether satisfying and tasty lunch and when they complimented her, she smiled and bowed her thanks.

She stopped by again, to see if everything was satisfactory and confided to them, "Papa is pleased you are here. He likes to come greet you, but he is so busy cooking. He does all cooking by self, you know."

"Please give him our Aloha and tell him we think his food is marvelous," Pua said.

"Arigato, that make him very happy," Keiko responded.

As they left, Pua whispered to Lucky, "I can't believe that dignified little man does all this cooking. I thought he must be an accountant or something like that."

"Surprised me too, but the food is great. We'll have to bring your mom and dad to dinner here one night."

At the butcher shop, Palani welcomed them proudly. "Here you see my place! What can I get you?"

"Steaks?" Lucky asked her and as she nodded, "two nice thick steaks."

"I have a fine tenderloin today. How about a couple of filet Mignons? Guaranteed to cut with a fork."

They accepted his suggestion and watched as he cut the meat to the proper thickness and skillfully wrapped each one with bacon, securing it with a small wooden pick. Before wrapping their order, he held it out for their approval. "There you are--anything else today?"

"Not today. Those are super," Lucky said.

As Palani packaged their purchase, he told them, "I'm going to slip a little of my own pate in with this--on the house. Just spread a little on top of the steaks before you serve them."

As they walked on, Lucky said, "I didn't know these little neighborhood places existed any more. It reminds me of the small town where I lived as a child. And Pua, we've got to do everything we can to keep them in business. Let's go get busy."

"I'm not trying to rush you, but now that you've had lunch, would you tell me what you found out this morning? About the signaling devices, I mean."

"The news is all good. This man, Chuck Henley, is an electronics nut and he has already built a system for his place that works on a remote control. And when he found out why we were in the market, he said he'd sell us all we need at cost plus. He's even willing to install them for us."

"I don't know how you do it, Lucky. Things just seem to fall in place for you. But what if some of the merchants don't feel they can afford them?"

"Oh, heck, Pua, a unit can't be all that expensive. We can work that out. I'll foot the bill for now and if they want to buy their own we'll let them, but the success of the operation depends on them, so I'm going to see that every association member has one and soon. Besides, I got a good deal on my car--and my TV was a gift--I'm rich, baby."

"How soon will this communication system be ready?"

"Henley says he can start installing by the day after tomorrow. Says there's nothing to it, but he wants to make sure they are right. Hopefully, by Monday, our key members will already have them."

As they reached the building lobby, they saw Albie waiting with an attractive middle-aged woman. She seemed pale and nervous, but there was a determined set to her jaw.

"Hi," Albie said. "Could you spare us a few minutes time? This is Mrs.Conley--Stella--."

"Yes, we met this morning. And this is my associate, Pua. Come on up."

The woman smiled tremulously and attempted to smooth the disarray from her hair, as they entered the elevator. Her gray eyes reflected a haunting kind of fear. Albie patted her hand.

Once inside the office, they moved to the round table and Pua excused herself to bring in iced tea for their refreshment.

"Lucky, we don't like to barge in before the meeting--"

"No problem. Go right ahead, Mrs.--"

"Stella," she interrupted. "Please call me Stella. Well, when the police wanted to take me to headquarters, I didn't want to go, but they persuaded me. So I went back to my restroom to freshen up and there, taped to the mirror, was a note. Here it is."

Lucky read it aloud. "Good morning, Mrs. Conley.

I was here yesterday to pick up that insurance money, but you closed early, shame on you. Too bad you weren't insured against what happened in the night, but that's nothing to what will happen if you don't pay. And I don't want to see any police around here either. When I call, you come--and you better have the money with you. Its signed GHPA."

Pua gasped. "Good Heart Protection Agency!"

"Has to be," Lucky agreed. "They must have figured you to burn this or throw it away, Stella. They wouldn't have left it around, if they had any idea you would fight back."

"I didn't know what to do; and the officer was waiting to take me to headquarters--so I just tore it off and shoved it in my purse. I was so frightened, I said as little as I could to the police--like some kids did that damage to be mean or something. I didn't want to lie, but--"

"You're not going to be in trouble with the police, Stella. You did what you thought best, under the circumstances."

"That's a relief. Anyway, when I got back, I talked to Albie--Mr. Keach--and he insisted on bringing me to you."

"We're glad he did. You know, this looks as if it were typed on one of those kiddie typewriters. See where it's smudged? The bottom is torn off, too."

"That tore when I pulled it off the mirror."

"Is that little piece of paper and the tape still on the

mirror?"

"It must be. I was so busy trying to get my shop back together, that I forgot all about it."

"Good. Maybe we have a thumbprint. The smudges on the paper smack of cotton gloves--but it would be no easy task to apply that tape with gloves on. Did you ever see him?"

"No. When he called me the first time, he told me to put the money in an envelope and stick it under the windshield wiper of my truck out back. And go back inside. The money was gone, when I closed up to go home."

"You didn't try to peek out the window?"

"There aren't any windows in the back."

"How often have you paid?"

"Just twice. That first time; and then when he called and told me my building was a firetrap and might burn down, he said the premium was $75 a week, starting that day. I said I couldn't pay that much and he just said, 'Pay it, silly woman,' and hung up. I really didn't have the money; so after sewing class was over a little before four, I closed up and went home. I was terrified. I didn't know what else to do."

"This last call came in yesterday?"

"Oh, no, day before yesterday."

"God, Stella," Albie groaned, "I wish you'd told me then."

"I started to, but you had customers; and then I
211

knew you had problems of your own, so I thought I ought to handle it myself."

"But we've got to stick together, or we're all going down the drain. Anyway, Lucky, that's why I brought her here today, while it was fresh in her mind. She wants to join our association. Right, Stella?"

"I certainly do. Things have been going so well until this happened and now I worry about the women who take my sewing lessons. They're in there for two hours, twice a week. What if he did start a fire?"

He conferred briefly with Pua and then said, "You both go back to your stores and Pua will visit you, Stella. If someone is there, she'll make like a customer; and then ask to use your restroom. She'll recover that piece of tape; and will hang around--maybe take a sewing lesson for cover, just in case he calls today. What time do you usually leave?"

"Five, ordinarily. Sometimes a little later."

"If the phone rings, let Pua answer it. She'll take it from there. Now you two go back to work--business as usual. Pua will be along soon."

After they left, Lucky said, "Now watch yourself, Pualani and call me right away if you hear from the creep. Don't get any fancy ideas and blow it. You have your gun in your bag, just in case--"

"Lucky, stop it, I was a cop, remember? I can handle it. And grinning impishly, to take away the sting from her words, she offered him a pert little salute and strolled, hips switching provocatively, to the elevator.

Chapter 21

The scrap of note was still on the mirror. Pua used tweezers, to be certain she didn't contaminate evidence, slipped it into a small bag and into her handbag for safekeeping. The mirror had been wiped clean.

When she returned to the sales room, a customer was there; and a glazier was repairing the front door; so she shopped around a little.

"I will have an opening for sewing classes next week, if you're interested," Stella told her, with a tiny conspiratorial wink. Feel free to examine my brochure there and I'll be with you in a few minutes. Turning to the woman, she said, "That is a becoming print for you and this deep turquoise is the same fabric as the print. It would be nice for the contrasting material called for in your pattern, don't you think?"

"They're perfect together. Thank you, Stella. Figure how much I need of each and add in the findings-- if you can find them in this mess. What a mean thing for anybody to do!"

Stella looked around, grimacing. "If you think this is bad, you should have seen it this morning. Mr. Keach put a lot of things back in place. No problem about locating what you need.

"I'm going to add a little extra of each fabric in case there's a soiled spot," Stella said, apologetically. Some of my stock was damaged. I don't see anything, but if there is something wrong, you bring it back." The woman smiled her thanks, paid and left.

Stella moved back to where Pua waited and with a sigh, slumped into a chair. "I'm exhausted. Nerves, I guess. Why don't I make us a cup of tea?"

"Let me," Pua said. "I saw your hot plate over there and put the kettle on."

"That's so nice of you. I just can't understand why I feel so pep-less."

"Being invaded that way takes the starch out of anyone. You try to relax a little. Do you take sugar or anything?"

"No, dear, but there's some there, if you do." Pua eyed the back door. Near it was an array of tumbled fabrics that had obviously taken the brunt of the vandalism.

"What do you plan to do with these materials?" she asked. "Surely you don't intend to throw them out."

Stella sighed again. "No, I'm going to take them home and wash them. Then I'll either use them myself for my classes, or put them on a 'as-is' sales table. Haven't really thought about it much." As Pua appeared with two steaming cups of tea, she added, "That smells so good. Tea is always so comforting, don't you think?"

They were talking easily, when the phone rang and Pua, with a silencing gesture, lifted it and listened.

It was a woman's voice and her first words were, "Listen, don't talk. We want you to get the money into an envelope--$75--and put it under the windshield wiper like you done before. Do it now and then stay away from the back. Don't go out there, or even look out there until five.

214

What's happened so far is peanuts, compared to what we'll do if you don't follow these orders. And no police! This is your last warning!" There was a click and then the dial tone.

"Someone is coming to pick up the money, Stella. Now don't worry. Put a few bills in an envelope and we may just catch him --or her--red-handed."

She dialed Lucky Seven. "Someone's coming for the money, Lucky," she said, as he answered. "I'm going to try something. Will you contact dad and the two of you pay a visit to your friend Albie--in his back room, around four o'clock? No police car, okay? Just wait for me to call you. I don't have time to talk now."

"Pua," he roared. "What do--" But Pua had already broken the connection.

As Stella handed her a manila envelope, she said, "I only have $35 in cash."

"Not to worry, just so there's some money in it. Are your car doors locked?"

"No. Something's wrong with one of them, so I don't bother. It's just an old Ford pick-up, with storage lockers on each side. It was my late husband's. He was a painter. It runs all right, so it's handy. Sometimes I pick up my own orders--saves me delivery bills."

"Great! Now listen, you grab a big armful of that cloth and toss it in the back of it; then put the envelope on the windshield; and come back in. I'll take out the rest. But I won't be coming back inside. Now don't argue, Stella and be quick. Timing is going to be important. Has

215

the glazier gone yet?"

"Yes. He finished just a few minutes ago. Should I lock up?"

"No, I don't believe so. It should all seem as normal as possible, just in case someone out front is watching. You're not expecting anyone, are you?"

"No. My customers are at home getting dinner ready, I should think." And she gathered up an armload of fabrics and went on her mission.

"When she returned, Pua told her, you stay put in here, until one of us comes for you. Don't admit anyone but Albie, Lucky, my father, or me. Promise?"

Stella agreed mutely, but her eyes were wide with anxiety.

Pua quickly removed her pistol from her purse, checked it; then caught up the remaining fabrics, drawing a length over her head and arms; and slipped out the alley door and into the back of the truck, burrowing under the stack of materials, trying to hide herself completely. The high sides of the vehicle were an unexpected blessing.

She made herself as comfortable as possible and, heart pounding, prepared for what might be an hour's wait. She grinned to herself, thinking of Lucky. She'd be in big trouble with him if this didn't pan out. Probably be in the doghouse anyway. But, blast it all, he'd promised to let her use her head. And this was her chance."

She felt no sense of peril. She figured she would probably be the only one with a gun and she knew how to use it and was a crack shot, at that. Time dragged by.

Cautiously, she did her isometrics to avoid muscle cramps. And then she heard it, a swishing sound and a clink of metal against metal, quite near. Then footsteps. Near, too. How come she hadn't heard them before? The steps stopped and she heard the snap of the windshield wiper. Now!

With smooth swiftness, she stood up, extending her gun firmly in both hands over the top of the cab. The man was stuffing the envelope into his pocket and looked up, startled into immobility by her sudden appearance.

"Move one inch and you're a dead man!" she said in a voice sure to carry authority. "Now slowly, slowly, I said, clasp your hands over your head. Do it now!"

He stared at her, mouth agape. "Who in the hell are you?" he growled, as he obeyed her order. "How'd you get there?"

"Never you mind. Just hold that position."

"You ain't gonna shoot me, not right here in this alley." He made a move to lower his arms. "You ain't got the guts."

"Try me!" Her voice and face were grim, the gun steady in her hands. He froze.

"Dad, Lucky? You there?" she called.

They burst out Albie's back door, guns at the ready.

"Police. Spread 'em," said her father and Lucky lifted her out of the truck bed and held her close for a second. Then he turned to Keoki, who was reading the

217

man his rights and searching him.

"He's clean," Keoki said. "Bring my car around, will you, Lucky and we'll take him in. Nice work, Pua."

"Thanks. Better cuff him Dad. He's got an envelope full of money that belongs to Mrs. Conley in his pocket. Don't want him to accidentally lose that on purpose."

"The hell it is hers!" the prisoner protested. "This seventy-five bucks is my pay."

"I don't remember anyone saying anything about $75, do you?" Pua smiled grimly. And Keoki, locking the cuffs in place, could not resist a grin of paternal pride.

"I'm going in to see Stella for a minute," Pua announced, with firm, unruffled dignity, "and then I'll ride in with you."

"Go ahead. We'll wait for you." Stella met her at the door and hugged her. Albie was right behind her, beaming.

"Are you all right? Is it all over? What does he look like?" Both Stella and Albie were questioning her eagerly.

Pua opened the door a crack. "Take a look. Do either of you recognize him?"

"I don't think I ever saw him before in my life," Stella answered, while Albie simply shook his head.

"You go along home, then, whenever you're ready, Stella. We'll be in touch with you after we hear what he has to say. This affair isn't over yet, but I doubt if you'll have anything to worry about tonight. Just leave a good night light on, okay? I'm sure a patrolman will check out the area from time to time tonight."

"Thank you, Pua. You were wonderful. Weren't you frightened?"

"Not really, Stella. It's all part of the job," she answered lightly. And she ran out and got in the car. As Keoki started it, the man in the back seat with Lucky said, suddenly, "What about my bike? I gotta have my bike." Keoki braked to a stop.

"What bike?" he asked sharply.

"The one I came on. There, behind the dumpster.

That's worth a lot more than any $75 and I don't want it to get stolen, or picked up with the trash. What you going to do about it?" Pua was choking back a giggle at his fears of becoming a victim of theft. Keoki grinned at her in empathy; then got out, hoisted the bike into the back of the station wagon and they were off.

"So that's why I couldn't hear him coming down the alley," Pua said. "I heard a sort of whoosh and then a metallic sound--that must have been bike meeting dumpster--and then he was there in a flash. I can thank my hula training for getting me to my feet in time. He almost caught me off guard. Know something? I'm convinced that a bike is the answer to the mystery of the sudden and strange disappearances of other suspects."

"How about that?" Lucky asked the prisoner, who merely grunted and looked morosely out the car window.

Once in his office, Keoki again asked, "Do you

219

want an attorney present?"

"Naw, I ain't done nothin' so why should I bother with one. She's the one needs a mouthpiece," pointing at Pua. "She's the one held a gun on me."

"And what were you doing with the windshield then?"

"I just happened to see some trash there and--"

You stashed your bike and decided to clean up the truck. Is that what you're saying?"

"You got it Dad!"

"And you just happened to be carrying this envelope with your pay in it? Who paid it to you? Who hired you?"

"I don't have to tell you that. I put my money in that there envelope myself. I ought to know."

"Let's take a look, then. I believe you said $75?" Keoki opened the envelope and pulled out three tens and a five. Silently, he spread them on the desk. "Mm, looks like your boss short-changed you."

"That God-damned bitch!" the prisoner exploded, staring at the bills as if hypnotized, his mouth twitching and his eyes glazing, while beads of perspiration formed on his pallid face. "She told me I could keep this for pay-- I needed a fix, man. And I sure as hell need one now and that ain't enough to buy me one." And he lowered his head on the desk and began to cry. "She knows damn well, thirty-five bucks won't buy me one," he sobbed bitterly.

"You mean Mrs. Conley, the owner of the shop? She told you that?"

"Hell no, man, that carrot-topped whore who sends us out." He was shaking and as he looked up, those pale blue eyes seemed to reflect like a mirror. Rather tall, thirtyish, sandy-haired.

Quietly, Keoki asked, "Do you know a woman by the name of Kimura at Keikoya Japanese Restaurant?"

The man stared at him in despair and said hoarsely, "I want a lawyer."

The major pressed his intercom. "Sergeant, come in." Kea entered. "Put him in the holding tank, until his attorney gets here. For now, set a charge of suspicion of attempted robbery and attempted rape. Advise the Medics he's an addict. Here's his ID, but you'd better run a check on him. Somehow I don't think Cyril Underwood is his legal handle. Oh, yes and let him call an attorney."

After they left, Keoki sat looking at Lucky and Pua, a half-smile on his face. "It's a start," he said. "I'll put a man on those two shops for the next few nights. There may be more trouble, you know. This creep is just a flunky though, as far as his bosses are concerned and I have a hunch he's in real trouble with them. They may just figure they lost one and let it go at that. They may move on to another victim, or cool it for a while. You have any input, Lucky? You're pretty quiet."

"I know. Frankly, I'm upset about Pua taking action without consulting us. I specifically ordered her not to do anything to foul up--"

221

"Ordered me! Foul up? I was under the impression we were a team, Lucky Gregory. If we're not, then this whole thing isn't going to work."

"But Pualani--"

"Don't 'but me'; I thought it all out and it went down with nobody hurt and--"

"I'm beginning to realize that. You thought everything out and handled it well. And there wasn't time to take any other course, without losing our mark. Okay, I over-reacted. I'm sorry. I'm proud of you, honey, but I did have this insane urge to turn you over my knee, too."

"Tell me about it!" Keoki laughed. "From the time she was three, she's had a mind of her own. She never was one to be coddled--cuddled maybe--but she craves responsibility like other women crave jewelry and $80 haircuts. You'll just have to give her, her head, if you want to get along with her.

It's a fact as identifying about this girl as her fingerprints."

"Thanks--I think." There was no trace of penitence in her response. Then her face softened. "Heck, fellers, I know you wouldn't be so jumpy about me if you didn't love me. This time I just had something I had to prove. From now on, I expect you both to trust me. If you can't manage that, I'll just have to find someone who will. I mean that."

The men looked at each other, grinned and swiftly raised their arms in surrender, a circumstance that seemed to unsettle Sergeant Kea as he entered the office.

222

"Major," he said, with a puzzled frown, "I have a note about a finger print, but I can't find--"

"Oh my Lord," Pua jumped up and grabbed her purse. "The tape. I got it off the mirror and put it in here. Yes, here it is. The tape looked a little greasy. Maybe the lab can get a thumbprint to match anyway. There was nothing on the mirror--wiped clean. At the least, this one should tell us if our collar is or is not the man who broke in and did the damage, right?"

"You bet. Sometimes, it's just as important for a print not to match. Send it on to the lab, Sergeant. And Kea, Pua wasn't holding us up. She just won a big argument."

"And then blew it by forgetting that blasted print," Pua pouted.

"Like I keep telling you, nobody's infallible," he said. "Frankly, I have a hunch that a different person did the store damage. Drugs haven't done this guy's brains any good. I doubt he's anything but a runner, a bagman perhaps; but you never know for sure unless you check it out. Agree, Lucky?"

"One certainty, in my book, is that this user is the same guy who robbed and made the trouble for the Kimuras. His reaction to it damn near proves he was the guy. We establish that and we've got him by the--by the--short hairs. "

This time, Pua laughed aloud. "Still protecting your little girl's sensibilities, I see," she teased.

Keoki glowered at her. "Pua, behave yourself," he

223

admonished. Then he added, "No huhu?"

"No huhu, makua kane," she responded, blowing him a kiss.

He winked at her and then turned back to Lucky. "In view of this arrest, I need to know a little more about the Kimura incident. Did they tell you how much money he got from them?"

"They sure did, nearly $800. That makes it a decent case, doesn't it? The $35 sure wouldn't do it."

"Right. Now we've got something to hold him on besides the assault on her person. I'd sure like to pin that attempted rape on him. But Japanese women would rather put up with the crime than lose face. God knows it's hard enough to get any rape victim to complain. The trials often result in the victim being treated as a consenting partner. And with the cultural problem--" He sighed deeply. "It's something that has to be resolved soon. Lack of prosecution gives rapists a green light. There are 'way too many of them."

"True," Lucky said soberly.

"Well, the ball's in the prosecutor's court now."

Lucky checked his watch. "You about through for the day, Keoki? How about coming by Lucky Seven for a cold beer?"

"I could sure use one. I've a couple things to check. Won't take long."

"We'll be ready, won't we, Madam PI. That is, if we're still friends?"

She stuck her tongue out at him and told him haughtily, "We are, as long as you both remember what you promised me today."

"We're not about to forget that," her father told her. "Am I correct, Lucky?"

"That you are. We have no choice. We need this gal in our business."

Chapter 22

"Want some cheery news?" Keoki asked, as they sipped their brew.

"Not business talk?" Pua asked.

"No, but you might call it joyous talk. I went to see Joy this morning--had to have her signature for release of her funds--and she was feeling great. She'll be released in a few days. Plus Herb's specialist came back from his mainland conference, convinced that some new laser technique he learned, will definitely return sight to Herb's eyes. Don't ask, Pua. I don't understand, but since the retinas are intact, this procedure should work, where what he had originally planned to do was kind of chancy.

"Anyway, when Joy gets home, Janna is going to stay with her for a few days, till Herb's home.

"You knew the friend he's been staying with is a retired carpenter and handy-man, didn't you. Pua, Jess Kukini? Well between them, they have fixed up the flower shop as a surprise for Joy's homecoming, when she comes out of the hospital. I stopped by and it looks great--new paint and the repairs completed. When they bring the plants back, no signs of their terrible experience will remain."

"That's fantastic! I expect that Herb is excited and nervous all at the same time, anticipating the surgery." Pua said. "What changes that can make in their lives!"

"Actually, he's quite calm about the whole thing. "I'll believe it when I see it," he said--and laughed at his own joke."

"Good for him!"

"Did you tell me the financial thing worked out for them, Dad?"

"Much better than they thought. The health insurance, plus Joy's stash, plus shop insurance they had never tapped--they're pleased."

Lucky stirred. "It appears that their misfortune had nothing to do with this gang activity we're working on, doesn't it. And yet I've wondered if there could be a connection. What do you think, Keoki?"

"It's occurred to me," he admitted, "but Anders swears the whole thing was his idea; and apparently it was. I'm inclined to believe it, for the simple reason that he had no place to go to afterward. There's no doubt in my mind that these other cases are pre-planned in every detail, from the way the crime is to be handled to the escape; and includes some kind of a safe-house. Each one seems to be a different pattern from the others."

"That's true. You know, in today's incident, the bicycle bit intrigued me. Do you suppose that is why no one has been able to track down any of the protection collectors? After all, a man running away has a completely different profile than one riding a bike. Actually, it's a pretty adequate disguise, when you come to think of it."

"True," Keoki agreed. "But we can't rule out a variety of escape mechanisms either. There's got to be a sort of planning board behind all this, designing a variety of modus operandi to confuse us all."

"Speaking of confusion, I'm curious about something, Dad," Pua said. "When the man we took in today blew his top about the money and said he was mad at--what did he call her? 'That carrot-topped whore,' you didn't follow up on it. What was your reasoning?"

"Well, if you remember, he turned paper-white when he was angry and I could see splotches, brownish ones like scalds leave, on his face. And then I was convinced that he was the man Mrs. Kimura described so graphically. And he was with a dye-job-red-head in their place for dinner before the Keikoya incident, you'll recall. What I really think is that the redhead is a key figure in this whole deal, sort of a liaison director for this particular area. Our collar said, 'She sends us out.' Remember that?"

Nodding, Pua added, "And it was the Kimura tie-in that panicked him."

"Exactly. He knows that attack made it a whole new ballgame--and that's when he asked for an attorney. After that I wasn't about to jeopardize the case with questions that can be asked and answered later. You know, honey, coming up with too much too soon can ruin a case. We have him for at least 48 hours and by then we should know a lot more about him."

"He's still a John Doe, though, eh? You still have no ID on him?"

"Not yet. He's given himself a time his bail is set, fancy name or two, but he forgets them immediately and comes up with another. We should have something from the mainland by morning, now that we have his prints."

Lucky snapped his fingers. "One other thing. I kept thinking that turtleneck jersey he had on was an odd thing for him to wear on a hot day like this. Could be he needed it for cover. His chest and neck must have terrible burn scars."

"They'll check that as they process him. I think that had a lot to do with his caving in and yelling for an attorney. He knows damned well that the burn scars could be a clincher--they could nail him good."

"The computer won't cough up information on the woman?"

"Nothing. We had a smattering of leads, but none panned out. So far as we can determine, she's kept out of any trouble with the law--that's probably her biggest asset to this syndicate. It's frustrating as hell."

"He called her a whore. Could she actually be a prostitute?"

Keoki scowled. "More likely to be a Madam, seems to me. Apparently she wasn't attractive in any way--looks or voice. I have a hunch that she's a relative newcomer here, her profession a cover for her real job of controlling the personnel for this whole operation."

Keoki walked over to the phone and dialed. "I'm calling the lab. They might have something on that print from the mirror by now," he told them. "Hi, Doc, Keoki. Anything for me on that print?... Uh-huh... I see... Anything else?... That's interesting... Okay, thanks."

He turned from the phone. "The tape you recovered had a thumb print all right, Pua--but it doesn't match our prisoner's. So we know for a fact we have at least one more participant in the fabric shop case.

"That's another scrap of evidence to support our gang theory. The sad part is, even when we get the boss--who I'd bet is a top underworld figure--and the liaison people, such as this Madam, then we can still only hope to apprehend a few of the peons--not all of them certainly. Some of those that escape us may have learned enough about the set-up to start up on their own. And some may just be terminated permanently.

"God, it's mind-boggling! It might even get worse. Small-time crooks are prone to use bullets instead of the few brains they possess and that means even more danger for the victims. The Lucky Seven concept may be needed here for a lot longer than you anticipated."

Lucky nodded soberly. "We'll stick with it. You can count on it."

"The lab is doing a tidy piece of work on the burn scar issue. The suspect is insisting that he got burned in a flash fire several months ago. But Doc says that the flakes of scar tissue residue, recovered from the inside of the jersey, show it to be more recent than that and they are characteristic of scald burns. They're still making tests and each one, so far, bears out his conclusions."

He glanced at his watch. "Auwe! I'm running late. Give mom a call, will you and tell her I'm on my way? I'll see you tomorrow." And he was gone.

For the rest of the week, no new incidents were reported. The signaling devices were installed in tandem at the butcher shop and Garcia's, Kimura's and Joy's store and Stella's and Albie's places of business. They tested out perfectly. Also, a monitor board was installed at Lucky Seven, a bonus aid that was the measure of Henley's electronic skills.

"The man's a wizard," Lucky told Pua. "He's even devised a simple code, in case an alarm is triggered by mistake. That's something I was concerned about. And now he is working on our monitor set-up, so it will operate automatically when we are out of the office. An alert signal will go automatically to headquarters. Then,--" The phone rang.

"Put Pua on extension for a late development," Keoki said. Pua came on, "What's up, Dad?"

"Our man in custody has just been identified as a Perry Ford, a Californian with a long record of petty crimes and one hung jury on a rape charge in that State," Keoki told them. "He had jumped bail on a felony charge and boasts a string of aliases that read like the names of heroes of Gothic novels. Has a record a mile long, according to California. And that's not all of it. He's also wanted in Vegas. We could lose him to California on the bail thing, of course. They're considering extradition proceedings. It's an expensive procedure and we'll have to wait and see what they decide. Meanwhile, he remains our prisoner. "I thought Pualani might be pleased to know what kind of vermin she bagged."

"All part of the game Dad," Pua said--and then giggled. "I am proud, Makua Kane. Now maybe I'll get a little respect from you guys!"

"Keoki," Lucky moaned, "We've got ourselves a

231

monster!"

By Sunday, Lucky and Pua found time to tour the island again, this time with Lucky at the wheel of the Golden Monster, as Pua called it, transformed into its convertible mode. He proved that Oahu geography was no longer a bugbear to him.

He even took a run out to the Banzai Pipeline to take in a surfers' meet, returning in late afternoon to keep their dinner-date with Pua's parents.

History repeated itself and when Malia caught sight of Lucky's sunburned face, as red almost as his wind-tousled shock of hair, she hurried out for spikes of aloe to put out the fire. Even Pua dabbed some of the healing gel on her nose and cheekbones.

"We had fun," she chuckled, "but I think we'll go back to the hard top for awhile."

"Well, just in case," Malia said, "on the lanai is a little gift from me to you, which I suggest you put in that sunny window at the office, for emergencies." She had potted for them a large, sturdy Aloe Vera plant.

It was an evening of good lighthearted conversation, excellent food and drink and afterward, the traditional Hawaiian music and hula dancing. The high point of the evening came in Pua's attempts to teach Lucky a few hula moves, an effort so unsuccessful that all four of them collapsed with mirth.

"What's the situation on our collar, Dad. Anything?"

"Nothing much. His attorney talked with him quite

awhile and an arraignment is scheduled for tomorrow morning. There's been no attempt to make bail."

"That's strange, isn't it?"

"Not really. I don't think he wants to be on the outside to face the people he's working for. And I don't think they want to identify with him, at this point anyway.

I'd make book he'd fight to stay right where he is. It's another case of wait and see. No trial date will be set until California makes a decision, anyway."

"Well, your meeting tomorrow night should be interesting. Good luck with it. Let me know what happens. Count on my kokua, any time."

Lucky gave him a comically quizzical double take.

"Lesson time. What's kokua, again?"

"Cooperation, my boy."

"Well, we certainly are getting plenty of kokua. We couldn't have begun to get as far as we have without it. Pua, we'd better hit the road, don't you think?"

Malia spoke up. "Why don't you stay over? You're more than welcome, you know."

"Thank you, Mom, but we want to be on the job early," Pua said, kissing her. "Ready, Lucky? And don't forget the plant." In the usual flurry of mahalos and goodnights, they made their way up the driveway.

"You know what I'd like to do now, Pua?" She shook her head. "I feel like cruising around down where

233

our clients have their shops. I want to get the night mood of those streets. See who's walking around down there. Check out which businesses have effective night-lights and perhaps get some other ideas for improving their protection. Want to go with me?"

"Certainly. I can even take notes. Have my notebook in my purse."

They started at the corner near Keikoya. They could see a soft light inside, but bamboo screens were drawn over the windows and the door, so that the light was barely discernible.

"Make a note to talk with the Kimura's about their windows, Pua."

Farther along they passed the butcher shop, its night-light creating a small pool of illumination over counters and register.

"Now that's more like it, the best so far! But look at this one. That's Garcia's Cantina, isn't it? Those wooden shutters covering the window arches are kept open in the daytime. Can you see a light inside?"

"No, just that decorative lantern by the front door."

"Make a note of that, too."

"What's next? Oh, the Mom'n Pop grocery stores. I think they're on Albie's list to come tomorrow night. Looks all right to me."

"Hmm, do you realize, Pua, that we've only seen a half-dozen or so people walking down here? What time is it--ten?"

"Eleven," Pua answered. "We're coming up on Stella's and Albie's places now. Oh good, there's a patrolman checking things out."

"Your dad is responsible for that. Too bad we can't have at least one officer down here all the time, but with the problems in Waikiki, there just aren't sufficient men to do anything but spot-check.

Albie's bare windows and night light were satisfactory as well. Three other shops caught their attention: the Malt Shop, a carpet store and a second-hand bookstore. All passed muster, except Stella's too concealing curtains. Pua made a quick note.

"That's enough for this time, Pua."

"Good thing, too. I'm running out of paper. "

"Tell you what. I'll drop you off and we'll call it a day--unless you could go for a cup of coffee."

"Not tonight, thanks. I'm all for shower and sleep.

We've had a big day."

 He waved to the guard as he pulled into an empty space by the elevator and held her close for a moment, kissing her eyes, her lips and her throat.

"May I see you to your door?" he asked softly. "

"No need, dear, I'll be fine."

He didn't make an issue of it. "I'll call as soon as I get in. Your shower will keep till then, won't it?"

"Okay, I'll wait; saying goodnight on the phone will be a very pleasant ending to a very pleasant day.

235

Now don't get out," she smiled, kissing him again. "You go get some rest and I'll see you in the morning."

But he walked her to the elevator, despite her protests--and watched until the indicator stopped on six.

Chapter 23

"I still don't get it," Pua admitted, as she prepared the agenda of the evening's meeting.

"Don't get what?"

"Well look, Lucky. With all the money on this island, why is it these goons bother with these poor little guys? Why not go for the big bucks?"

"They are going for big bucks and getting them, too."

"It still seems to me they're running awfully big risks for very little take."

"Look at it this way, honey. Let's use $100 a week and 100 victims. If they are working their own racket successfully, that's $10,000 a week and $520,000 a year. And we have already learned that if any of their prey doesn't follow their instructions to the letter, the ante is raised.

"I'd be willing to bet you can multiply the number of businesses by hundreds--thousands maybe--of terrified merchants, too afraid even to report what is happening to them. It's terrorism at its worst. And I'd bet that the $20,000 is more than enough for their overhead--i.e. A cool half million net--no taxes--and that's just a hundred victims!

"There are thousands of possible victims right here on this island alone. Pua, think of that! Think of all the towns in the islands--and don't count out the upper-middle income shop-owners either. You can bet your bottom dollar, they're hit for more than $100 a week. Tragically, the victims pay up, fearing if they don't, they'll be vandalized, robbed, beaten up and even--this is the biggie--endanger their families if they resist."

"In other words, they hit for what they know they can get with a minimum of pilikia--trouble."

"Right. And I believe what we're doing now is just scratching the surface."

"That's scary, Lucky. But I can see where you're coming from. It's like a plague."

"And point two: If this Ford is an example, I agree with Keoki that the ringleaders are purposely hiring petty criminals, addicts, ex-cons and other dregs of society to do the terrorizing--actually blackmailing them into doing their dirty work. As for taking care of the flunkies when they take a fall, they don't. They just let them take the rap--or get rid of them one way or another."

"That being so, Lucky, why aren't the big wheels concerned that the racket may be exposed by the ones who get caught? Could it be that guys like Ford don't really know who they're working for; don't know who to rat on?"

"That's got to be part of the answer. See how devilish it is? Both their crew and their victims are caught in an economic bind; and both are in fear. The hirelings are expendables and they know it. And if, as we suspect, the bulk of them are users, they stay in this racket until they OD or get caught--or are killed."

Pua shook her head. "Seems to me that with such a

system, the big bosses would need a constant supply of new help. The attrition could be awesome. I wonder how they recruit enough of them to do their dirty work."

"Oh, Pua, that kind of scum hang out together. One guy can afford a small bag of crystal meth, say and his buddy can't. The one with the cash tells the other how he's making it and tells him how to get a job with the same outfit."

He paused, considering. "My God, Pua, if this ring is operational all over Oahu, we're talking well over millions in annual take. It's vicious."

"And if we don't play it pretty cool, we're expendable, too, right?"

"That's been worrying me some, since I figured all this out. Maybe I was wrong to let you in on it."

"Lucky! 'Whither thou goes that's where I want to be. I'm not afraid. Together we can handle it. I know we can. Stop it before it gets completely out of hand. Isn't that what we're all about?"

"You're the best, Pualani."

This night, there were new faces among the merchant group. By half past eight, nine people had already come in. A half hour later, five more had arrived and Lucky called the meeting to order.

As Lucky began to explain, for the benefit of the newcomers, Albie raised his hand.

"Mr. Kimura and Stella and I have gone over that part with the new ones already, Lucky," he said. "And we've already agreed that the $25 per week per store you mentioned is more than fair for your services and membership in the association."

"Wait a minute, here," a craggy-faced little newcomer interrupted. "I'm Bundy and I own the Package Store. I get hit for a bottle here and there and cash from the drawer--doesn't amount to much. I keep a few bucks for change in the till and the rest goes directly to my floor safe. I never was threatened, really, just robbed now and again. I never fight 'em. I'd rather be poor than dead.

"Now then, Palani thinks I ought to go into this, but I don't know. No matter what, I'm going to get hit now and then and I don't see how any association is going to do me any good."

"Bundy!" the big butcher roared. "Where were you when they handed out the brains? What I told you is, what's good for one of us is good for all of us. Now you shut your face and listen. Nobody has to join as doesn't want to. I told you that! Anyway, you and I both know you've been hit regularly; and a couple of times, gunfire--."

"Okay, okay, I'll listen. 'Nuf said, Palani." Lucky had sat in silence throughout the exchange. Now he spoke up. "First, let's explore what will make it work and how we plan to go about it. We want to set up a mutual-watch system among you and a simple inter-communication, so you can alert each other when one of you has a problem.

"Your association of merchants can keep us on, or cancel our service and continue to help protect each other, under your own leadership, whenever you feel you are ready. What I want all of you to understand is that in no way are we trying to exploit you people."

"What about the storekeepers that don't come in with us? They get a free ride, huh?" Palani asked.

"You said it yourself, Palani: What's good for one of you is good for all of you--the whole of your business community is bound to benefit. And that's why the more active members you can get, the quicker we can wrap this thing up, get rid of these leeches, wherever they strike; and prevent their striking whenever we can."

Albie raised his hand again. "You'll join in with us in the association, won't you?"

"Of course. But when you get your problems solved, we will move on to others who need the same service--and you can carry it on here."

"All right, I move that we agree as a body that $25 per week, per store, is a fair amount to pay for the services of Lucky Seven."

"Would you add, 'as long as those services are required'?"

"As long as those services are required," Albie repeated.

One of the newcomers raised his hand. "If it doesn't work for us, can we get out?"

"Absolutely. No questions asked. After all, what it amounts to is your mutual protection group versus the protection racket. If you feel you don't need that, no hard feelings."

"Then I second the motion." The vote was unanimous.

"What about your expenses?" Bundy inquired. "All you Pi's have added expenses."

"That fee covers all except one. We have already begun installation of a tandem alerting system, which is basic to our plan. We will continue installation this week and it is optional as to whether you wish to buy the units outright, or add a little to your fee each month until they are paid for. They will only run about $25 to $30 per store, installed. I have one here to give you an idea as to what they are and how they work."

"We don't want something for nothing. Let's see it." It was Bundy who spoke up first and the others echoed his sentiments.

"Pua?" She crossed to stand behind the desk, as if she were behind a counter, identifying the file cabinet beside it as a cash register.

Lucky, slouching a bit in his role went over and, pretending to draw a gun, said, "Okay, Lady, you held out on us this week. Now you can give me all you've got in your till. Keep your hands in plain sight."

Pua feigned dismay and put her hands on the top of the file, while he reached around to open and empty it.

"Please don't shoot me. Just take it. I don't want trouble." she moved slightly as if to avoid his hand. And suddenly, a bell rang in the far corner of the room."

"How'd she do that?" It was Bundy again. "She hardly moved, I was watching close."

242

"Well, Mr. Bundy, straighten that picture just a little, will you?" And when he did, the bell by the file sounded. "I'll be damned," said Bundy.

"The contact isn't as thick as a dime and can be concealed very easily. A slight pressure is all it takes.

If you touch it by mistake, just touch it twice and it will cancel the alert. Mr. Henley will help you place it, where such a mistake is unlikely.

"Now then, when you hear a triple--ding-ding-ding--that alerts every merchant, except the one in trouble; and that is when you get out on the street, if possible." And Lucky went on to explain the purpose and the value of their casual walk toward the victim.

"When he installs your signal, Mr. Henley will explain in detail; and give you a card, with the name of your group's leader, as well as your proper procedure."

"Who makes that triple signal?"

"This monitor will do that automatically. In the unlikely possibility that it should fail, then the one who received the signal can press three times--and accomplish the same alert. The one in trouble need not worry. His receiving signal will be blocked out, temporarily, as soon as he completes that one touch."

"If you receive the single signal you heard in the demonstration, you'll know it is your tandem-buddy who's activated it and is in trouble. If you hear two, it's a false alarm.

"Mr. Henley will also advise you as to your behavior on the street. Observation is the key word

243

there."

A few of the merchants seemed a little bewildered, so Lucky added quickly, "Don't worry about it, now. When we have a dry run or two, you'll see how simple it really is."

"Can you clue us in on special things to look for?" Albie asked.

"Just walk casually along the street, together or singly, but walk, don't run and keep your distance from other groups--just be normal sidewalk traffic. Look for such things as a car parked in an unlikely spot, a person running, or a stranger riding a bike. Pay particular attention to strangers who seem to be idling on the street. Get a mental picture of their faces, particularly those that are not familiar to you. The thing to remember is to do it discreetly. We certainly don't want any innocent bystander accidents. So far, as some of you know, these culprits have a way of disappearing into thin air as soon as they leave. Some of you here can testify to that. But since apprehending the one man at Stella's Fabrics, we have a strong hunch that bicycles are used for some of the escapes. You, who have already been hit, be extra alert. You may just recognize the very person who victimized you. We suspect that they use outside henchmen, in addition to the individual who pulls the heist.

"When you get back to your store, jot down anything at all you feel might be significant on your report form. If you have a hot tip, telephone Pua or me here, or the police."

Mike, from Mike's Malts, had become suddenly

244

alert.

"That puts me in mind of something I saw the other day," he said. "It struck me as weird at the time, but I forgot about it. I was on my way up to the bank and a dry cleaner's van was pulled into the alley where I make a short cut. A man was opening the back and he pulled a bicycle out of it. It struck me funny to see that wheel coming out of a dry cleaner's truck."

"When was that?" Lucky asked.

"I don't remember; I go every day. Tuesday or Wednesday I think. I'm just not sure. Maybe it was last week even. I'm sorry. I'm just not sure."

"What time of day?"

"Afternoon, close to four, I should judge. I was in a hurry to get to the bank before it closed."

"Did you notice anything about the man's appearance?"

"He wasn't a kid. Frankly, I didn't pay much attention."

"Any sign on the vehicle?"

"Let me think. It was a dirty tan, as I recall; and I saw the word Dry and part of the word cleaner on the driver's door, which was still closed--oh and some stars, two on that side, dark blue ones. That's about it. The guy with the bike just closed the door at the back of the van, slapped it a couple of times and off it went. Then he got on the bike and rode away. I didn't see the driver."

"License plate?"

245

"Sorry, Lucky. It didn't even occur to me."

"What you did is very helpful. That is the kind of observation we're talking about. Remember, all of you, don't try to decide if something you see is important or not. Jot it down and let us be the judge. We'd a lot rather have too much input than too little. One tiny little detail, such as Mike just gave us, may be all we need to solve a puzzle. Now, if there are no other questions, we have one more order of business.

"Last night, Pua and I cruised around down here and came up with some weak points in night safety measures. She made copies for all of you.

As she passed them out, they read them eagerly.

Garcia looked up. "Our insurance company told us to fix them shutters. We're getting them changed for wrought iron bar things this week."

"We goin' fix, too," Mrs. Kimura said.

"Stella gasped, "It never occurred to me my curtains were too concealing. I'll fix them tomorrow and I'll pick up Joy's and fix them, too."

"Now that's what I call real Kokua," Lucky said.

Pua was checking her notes. "The rest were night lights."

"Some of you are okay, but be sure you get good strong illumination in your stores after dark. Take a look at the butcher shop, if you want a fine example."

"I'll be glad to help anyone who needs it," Palani said proudly. "Just ask me--no charge. I figure each of us is safer, if all of us do our best to keep safe. It sure relieved my mind, when I got mine set up, after my trouble and all."

Lucky smiled. "More kokua, eh? Thank you. Now there is one more very important recommendation. If you don't have them, invest in deadbolt locks for your doors, the kind that requires a key to unlock them from the inside as well as the outside. Your locksmith will advise you and you can double the security of your property after hours, in this simple and relatively inexpensive way. Some insurance companies offer discounts if you install them."

"On that note, we'll adjourn so you can enjoy a little refreshment and chat among yourselves. That's the way good ideas are born."

"Is okay to pay tonight?" Mr. Kimura asked. "If you like. I'll be at my desk." Kimura was the first to approach the desk and the others followed, one-by-one, as each transaction was completed. The last was Mr. Nello, proprietor of the second hand bookstore, who had listened attentively throughout the meeting.

"Could I stay for a few minutes after we disband?" he asked, as he pocketed his receipt. "I won't keep you long, but I think I'm in trouble."

"Stay, by all means. No problem at all," Lucky told him.

Chapter 24

Clyde Nello was a small man in his sixties, bespectacled, with tidy gray hair and laugh lines that belied his almost pedantic appearance. But he wasn't laughing as he began his story. "I find myself in a very peculiar position," he began. "I have to give you some background, so you can understand it, however. It may seem tedious."

"You take all the time you need, my friend," Lucky said.

Nello took a deep breath and began: "I was a professor of literature in a small college back East for many years. It had never been easy sledding there for me, because it was my view that my students should have the opportunity to read and assess all kinds of literature, from the old classics to the new, regardless of subject matter--a view not received with approval by the Board of Regents."

"Unfortunately, what they felt to be the more prurient--sexy, if you like--classics finally brought their wrath down on my head. When I insisted on my right to teach and my students' right to learn from whatever I deemed appropriate and valuable--indeed necessary to the literary education of these young men and women--they gave me the option of resigning my chair or using, as teaching materials, only the books in the list that they, in their questionable wisdom, had made up for me."

"I refused to compromise or equivocate in any way. It was a point of honor with me to offer my students the opportunity to explore and understand the entire wonderful tapestry of literature. I knew fighting would make a destructive issue of it. So, reluctantly, I resigned."

"My students and graduate students kicked up a terrible rumpus over it and the affair became widely-publicized. My wife left me over what she termed my stubbornness. I was actually stoned to unconsciousness by townspeople--on my way home from the market one night. That prompted my students to riot--two of them were badly hurt. What was happening was not only bad for me, but for the entire community. I moved to California; but soon learned that the press had already branded me as a maverick, negating any chance I might have to teach again.

"Then I remembered an old colleague, who had retired and come here to Hawaii to open a book store--specializing in rare books. I wrote to him and his answer was to invite me to come here to manage his store, because his health was failing. And that's how I happened to make my new home in these marvelous islands. Sorry to be so slow about getting to the point, but it all has a bearing on my present problem."

"When the old man died a few years ago, he left me his books, among them a treasury of collectors' items. So, I rented this street-front store down here and decided I would specialize both in very old books, first editions, signed copies, which I would buy at the auction sales of various estate assets; and in an omnibus collection of new and used books--my bread-and-butter items. They included serious novels, mysteries, Westerns, romances--as well as a good selection of non-fiction."

"I've made a good living at it and have a nice clientele of collectors and other people who still cherish the old and the worthy writings of days past and can afford to buy them. And since I included in my stock, a good many second-hand books that came with the estate collections I purchased, I also enjoyed an ever-increasing clientele, who browsed frequently in hopes of finding a super-buy among them.

"My prices run from a quarter to several dollars and on up to several thousand dollars per copy, in some instances. My browsers are frequent callers and usually find something they'd like to buy."

"Now then, about three or four months ago, in checking over my stock, I discovered that somebody was lacing my shelves with pornography. In fact, I lost one of my oldest customers, who inadvertently picked up a handsomely bound volume and found inside, not its original material, but an incredible collection of filth. Later, I discovered another of my older books, mutilated in the same way, its original text removed and replaced by what I can only refer to as depravity.

"So I began a book-by-book examination of the stacks. I'm still at it. It is slow work. I found other unsavory material--one enclosed in a copy of Tom Sawyer, another in How to Win Friends and Influence People and even one in The Pictured Scriptures, which had been rather a valuable book until it was destroyed in this way."

"Other customers would come upon the same type of thing, pornographic books shoved in between volumes of light reading material. Some even wanted to buy them and one man threatened to take me to court if I didn't sell his find to him. I told him it wasn't mine to sell and he left grumbling, but he didn't sue. Yes, Lucky, you have a question?"

"You have had this trouble how long?"

The distraught man threw up his hands in despair. "I can't be sure; but none was ever reported before that. And I do go through the stacks constantly, filling in the spaces left by previous book purchasers. It didn't occur to me to leaf through each one, until this began to happen."

"I watched the shop as best I could, but not once have I observed any suspicious activity. I really can't say when it started, or if it is still going on, for that matter.

"Now then, three weeks ago a man came in to my shop and showed me a file of newspaper clippings about my mainland trouble. He told me he was a police detective and asked me if I didn't know that porn bookstores were illegal and that a 'geezer' with a reputation like mine should have to pay for breaking the law. That's when he fed me his line about buying protection."

"He claimed to be a police detective?" Pua asked in dismay.

"Yes and he flashed a badge, but when I asked to examine it, he said he was working under cover and had to keep his identity secret. I didn't believe him, of course, particularly when he offered me protection for $100 a week, beginning that day. He said he didn't like to take an old man into custody on porn-selling charges if he could help it. And when I tried to explain what was happening, he held up his hand and said that this was something for a judge to hear. But that he'd give me an option."

"He went on to tell me that every Wednesday, I must put $100 inside the back cover of an old dictionary I keep on a table near the front door. I was to stay back in the files between Noon and 2:30 p.m., or he'd see to it that the old story made headlines again; and that, along with this porn scandal, would ruin both my business and me.

"God help me, I gave him $100. He told me not to report him to the police, because, as an under-cover man, he had access to the files and would know about it at once."

"And you didn't report it?" He shook his head, helplessly. "I went over there to report it, but lost my courage. Last week, I separated some of the books, so I could see out to the sidewalk on each side of the door and I watched, but he didn't show up. Some tourists came in to browse around and I just called out to them that if they found something they'd like, to bring it back to me. They didn't buy anything much, but later, when I went to look, the money was gone. I don't know. Perhaps he came in when the tourists did."

"And you're due to pay again on Wednesday?"

"I'm supposed to. Great Heavens, in the old days, I would have defied them and probably would have been beaten or killed for my pains, but I would feel more like a man than I do now. I feel ashamed and angry--but I seem to have become a coward. I need help."

252

"Can you describe the man claiming to be a detective?"

"Not very well, I'm afraid. I saw him only once. He was about my height and not thin exactly, wirier, I should judge. He wore tinted glasses and had a Band-Aid or bandage of some sort on one cheek. He had on one of those hats with a bill, the kind sports car buffs wear and it was pulled down low in front."

"What about his clothing?"

"It was a faded aloha shirt and old jeans, if memory serves me."

"Can you describe any of the tourist group that came in last week? Anybody resemble him?"

"Oh, no. My tourists come down here on a bus, most all wearing those his-and-hers aloha shirts and muumuus." A half-smile flitted across his anxious face. "I get quite a few tourists, so I only looked that once and quit spying."

"Then perhaps he came in after that group had entered."

"I doubt it. I have a bell over the door that tinkles when it is opened. I didn't hear it but the once. I suppose he could have come in after they entered and caught the door before it closed, though. I couldn't see the door, itself."

"Could be. Whoever picked up the money was probably not the same man who threatened you.

"Tell you what," Lucky said, smiling

253

encouragement, "you go on home now and try not to worry. We'll come in the shop tomorrow and if anyone is there, you simply treat us as if we were new customers. If you're alone, we can discuss plans then. Otherwise, we'll be in touch by phone. If anything happens between now and then telephone 555-7777." and he gave him a card. "Where do you live, by the way?"

"Right here. I have an apartment on the ninth floor, 97-E."

"Good! You are the first new neighbor we've met," Pua cried, as Lucky shook hands with him and gave him an encouraging pat on the back.

As they were leaving, Nello hesitated and said, "You know, what bothers me more than paying the money, is how they found out about my past in the first place. I've never talked about it and I'm sure the old man--my friend who owned the store before me--never did. I just can't figure that out--let alone why they would think I was that important."

"This organization is like a spider's web, Mr. Nello. They must have vast sources of information to build their racket on. But my guess is that one of them recognized you and realized you were vulnerable. You let us sort it all out. We'll start tomorrow."

It was their first visit to the bookstore and they were both amazed at the number of volumes packed into a small area. Three rather narrow aisles of bookshelves about six feet in height used up most of the floor space. At the back, partially screened from view, was an old-fashioned roll top desk and a deal table, apparently the office center of the store. Nello was back there packaging books; apparently purchased by a tall woman, who seemed to be one of his regulars, judging from the threads of conversation they were able to pick up.

"Be with you in a minute, folks," Nello called out. "Make yourselves at home."

While they waited, they leafed through a number of books on the shelves. "Oh, look at this," Pua gasped, holding out a slim volume. " 'Sonnets from the Portuguese'."

"What about it? Looks old."

"Look inside the cover. No. Here, give it back. This inscription is written in faded, spidery script and it says, 'What I do and what I dream include thee, as the wine must taste of its own grapes,' and it's signed 'to my beloved Phoebe, so much a part of me, on this our wedding day and forever, Simon.' It's dated June 11, 1861. How precious! I'm going to buy it."

Lucky smiled at her radiant face. "No," he said. "I'm going to buy it for you. I've been hunting for a gift that would make your face light up that way."

The sound of the bell indicated the departure of the customer and Nello joined them.

"So you discovered my little treasure, eh? It's not a first edition, but it is very old and I found it when the Simon Deering estate across the island was sold at auction. He and his Phoebe lived long, full, happy lives together there, and I am told."

"I'd like to buy it for Pua," Lucky said, glancing at

255

the tag inside the back cover.

"Fine, but I didn't pay that much for it. I paid $50. I want you to have it at my cost."

"Not this time," Lucky told him with a warm smile. "It's worth a lot more than your price. Just look at this girl's face."

"I understand. I understand," he said softly. As Pua held her gift close, she murmured, "Thank you, darling. Nothing could please me more."

"Well, have you anything new to report, Mr. Nello?" Lucky asked.

"Yes, I have--and Lucky, I'd like you and Pua to call me Prof, if you will— that's what I'm known as here. As for the latest happening, I had a telephone call this morning from a woman who growled--" He paused to adjust his glasses in order to read a note. "Ah, yes. She said, 'Tomorrow, put the money in a large manila envelope and mark it Special Delivery in red. We'll have it picked up around two o'clock. Have it ready on the small table beside the door and don't dare show your face out front. No police!' That was it."

"You couldn't recognize the voice? Seems she knew a lot about your set-up here."

Nello shook his head. "It was so muffled--yet something about it. I don't know. Sounds crazy, but I had a feeling that she knew me."

"Tell me, Prof, do you happen to remember seeing a red-headed woman in here recently?"

256

"Only the one they call the Madam," Nello grinned. "She's a book nut, buys lots of them. I guess she gets bored waiting for her girls to change clients. It wouldn't be the Madam, though, the one you're after. She's been a stable boss for years and years, so I've been told."

Lucky and Pua stared at each other, a dawning possibility in their eyes.

"Where's her stable, do you know? I think I'd better pay a visit down there."

"Lucky! Come on!" Pua protested.

"I warned you this business takes us to strange places," he teased. "But all the girls really care about is getting their money. Nothing's going to happen, except I might buy a little information. Satisfied?"

"Not entirely," she pouted. "I thought you promised I could get in on everything."

Lucky hooted with laughter. "Hey! You were the one that copped our first collar. Do you remember? And somehow I can't see you wanting to get a job at a brothel as an undercover assignment."

She blushed. "I see what you mean. Guess I have to trust you on this one. Now stop laughing at me!"

"Okay. So where is it, Prof?"

"Down on Hotel near Maunakea. Up on the second floor,

I believe. You can't miss the O.K.R&R Massage Parlor sign, blinking away in glorious neon! That's what the Madam named it. She used to give me scrip, but I've never cashed any of it. Too old or too particular--I'm not sure which," and again they saw one of his rare smiles.

"I do have an assignment for you tomorrow, Pua, if it's all right with Prof. How would you like to help him check his shelves for three or four hours. You wouldn't mind, eh, Prof?"

"Not at all. I'll welcome her help. I don't want her in danger though."

"Nor do I."

"I'll be delighted to help you. Sir," Pua said, with a graceful bow.

"That's settled, then. Prof, follow the instructions exactly. Will eleven be early enough for Pua to come in? There's something else I'd like her to work on earlier."

"Any time is fine with me."

Walking back to the office, Lucky told her, "In the morning, I'd like you to go to the News Building and do some more reading. See if you can find coverage on that college scandal."

"Will do. I'll call the Prof and pretend I need dates for our work-up or something. Just think, I'll be out from underfoot most of the day." She grinned wickedly. "You'll have lots of time to rest up for your evening's exertions at the O.K.R&R."

"Pua, you really are the limit!" he remonstrated. But she was already running into their building, her laughter reassuring and, he thought, nice--very nice.

Chapter 25

Breakfasting on her lanai, Pua half-wished she didn't have such a full day planned. It would be nice to just relax today. Then she grinned to herself. That thought would last only as long as the last drop of coffee. There was no way she could ignore the lure of the current mystifying puzzle.

Well, she'd better get going if she was to make it back from the News Building in time to go to work in the bookstore. But she had a call to make first, one that would take a certain amount of finesse if she were to get the vital information she needed for her research, without tipping the Prof off to her real goal. Nello answered the first ring, his voice uncertain, insecure.

"Good morning, Prof," she said. "This is Pua."

"Oh, it's you," he answered in obvious relief. "I was afraid it might be another--I'm sorry. Good morning, my dear. What can I do for you?"

"I'm just getting your file in order," she said. "When did you come to Hawaii? And when did you take over the book store?"

"Let me see. I left Claymore in 1980--April 1980; left California in November of '81; and actually opened this shop as my own, in 1984--also in April. Do you need the exact dates? I was having a rough time getting my life back together and I honestly don't remember the exact date I left California. Is it important?"

Pua was contrite. "That's all I need, Prof. We just want to get a time frame bearing on the case. We've got to

259

find out how and when the person who set you up discovered you were here. This is all I need, thanks. I must run now.

I'll see you around eleven."

"I'm looking forward to it, Pua." She put the phone down and sighed. It wasn't really snooping she comforted herself. The dates might prove important.

Driving the Fiat through the busy streets, she shook off her sober mood and regained the sense of well being she'd had at the beginning of the day.

The same clerk who had helped before greeted her warmly and set up the monitoring system. Pua began with March of 1981 and found nothing. April 6--there it was, his picture and all. She began taking notes. Good Lord, she thought, the students had actually rioted for his cause. The police had been called to restore order on the campus of Claymore College, located near Kansas City, Missouri. They had tried to force the students back to their classrooms, but they had resisted and fighting broke out. In the melee, two of the young men and one co-ed had been seriously injured. Their identities have not been released.

Ah, here it was. Clyde Nello, who had been professor of classical literature at Claymore until his resignation on Friday, was summoned to the scene by the police, in an effort to quell the near-riot. He pleaded with the students to let the matter drop and return to the pursuit of their education. Still protesting, they had acceded to his wishes. The photo pictured him, surrounded by policemen, talking to the massed students, using a bullhorn.

There was more. Pua copied it word-for-word. "The protest was in support of Nello, whose leaving was considered by the students to be an ouster, because of his insistence on using books in his classes that were considered by the Board of Regents of Claymore College to be unsuitable for co-educational discussion.

"When approached by this reporter, the professor stated that it was his firm conviction that both his rights and those of his students were being denied and that he could not, in good conscience compromise those rights. He declined to comment further."

Pua shook her head and kept searching for a follow-up. She found one short article, published a week later. "Clyde Nello, whose recent removal from the faculty of Claymore College made national headlines, was hospitalized today with injuries resulting from stones thrown at him by a group of townspeople, who demanded that he leave the college town. No arrests were made.

"The following statement was issued by Mayor George Ellis of Claymore Village: 'The stoning of Mr. Nello is most regrettable; but it should be considered only as the rash act of people angered beyond control, by fear that their children's moral judgments had been defiled by their exposure to improper reading material in his classroom.'" Pua snorted with disgust. "Sanctimonious old bag of wind," she grumbled.

"Are you all right?" The clerk was eyeing her anxiously.

Pua looked up and realized for the first time that

261

she was crying. "Just angry," she said, drying her tears. And thanking the girl for her help, she gathered up her notes and hurried back to her car.

On impulse, she stopped at Lucky Seven. She caught Lucky, as he was about to leave and burst into tears. "Look at this," she sobbed. "That poor dear man was absolutely crucified for standing by his honest beliefs."

"And so was Christ and so many others, Pua. There's nothing more cruel than ignorance." He read her notes through and then smoothing back her hair, he tipped up her chin and kissed her gently. "Go wash your face, sweetheart. You'll be late for your job."

When she returned, she was composed, but she asked worriedly, "Does Prof have to know we read this?"

"I don't see why," he answered simply. And hand in hand they walked down the hall.

"Where were you headed?" she asked.

"I'm helping Henley install the signals and this afternoon we'll be completing the monitor board up here. You call if you need me, okay?"

"I will." As she walked to her car, she was smiling smugly. He was learning. He hadn't given her the do's and don'ts treatment this time.

The Prof was busy with customers when she arrived, so she went back in what he called his stacks and began checking the books along the rear wall. These were not sorted by category yet, so she didn't expect to find anything; but she kept at it, leafing through volume after volume. As she took one large book out, a smaller one fell to the floor and she stared in shock as a sheaf of photos slid out of it--porn, explicit porn--somehow the more disgusting because they were Polaroid's.

Quickly, she swept them back into the book and set it aside. How on earth did anyone have the gall to do such a slimy deed, clear back here, she wondered--not five feet from the Prof's desk, too. She sat down on the step stool and thought about it. Could the pictures have been in the book at the time he bought it without his realizing it? Not likely, the way they had scattered on the floor, too slippery to have been there long. The question was when and how? The more she thought, the more confused and angry she became.

Then it hit her. The Madam. If she was a frequent customer here and an avid reader, she probably had the run of the place, even the books that hadn't yet been processed. She could come back to see what new things he'd picked up. Throughout the store, she'd have ample opportunity to set the stage for the extortion, a little at a time. She could have been at it for weeks--maybe longer than that.

When Nello joined her, Pua asked him, "You say the woman called the Madam is a good customer?"

"Ruby? Sure. She's in every week or so, sometimes oftener. Why?"

"Does she always buy?"

"She certainly does. She gets three or four every time, pays me, puts them unwrapped in her big shoulder bag and off she goes. She likes mysteries, spy stories mostly. And she's forever ragging me to buy more of them."

"Looks through these unsorted ones occasionally?"

"Yes. But Pua, if you're suspecting her of making this trouble, I find it hard to believe. She's always nice to me, as if she considered me her friend. Sometimes she even turns in books she has purchased to be sold again, after she's read them--even places them on the shelf. I don't approve of her profession, needless to say, but it's difficult for me to believe she'd do anything as dreadful as what's happening, especially to a friend."

"Does she come in at any given time?"

"Usually mornings, as soon as I open up. Says her girls sleep late, so she has a little free time then. Do you really believe she has something to do with this?"

"I'm not sure. Does she ever come back here and look through these books that aren't classified yet?"

"Occasionally. Why? Did you find something?"

She handed him her find; The Case of the Black Pearl. Some of the photos slid from it. "My God," he said. "I'm sorry, Pua." He shoved the pictures back into the book and added it to a carton nearly filled with others he'd found. "These have got to go to the incinerator."

"Oh, not yet, Prof. Seal them up or something, but don't burn them. They may be needed as evidence."

"I still can't figure Ruby for this."

"Perhaps she had no choice, Prof. She may have been ordered to do it."

264

"Ruby the Madam?" He shook his head, firmly. "She's a tough old bird, that one. No one's going to tell her what to do or not to do." He hurried away as the bell on the door tinkled.

"I'm supposed to pick up this here for delivery," she heard a young voice say.

"You come back here right now!" the Prof shouted. "Pua, did you see? It was a boy, a youngster. He had a bike out there. He's riding toward the canal."

She got a glimpse of the boy as he was momentarily held up in traffic. At the same time, she noticed Sergeant Kea in pursuit; in the unmarked car he used for stakeouts; and beside him--no doubt about it--the familiar red head of Lucky Seven Gregory.

"Don't worry, Prof. Detectives are following him. They'll handle it."

Nello was shaking. "A little kid," he moaned. "They're using a child now! I don't understand all this. Could it be a coincidence?"

"The boy knew where to look for the envelope, didn't he?"

"You're right, of course. But when I yelled at him, he seemed to panic--as if he didn't expect my reaction. I hope he isn't in on it, but he must be."

"Not necessarily. Let's not jump to conclusions. He may believe he's making an innocent delivery to whoever hired him. We'll have the story in time. Anyway, we can do nothing now. Let's get back to work." Within the next two hours, they had found a half-dozen more, well thumbed objects of their search. Two were hidden between the covers of books from which portions of the text had been cut away to accommodate the trash.

Nello grabbed up one of them and gesturing with it grimly, he said, "Funny thing, Pua. The Liquidators. I would have sworn I had only one copy of this and it was sold."

"Can you remember who bought it?"

"I can't be sure, but if memory serves me right, it was Ruby." He heaved a sigh. "One never knows--" The telephone interrupted him and he braced himself as if to receive still another blow. "Will you answer it, please?"

"Nello's Book Store," she said. Then she cried eagerly, "Lucky! What's....Yes, I saw you. We've been on pins and needles ever since.... What?.... Just a second. I'll see. "

She turned to the Prof. "How soon can you close up? We're both needed at headquarters."

"Any time. I have no appointments today."

She passed on the message and then listened attentively. "I see. Okay, we're on our way."

"We're to walk over to our building and meet them at Lucky Seven. They want to brief us there first."

"Let's go then. Just bolt that back door for me, will you please?" He reversed the sign on his door and they left.

When they reached the office, the door was slightly ajar and Kea and Lucky were waiting for them.

"We're getting some action at last," Lucky said. "You caught the boy?" Nello's voice was sad, his eyes pain-filled. "He seemed like a nice, clean-cut little boy. I hate to think of him in trouble."

"He's all right," Kea smiled. "He isn't in custody. We followed him and saw him pass the envelope to a man in a parked car, then take off. We'd radioed the info on the car, while the exchange was being made and patrol cars were stationed on the ready to make the chase. The guy caught himself, in a way--tried to make the turn into Aloha Motors and crashed into a couple of used cars in the lot. As if that wasn't enough, he tried to throw out the envelope and it sailed right inside the broken window of one of the cars he'd hit."

"But the boy, what about him?" Nello was still deeply concerned.

Kea grinned. "I know that kid, Prof. Used to be my paper boy, as a matter of fact. He's an all right kid. Name's Joey and we found him within minutes at the Fun Factory, playing electronic games. I had a hunch he'd be there, if he had money on him.

"The man in the car had asked him to pick up the envelope and bring it to him. Gave him $5 to do it. Joey asked him why he didn't pick it up himself and the man told him he had a game leg and didn't want to lose his parking space. Sounded okay to Joey, so he did the job. Simple as that."

Lucky chuckled. "That was one scared boy, though--when we showed up. 'Don't tell my mom,' he pleaded. 'She'll ground me for a month. And when I gave that guy the envelope, he told me if I told the police what I done, they'd let me rot in jail and if they didn't, he'd come after me himself. That must have been a bad thing I done.' The kid's eyes were as big as saucers."

With a sigh of relief, the Prof relaxed. "So, I gather that if I'm able to help you, that evil man's chances of getting out of jail to do any more damage are practically nil. Is that right?" At Kea's nod, he took a deep breath and said, "Let's go, then. What must I do?"

"Well, Sir, it may be that at some time you've known the suspect and we'd like to take you in for a line-up identification."

"I don't mind, but I don't know many people here. Women are the big book buyers. The men are usually collectors and call me for appointments."

"This suspect apparently knows you. When they recovered the money, he yelled, 'That stupid, damned, shit-head school teacher will be sorry he ever crossed us!'

Sorry, but those were his exact words. He ranted all the way to jail--something about his sister and some riot."

The color drained from the Prof's face. "How do I go about this?" he asked.

"You ride with Lucky and follow his instructions," the sergeant told him. "We want to protect your own identity down there, if possible. Pua, you can come with me."

No one was in the viewing room when Nello got there. He sat down, tiredly and wrestled with his conscience. "If he's who I think he is, I'll know him. And if I know him, I've got to speak up. I have to live with myself. And then it will all come out, all over again. I can't help but hope he isn't--" He buried his face in his hands.

Within a few minutes, Lucky, Pua and Sergeant Kea entered the room. Nello was informed that the glass between them and the line-up area was one-way, that the men in the line-up would not be able to see him or hear anything he said. And before he knew what was happening, six men walked into that brilliantly illuminated area beyond the glass and stood facing them. Nello gasped, as if in pain. The men turned and took the stances directed by an officer somewhere in the shadows of the room; and Nello fought off the temptation to plead ignorance.

Then, squaring his shoulders, he rose to his feet. "I can't forget that face," he said quietly. "Number three is the brother of the girl who was crippled in a student riot staged in my behalf at Claymore College, Kansas, in 1980. His name is Jackson Steele."

Chapter 26

"It's all going to come out, isn't it," Nello sighed. "The whole miserable story. Steele was still in high school when it happened and he was heartbroken about his sister's injury. She had been a promising dancer, you see. He told me that sooner or later he was going to find a way to punish me."

"It took a lot of courage to make the identification," Pua said gently.

He gave her a twisted smile. "I was tempted not to," he admitted, "but when it came right down to it, I had to--it was a matter of principle, you see, just as my resignation was. I realized I had no choice in the matter."

"I can understand his locating you here in Hawaii," Lucky said, "but I can't figure out how he tied in with the extortion people. Brace up, Prof, your situation may not be as bad as you think."

"Oh, I'm not afraid for myself. I'm a fatalist of sorts," he said. "Do you think I should try to see him, talk with him?"

"No, not now anyway. He will be undergoing psychological evaluation first of all. At this point, his sanity is in question and no one but a psychologist will be able to talk with him until his mental health is determined. My advice would be to just let it ride, for now."

Nello nodded, soberly.

"Come in with us for a cup of coffee," Pua suggested, as they reached their floor.

"Another time, thank you. I'm just going to relax and listen to the classics for a while. I'm not going back to the shop today. The sign on my door has no time indicated, so that's no problem."

"I could use a drink," Lucky said as they entered the office. "Bet you could too."

"You'd win. You fix them while I do pupus. How about some crabmeat with red sauce and those little sesame seed crackers you like?"

"Super!" And they set about their preparations. Lucky tasted his concoction and, pleased, suggested, "Here, take a sip. Is this good, or what?"

"Good! That's fantastic, Lucky! Let's have them here at the bar. We haven't once used the bar stools yet."

"Good idea."

"I wonder what's next," Pua mused. "I keep getting a breathless kind of feeling that everything is moving too fast. "

"So do I. Keoki told me the suspect was asking for an attorney. He apparently wants to get out on bail. That's a change in the pattern. I don't think he'll make it, however.

If I were he, I'd stay put, I think. After all, he blew his assignment and those people he's working for apparently have a sink-or-swim policy."

"I'm inclined to agree with you. Honey, I want to talk my assignment tonight."

"Please! I'm eating." Her eyes were twinkling. "I

271

want to think about you with another woman."

"You don't trust me?"

"Of course I trust you, silly, but I don't have to like the idea, do I? Seriously, if the Madam turns out to be the liaison in this ring, I think she's smart and dangerous. I'm-not crazy about the idea of you going in there alone."

"I can handle it; but if you don't mind, would you stay here till I get back? We can have late supper here, or go out, whichever you prefer. I don't feel like dinner now, do you?"

"Golly, no. And don't you worry, I'm not about to leave until you're back--safe, sound and ready to tell me all about it--and I do mean all! Right now, I want a nice big hug and kiss and then you skedaddle!"

When he had gone, though, she felt lonely and nervous. Finally, she settled down at her desk; and picked up the telephone to call her mom. She always felt better after she talked with her.

As Lucky parked his car at Municipal, he toyed with the idea of taking his gun with him; then discarded the idea. It was possible he might be searched and if he was heeled, his visit to the OKR&R Massage Parlor might backfire. He locked it in the trunk.

The night people were out in full force, as he picked his way along Hotel Street and while he caught a few curious stares and was approached by a few hookers it all seemed pathetic, rather than dangerous. Every city he'd ever been to have a section like this--and there was a weird sort of fascination about it.

272

The steps up to his destination were dimly lit and dirty, but to his surprise, when he opened the door, the reception room was well furnished; and the decor, if bizarre, at least made a stab at being attractive. Seated there were a trio of the girls, the rosy lamplight softening the telltale hardness of eyes and mouth so characteristic of their trade.

They greeted him warmly and motioned him to an alcove toward the rear of the room. And there, for the first time, he met the Madam face-to-face. She was reading and behind her, stacks of books evidenced her fascination with the printed page.

She looked up, her elaborately arranged hair flashing orange-red in the cone of light from her reading lamp. If she had ever had beauty, it was ravaged by both time and a soul that had none. Her eyes were a cold gray and her mouth a narrow line, its lipstick, spilling out untidily into the creases that bordered it.

"This is your first time here, right --tourist, eh?" He shrugged. "Does it make a difference?"

"Only if all you want is a massage." He grinned and let her comment ride. "Well, I have three of my girls free right now, or you can wait."

"How about that blonde one," he suggested.

"The blonde is $25 for up to an hour; $80 for the night. You buy your own booze. If you're kinky, double the price. Pay in advance," and as he reached for his wallet, "You pay her."

"Fine."

"Brenda," she called and as the girl appeared, she went back to her book.

"Good evening, will you follow me?" And, in silence, the girl called Brenda led him to a door down the hall. "I was hoping you'd choose me," she smiled, her eyes world-weary, but her voice sweet and gentle, compared to the Madam's harsh tones.

"Make yourself comfortable, baby," she said. He looked around the small austere room. It contained only a bed, a dresser, a massage table on which rested a small radio and a stack of books. A single floor lamp made a half-hearted attempt to give light to the area. She caught his grimace.

"Not much is it, baby; I'm pretty new here and this is all I got. You didn't come to look at the room, though, eh? What do you want, an hour or a night? I recommend the night. I'm pretty new in this place, but I'll tell you this. I never get any complaints."

"I'll take the hour rate. I have to be someplace later."

She pouted, coyly, "Whatever you say. What's your name, dearie?"

"Blake," he answered.

"You'll have to give me the money now, Blake. I have to take it to the old bat." Her hand flew to her mouth. "You won't tell her I said that? It just slipped out."

Lucky grinned at her and gave her the money. "No way, Brenda. I've had bosses I didn't like, too."

"Be right back. You go ahead and get your things off."

As she came through the door again, she was already unzipping her long dress. He went to her and zipped it up again. She looked startled to find him still fully clothed. "Look," he said. "All I want is an hour of your time, just talking--okay?"

"You some kind a freak?" she asked, eyes wide with astonishment.

"No, but right now I need to know some things much more than I need sex."

"You're Fuzz?"

"No. I'm not, but I need some information, that's all."

She sucked in her breath. "About me?" Her eyes were frightened.

"No, Brenda. It's about someone here, though. The one you called the old bat. How long have you been working here?"

She relaxed. "Three months and as soon as I can afford a ticket, I'm moving on. This is a dump!"

"Ruby tough to work for?"

"You're damn right. She takes a whopping cut and then doles out our pay in dribbles. Sits there reading her blasted books and raking in the dough. But she's a rough one. Nobody ever argues with her for long, unless they want a good cuffing."

"She's always there?"

275

"Not in the mornings, usually. A woman named Belle is here mornings and she fills in when Ruby goes out. We're supposed to get our sleep then. But sometimes we get called for an early-bird John."

"I gather that one or the other of them is here all the time. Is that right?"

"You got it. Mister. Like guards, to make sure none of us get ideas about taking off."

"Every now and then Ruby has meetings with some guys in the room around the corner, at the end of the hall. I don't know if they're business partners or what, but sometimes I hear them yelling a lot."

"Yelling? What about?"

"God, I don't know. Just arguing like. It's no orgy if that's what you're thinking. She retired from active whoring a long time ago."

"Can you describe these men?"

"I never had a look at them. They come up the back way, for one; and the other girls warned me to leave the whole thing alone. One girl popped in on them, before I came here. She got one of Ruby's beatings and ran away. She was found a few days later--her body floating in the Ala Wai Canal, they told me." She shivered. "That was enough for me. I don't need that kind of trouble. I just mind my own business and do what she tells me. God, I don't know what I'm doing all this talking to you for. I could really get creamed if Ruby found out."

"Don't worry about that. Believe me, I won't talk, Okay?"

276

"Okay. But, damn it all, I'm scared."

"I'll keep my promise, Brenda. Now, other than what you've told me, Ruby just sits there and reads and makes your--er--appointments?"

"That's about it. It's a funny thing about those books of hers. She won't lend them to us; but one day I saw her cutting one up. She screamed at me to get back in here and not to come out until I was called. She scares me. I think she's crazy-mad. That's why I want out. But she won't let us quit.

"When I get the money, I'll just have to make a run for it. I've been keeping half my tips. If she finds that out, I've had it."

"I hope you make it, Brenda. And I want you to take this and add it to your getaway fund." He extracted a $20 bill from his wallet and gave it to her. "You've been very helpful."

"Thank you. Believe me, I'd spill more, but that's all I know. Hey, can't you stay? We could have a great time, Blake honey. I'm good, I'm really good; and I bet you are too. I--I think it would be fun for me, too, for a change."

"No, Brenda, I'm running out of time. What we've talked about is our secret, right? That way neither of us will get into trouble."

"That's for sure and I'm really sorry you can't stay. I better make it look good." She tousled her hair and smeared her make-up; then unzipped her gown a little. "Come on, I'll show you out. Oh, wait a minute." She went back to rumple the bed. "There now," she said with satisfaction.

As they passed the alcove, Ruby called out, "She treat you all right, Mister?"

"She sure did," he said, with a secret smile for Brenda.

"Come back again, then. She's on regular." Lucky hurried down the stairs. He felt as if the sordid aura of the place had infected him. His depression lasted until he reached his car. It had a ticket on it.

He'd neglected to feed the meter. Looking at it, he began to laugh. Tonight was his night to pay and pay and pay. His mom had warned him long ago to stay away from what she still called "houses of ill repute." And still laughing at that memory, he headed for home.

Pua's greeting was like a breath of fresh air; but he didn't touch her. He said, "Make me a drink, will you please, my love?" and went to take a shower. She sensed his mood and when he returned, she placed his glass on the bar and asked, "Want to tell me about it?"

He put his arms around her and reveled in the fresh scent of her hair, the guileless velvety dark eyes, the clean wonder of her, as they clung together. Pua broke the spell by tipping his head down to hers, so she could kiss him lightly on his nose. "Information before hanky-panky," she said and spun out of his arms.

As she listened to his story, she felt an unexpected pang of pity for the girl Brenda.

"From what she told me and what I saw, I am sure

278

that the Madam did in fact salt the Prof's store with porn; and I have a gut feeling that she has meetings with some of her associates in the extortion racket right there. Maybe the top man is among them. I'll brief your dad on it and also check on that dead girl they found in the canal. I want to read the file on that case. We're talking murder, here."

He took a long pull at his glass. "What shall we do? Go out to eat?"

Pua shook her head. "Not unless you're starving," she said. "I made an enormous tuna salad and all I have to do is pop some rolls in the oven. And, my dear, I made a chocolate cake—we can have that for dessert."

"You did all that since I left? It sounds great, but how come?"

"I felt lonesome, so I called mom and she said the best remedy in the world was cooking, so I cooked, if you can call it that. I enjoyed it, too, smart lady my mother. Give me ten minutes for the rolls, okay?"

"Sure. I'll pour us a refill. And Pua, I've got a confession to make. Now don't look so upset. I'm only telling you because you will be writing the checks around here. I got a parking ticket tonight."

"Lucky, you didn't! I'll have to dock you on your next paycheck, you know." And laughing, she escaped his playful karate chop and ran into the kitchen.

He was finishing a second piece of cake when the phone rang. "What now," he muttered and answered it.

"Oh, Hi, Keoki, what's up?... He did?... How?...

279

But I thought.... I see. Where does that leave us?... That's for sure. Who made the bail?.... Wow, that's heavy... I'll see you about nine then in your office. I'll have Pua tell the Prof. "

"Tell the Prof what?" Pua's face was a study in anxiety.

"Steele got out on bail tonight, through an attorney who got some judge to set it, early this evening. Keoki is steaming about it. That happened around seven."

"So what does that--"

"Oh, that's not all. At ten, Steele was thrown from a car down in Ala Moana Park. A couple of kids who were walking back from a beach party saw it happen. They didn't know what it was that was dumped, but they were curious and went to investigate. He was still alive and they called an ambulance, but he died on the way to the hospital without regaining consciousness. He'd been shot twice, in the stomach. No doubt about this one--it's definitely homicide."

Pua was listening open-mouthed. "I'll bet there'll be some butt-burning down at headquarters tomorrow, if they didn't let dad know what was going on. He'd have had a tail on him from the moment he walked out of jail. He figured from the first that he was a marked man, you know. Well, I hope that will at least take the heat off our poor professor.

It's no longer a question of revenge. I doubt if Steele's murderers knew or cared why he was set up. Just followed orders. Do you agree?"

"Absolutely. Oh! Keoki suggested we tell the Prof about it. It's late and I hate to disturb him; but he's probably lying awake worrying, anyway. Let's run up now. What do you say?"

"I think it will relieve his mind to have it resolved, but I know it will sadden him. He's felt so involved.

"I know. But Prof must realize, down deep, that he had no control of the situation. He can't be blamed for what happened. Let's go break it to him and see if we can help him understand that."

When they approached his door, they could hear the music of Beethoven coming from Nello's apartment. Lucky rapped lightly and said, "Prof, it's Lucky."

"Just a minute." The music was turned off and Nello opened the door, tying the belt of his robe.

"Has something happened?" he asked. "Come in, come in.

"Its pretty shocking news, Prof. Steele was murdered tonight." Nello paled and sat down suddenly.

"Oh, no--It's too bad. Was it because I identified him?"

"That made no difference at all. Prof," Lucky told him. "He was a marked man the minute he failed his assignment at Stella's. You had nothing to do with it."

"I suppose I could just as well blame Tolstoi, Balzac, Fitzgerald and the rest, when it comes right down to it," he murmured ruefully.

Lucky's jaw dropped. "Do you mean those were

among the authors of the books you were ordered not to use?" he asked incredulously. "Those and their ilk. Even Harriet Beecher Stowe was banned as racist, along with Mark Twain."

"Unbelievable!" Pua gasped. "With that mentality, I'm surprised they didn't burn those books."

Prof's smile was twisted. "They did--some of them."

"My God! Here's better news: Major Kanai asked us to tell you that what happened to you before is in no way relevant. Do business as usual, but keep an eye on Ruby, when she comes in, without letting her know she's under suspicion. I have reason to believe that situation will be settled in the next week or so."

"If they call me for more money, do I follow their instructions?"

"Major Kanai will let you know how to handle that."

"Thank you for coming. My mind is relieved and I think I can sleep now."

Back in Lucky Seven, they viewed the mess they had left, with some dismay. Pua hesitated and said, "I guess I can clean up the kitchen in the morning.

" Lucky drew her into his arms. "Pua, darling Pua, I love you," he whispered, "and I need you. Please don't leave tonight."

Her arms went up and around his neck and tilting her head back, she smiled up at him, eyes luminous, face radiant and whispered, and "I know that my darling and I love you too

As she raised her lips to his, she whispered, eyes filled with promise, "I hadn't the slightest intention of leaving you tonight."

Chapter 27

Still half-asleep, Lucky reached out for Pua, but she wasn't there. Had he dreamed it all? Were the loving, the touching, the exploring and the ecstasy all fantasy? It couldn't be. The scent of her was there and as he became fully awake, he was aware of other delicious aromas, the rich temptation of coffee brewing and bacon frying. For a moment he lay there savoring the pleasant sensations this morning had brought. Then he stretched luxuriously and groped for his robe.

"Good morning, sleepy head," Pua cried. "Breakfast is almost ready and you're going to have to hurry, if you meet dad by nine. What's funny?" He was laughing as he slipped his arms around her and, spatula and all whirled her around and around. He held her at arms' length; then laughed again and kissed her.

"You are, my sweet; you give a whole new meaning to the word glamour." She looked down at herself and grinned. She was wearing his pajama top and its shoulder seams were almost down to her elbows, the sleeves rolled up somewhat untidily, its hem well below her knees and its V-neck offering him a generous glimpse of firm golden-tan breasts. To complete her ensemble, she had donned his kooky 'Here come da chef' apron--and the whole effect was hilarious.

Seeing herself through his eyes, she was laughing too. "At least I'm decent," she crowed. "Now let me go. The bacon will be burned. You have time for about a three-minute shower and everything will be ready."

They ate hungrily and as he finished his second

cup of coffee, he said, "Terrific breakfast, my love, but I'm running a little late. You going with me?"

"How about if I drop you off at headquarters and go get some fresh clothes on? I'll be at dad's office in a little while and we can play it by ear from then on."

"That's a good idea. Too bad you can't go just as you are, though," he added, wickedly.

Keoki was already at his desk and it was plain that storm clouds were brewing. "Glad you could make it," he said, his voice agitated. "This is one hell of a mess! I don't know how it happened, but Judge Araki says he not only didn't set bail, he was at Oahu Country Club from about four until late in the evening. And get this; the man who bailed Steele out is the attorney who visited him earlier. To cap the climax, bail was set at a mere $1000 and paid in cash."

"If it wasn't the judge, who did set it?"

"Damned if I know The only thing we have is the envelope which the order form came in--it's faked--and the bills, ten hundreds. It has the court's return address, all right. But Rodgers accepted it. Damn, I can't figure it all out. Oh, here he comes. Will you wait outside Lucky? This had better strictly one-on-one. Come on in, Rodgers."

Lucky tried not to stare, but he was fully aware that the conversation going on inside the big glass windows was anything but amicable. Keoki's face was drawn with the intensity of his anger, as the red-faced officer talked. Finally the major threw his arms in the air and waved him out. Lucky returned to the office.

"This is incredible!" Keoki sputtered. "He says he got a call from the judge's clerk Emma about five, just after I left, as a matter of fact; saying that Steele's attorney had asked that bail be set immediately; that Steele was a diabetic and was likely to go into insulin shock if he wasn't taken to the hospital at once. She claimed that the judge was at that moment signing an order for release of the prisoner on bail reduced to $1000, effective immediately. And she said Steele's attorney was bringing the order and the bail money was enclosed. Said the judge advised him to expedite the release."

"Rodgers, who had just come on duty, bought the story--thought it was 'reasonable bail for shoplifting.' "Shoplifting! For God's sake! Didn't bother to check the charge, even. Just believed what that woman told him on the telephone, slit the envelope, saw the bills and released Steele to his attorney. And he didn't call me because he thought it wasn't enough to bother me about. I keep telling them to call me--radio or phone--whenever something odd goes down in one of my cases. My God, that's standard procedure.

But he has a high opinion of his own judgment and did, as he said, 'what I thought you would have done.'"

"How did Steele react, do you know?"

"Rodgers said he looked scared and sick and pleaded with the attorney. 'I'll be all right' and 'you don't have to take me out; I feel fine now,' something like that." Keoki shook his head, wearily. "Steele must have had a lot to tell, if they were willing to pay $1000 to get him out just to kill him."

His phone rang and he grabbed it up. "Kanai." He listened glumly. "Figures. Well, thanks for trying."

"No definable fingerprints, except Rodgers'. Damn! And how the hell did they get that envelope, do you suppose? Sure as the devil it wasn't from Emma. The bailiff's sign-out sheet confirms that. Both he and Emma get the afternoon off, when the judge has his weekly date at the club.

"I have to believe somebody went in that office earlier in the day and lifted that order form and envelope--when the clerk was in chambers with the judge, perhaps. Maybe it was Mr. J, himself."

"And when the coast was clear, they got in a woman to pose as clerk--one of the gang, no doubt." Lucky suggested. "Do you read it that way?"

"I don't see how it would work any other way. Took a chance, though. Any other officer would have called for confirmation. Rodgers says he called, but it was after five and he figured the court was closed, when there was no answer. This isn't the first time he has taken over authority, instead of checking things out.

"This time he's bought himself a big suspension. We can't afford sloppy police work like that around here. He should have sensed that something was wrong, when Steele didn't want to get out, for Pete's sake."

Lucky thought a minute, and then made a suggestion. Did Rodgers describe that attorney?"

"Sketchily. Let's see. I made a note. Here it is. Taller than average, thin, in his 50's, gray curly hair,

287

slanted dark eyes, hapa haole."

"Hapa haole?"

"Half-half haole and Polynesian, in this case. Will you go down the hall to our artist? Rodgers is describing J to him--should have a sketch by now. Pick it up for me, will you? I'd just as soon not see Rodgers right now." Lucky nodded.

As he reached the artist, Rodgers was saying, "That's about it--maybe a lower hairline. Except, he had on round-shaped tinted glasses. There you go; that's him. "

"Fine. You want to take this in to Major Kanai?" Joey asked.

"Not particularly. He chewed my ass a while ago. I'd just as soon he cooled off, first."

Lucky spoke up. "I'll take it. He sent me for it."

Pua had come in and Keoki was briefing her on the developments. He stared at the sketch, his brow wrinkling. "Dear Lord, I remember this face from somewhere. Can you kids spare an hour or so?" Pua glanced at Lucky inquiringly and he nodded. "Go check through the mug shots, will you, '83 and '84? See if you come up with something. I'll call them to expect you."

The rather distinguished face bore little resemblance to the hard-bitten visages that made up the bulk of the big book. In less than an hour, Pua found him. "Martin Jessop, alias Mark Jones, alias Miles Joss, alias Mr. j, it's a make. Lucky."

"Great! What's his record? Aha! California again, convictions for fraud; for practicing law after he was disbarred; served 18 months of a one-to-ten sentence for-- Qh! Look, here's an Island case, August 1983. It was fraud on Elsie Church at Banyon Rest Home. Charges dropped. Come on; let's go see if this rings a bell with Keoki. What's the number on this photo? We can sign out a copy—87670."

Keoki stared at the face, listening to Lucky's report at the same time. Suddenly, he slapped his forehead with the heel of his had. "Of course," he said. "He called himself Miles Joss and his scam was on an old widow out at the Banyan Rest Home. It was a get-rich-quick deal and she was ripe for the scam, because she thought she was getting low on funds. That's an expensive place.

"She wrote him a check for several thousand dollars and called her banker to tell him to cash it. I guess he didn't like the sound of it and explained why. She got scared and changed her mind wiki wiki. We got him-- don't recall the details--but he was arrested at the bank and we recovered the check. Held him on suspicion of theft."

"Then she wanted to talk to him. A deputy from the Prosecutor's office took him out there, let her have her private talk and by the time they got back to the station, she had called in that she refused to press charges. Just wanted her money back. She said it was a misunderstanding, 'all a mistake.' Mistake, my eye! But we had to let him go. And he kept going, as I recall— back to the mainland. Well, I'll get my men on it and you keep your eyes peeled as well. He's a slippery one. But we've got him cold as an accessory to Steele's murder."

Armed with copies of the mug shot, Lucky and Pua worked on opposite sides of the streets where their clients did business, to see if anyone recognized the attorney. Not one of them did.

Pua said, "Let's stop at the Mom n Pop Grocery and pick up a few things. While we're there, we can see if they recognize him."

"Good idea. I want to talk with them about the association, too, Pua. They haven't come to a meeting yet." Mom and Pop Hanohano had been in the same location for some forty years and enjoyed a regular trade from the residents in the surrounding area. At the moment, they had no customers, so Pop was trimming vegetables, while mom cleaned the glass-topped frozen food case.

"Fingerprints, fingerprints," she said, smiling. "Reminds me of my windows when the keikis were small. Couldn't keep their sticky little fingers away from them." She took a final swipe and put away her cloth. "There now, what can we do for you?"

Lucky stepped forward. "We're the people from Lucky Seven. You've heard of us?" She nodded. "This is Pua Kanai and I'm Lucky Gregory. We were sorry you couldn't make our meeting the other night."

She glanced quickly at her husband and her eyes shifted uncertainly as she answered. "We were sorry, too." She looked toward the cash register. "Your man Henley was in this morning and put in that signal thing. Pop said it was a good idea. He explained exactly how it

290

works. Mike's Malt is our tandem." She stopped suddenly.

"Pop," she said, defiantly, "I'm going to tell them, Pop thinks we should take care of it by ourselves, but I'm worried. A man came in here a few days ago and got two big bags of groceries. Expensive things. After I sacked them, he told me to take out the money in our cash drawer and put it in one of his bags and told us to keep our mouths shut about it, or he'd shoot me. It wasn't much, about $50 cash and roughly $65 wholesale of groceries, but it made me mad."

"He said someone would come in one day every week and if we followed the same orders, he'd guarantee we could go on doing business as usual. He said we could put it on our income tax as insurance. Insurance!"

"That is the kind of thing we're trying to fight, Mrs. Hanohano. Can you describe this man?"

"Oh dear, he was sort of ordinary looking, wore a cap pulled down on his forehead, had very pale skin and wore glasses, the kind that have darkish lenses; and he'd cut himself or something--had a bandage on one cheek. Otherwise, he was just sort of medium everything. Isn't that right, Pop?"

As he agreed, Lucky and Pua were nodding at each other in mutual agreement. "That man won't be bothering you again," Lucky said. "He was killed last night." And as they expressed shock, he added, "But he's just one among many, who may give trouble. I'm afraid his murder doesn't let any of you merchants off the hook. We'd like you to meet with us, whether you decide to use

291

our services or not, Mr. and Mrs. Hanohano."

"We don't get out of here until about a quarter of nine," Pop said.

"That's fine. You know where to go?"

"Yes, Albie told us. He thinks you're going to make a big difference around here. Actually, this is the first trouble we've had, but poor Mr. Bundy was robbed again last night. You knew that?"

Lucky's face tightened. "No, he didn't say anything about it," he said grimly. "We'll look into it."

Pua extended the mug shot. "One more thing. We would like to know if you recognize the man in this picture."

"Why yes, that's Mr. Jones. He's been in quite often. He buys frozen dinners and things like that. I think he must live alone. He only buys one of a kind, you know. He seems nice, but lonely-like. I feel sorry for him all alone like that."

"Well, watch yourself when he's in. We think he may be a key man in all this trouble. Just give us a call at this number if he returns, will you please? Does he drive or walk--did you happen to notice?"

"I'm sure he walks. He has a little folding cart-like thing he puts his groceries in and trundles it along. But he seems so nice. So gentlemen like. I can't believe he would be involved in anything wrong."

"Trust us, he doesn't deserve your sympathy." As she rang up Pua's purchases, she said, "You can be sure we'll be there Monday night, right, Pop?" And he looked a little sheepish as he nodded agreement.

"Don't hesitate to use the signal--just a touch will set it off--your contact is the Malt Shop? --Good. By the way, where did Henley place your signaling device?"

"Right here by the No Sale key. It's fastened under that little plastic calendar. I was afraid to put it on top of the register, for fear I'd trip it by mistake. This way, if we have trouble, he showed me how easy it is to move my hand to the right and nudge the calendar when I use the No Sale to open the cash drawer. I'm glad Mike is our tandem-partner. Such a fine, helpful young man!"

"All right, we'll look forward to seeing you on Monday night."

"We'll be there."

"And if Jones shows up, act natural. Don't let him know you suspect him, okay?"

"That's easy. You see, I still can't believe he's anything but a nice gentleman. But I'll be careful."

Hanohano spoke up. "Look here, if you and Pua don't mind, would you call us Mom and Pop? All our friends down here do and I think you folks are going to be very good friends to us."

"Thank you, Pop, we'll do that."

Chapter 28

The more he thought about Bundy's failure to mention being robbed again, the more perturbed Lucky became. He had to know why.

When he walked in, Bundy was sweeping out. He looked up and went back to sweeping. "I see you heard," he muttered.

"Sure. But I don't get it. You didn't--"

"'Cause it wasn't much!" Eyes intent upon his sweeping, Bundy said, "Some stoned kid took me for a few bucks and a few bottles of V.O. I don't argue with a user. You never know what them guys will do next. Had a buddy with him, but he just watched. In training maybe."

"But that's the point! You just gave him a free ticket to try it on someone else. Made it seem easy. Suppose he went over to the Mom n Pop store or to Mike's Malt Shop, afterward; and pulled some kind of heist, maybe hurt someone.

Don't you feel any responsibility for your neighbors?"

"I don't want them to get hurt. I'm gonna use the system, but this was just a piddling' little--"

"In your case, maybe. But getting away with it so easily might have given him the idea he could get more next-door.

"All you had to do was press your signal contact; and let him take what he came for--at that point your neighbors take over for possible identification and the police might well have had him in custody by now. You seemed to be with us at the meeting. Have you had a change of heart?"

The man shook his head, but wouldn't meet Lucky's eyes. "You made it sound easy, but when you're looking down the stumpy barrel of a Saturday night special, man, you don't think of anything but your own hide!"

"He pulled a gun on you?"

"Yep. Most of them do. This isn't a part of that protection business you folks were talking about. This was just a dumb hype kid; and each time it happens like that, it scares the hell out of me. I just want to get 'em out of my place. If I have to admit it, I will. I'm a coward." For the first time, he looked directly into Lucky's eyes.

"Why do you think you get hit so often? You have the reputation as an easy mark, that's why. And one of these days, one of them is going to put a slug in you--and maybe in one of your neighbors. Can't you understand that? Your type of business is more vulnerable of course; but you're being offered the support of your friends and neighbors; and don't you think you owe them support in return?"

"Never thought about it that way. You could be right." He looked thoughtful. "I could be looking at it all wrong."

"I believe you are."

"Yeah. Now that I think of it, I've really been

telling them to keep coming back--take my money, or booze--no huhu. Okay, count me in. Next time, I promise I'll signal." Slowly he rolled up his sleeve, revealing an ugly scar. "I got this when I hit my silent alarm one time last year. Kid about like this one got off a shot at me, while I was emptying the till, for God's sake. Can't blame me for being a little skittish after that, can you?"

"Of course not. But remember this. Go ahead and give 'em what they want; tap the signal and let your neighbors and the police take it from there. Where's your signal, anyway?"

"He set it on the side of my cash drawer panel."

"That's good. You can touch it in the very act of opening the drawer to take out the money."

"Good, unless one of these hypes opens the till while I'm standing there with my hands on my head, helpless."

"But even then, you could signal as he leaves, couldn't you?"

"I could do that all right, but wouldn't it be too late?"

"Perhaps, but in less than two seconds, the triple signal alerts all of our people and the police. We would have a good chance of identifying and perhaps arresting the suspect and he'd never be the wiser--that's the beauty of our system. There's no sound to give you away."

"That's right. Okay, I promise." He extended his hand tentatively and they shook.

"As Lucky turned to leave, Bundy called after him. "Oh, I can't be with you at the next meeting. My daughter's coming in from Maui. It's my birthday." He grinned. "She comes over every year to celebrate with me."

"Have a happy one! We'll let you in on anything that comes up."

Back at the office, a breathless Pua met him. "I've been trying to locate you. Dad called. One of the patrolmen out near Aina Haina caught sight of Ruby driving out toward Hawaii Kai, in company with three men. They were held up in traffic by an accident he was covering and he recognized her from this morning's ready-room briefing. She and her companions complained that they'd be late for their lunch date at Pat's. "Dad wants to know if we'd ride out that way and see if they're up to something. They're in a blue Buick sedan with a silver stripe, Oregon plates--we don't have the number. "

"Call him and tell him we're on our way, Pua."

Midday traffic along the beach was negligible and the powerful car had a chance to show her stuff. Lucky grunted his satisfaction.

"Dad figures the car may be stolen and is sure the Oregon plate is. If they're trying to be cute, they'll probably drive off on a beach frontal road and change it for a Hawaiian one--especially since the incident with that patrolman. He thinks we should concentrate on the car--how many Buick's sport a silver streak anyway?"

"Tell you what, Lucky, when we get to Pat's, why

297

not drive on past a little ways and turn around. Then we'll appear to be coming from the other direction, when we enter the parking lot--just in case they're edgy about being followed. Only takes five minutes or so more."

"Good thinking. We'll do it." As he parked, Pua said, "There it is, a blue Buick sedan, silver stripe and all. And they've changed to Hawaii plates. I'll jot down the number for what it's worth. Now what?"

"Now, we'll go in and have lunch."

"That woman has seen you before, darling, if you'll remember. Isn't that risky?"

"No-way. To her I was just a horny, hasty John. And so what if she does recognize me? A nice tourist type like me has a right to pick up a local wahine and take her to the famous Pat's at Punalu'u for lunch, for Pete's sake!"

"I suppose," she said, dubiously. Seated at a garden-side table for two, they looked around casually and found their quarry across the room at a large table. In addition to the four they expected to see, there were two other men and it looked as if they were all involved in a bitter argument, even though their voices were hushed. The convivial martinis in front of each of them seemed curiously out of place. While Lucky ordered, Pua was surreptitiously making descriptive notes of the faces she could see. The heavy-set man at the end of the table was apparently conducting the luncheon meeting; and his bearing of authority caused her to take special care in his description.

"I've seen that big guy somewhere before. Want to

298

bet he is not the big boss?" she whispered.

"Not a chance I'm going to bet with you, lady. Now put that away and let's make like the sweethearts we are.

Holding her hand and looking deep into her eyes, he said softly, "It looks to me as if the Madam is on the carpet. She's angry and she's scared." He kissed Pua's fingertips and with her most alluring smile, she answered, "I wish I could remember where I saw that man before-- maybe his picture was in the paper or something."

Touching glasses, they pretended a toast and Pua lowered her eyes shyly as he told her, "Go to the lady's room, over there, beyond where they're sitting. When you come back, pay close attention to the faces of the men who have their backs to us." And as she stood, she blew him a kiss and whispered, "You, my dear, are Mr. Excitement. I adore these tough assignments." As she passed the big table, he noticed an admiring glance after her from one of the men, but other than that, there was no reaction.

They were all trying to talk at once when she returned and as far as he could see, no one was even aware of her brief pause on the terrace before making her way back to the table. "Lucky," she whispered excitedly, as he rose to seat her, "the thinner man at the end of the table is Mr. J. I'm sure of it." She gestured, as if complimenting him on his choice of the foods, which had been served during her absence.

"The other man is balding and scarred."

"That's it, then," rolling his eyes appreciatively

over a forkful of food. "Now let's enjoy our meal."

"Are we going to tail them from here?" she asked. "No, I think we're home free so far and I'd like to get our report back to Keoki as soon as possible. Besides, they're just beginning to eat. We'll be finished before they are; and we're here to observe only, remember. Mmm, this Opapapapa fish is great, don't you think?"

She chuckled. "Opakapaka, my dear. I love it--so moist and tender. For dessert they chose Pat's world famous coconut cream pie, made with fresh shredded coconut and genuine fresh coconut cream and rich Kona coffee. As they ate, both kept track of what was going on at that big table. As Lucky seemed to be concentrating, she gave her whole attention to the food.

When they were homeward bound again, she said, "Ruby's face was as red as her hair. She didn't, repeat didn't, enjoy her lunch."

"I know. I've got a job for you. Did you get another notebook?"

"Right here."

"Good! Divide it into five columns across. Got it? At her shaka sign, he said, "Label the first column Big Man, below that, exactly what I say. Ready? 'Damn stupid to take a chance like that--clear with me first on any change in plans.' Then 'I can't afford to take a fall on this.' And two more: 'No, not the office--use the beauty shop line' and 'You mess up, you're out of it I'll call you if I have to, but I better not have to--I trust you get my meaning.'

"Now Ruby sat next to him, so use her name for the next column and under it, 'but I didn't do it obviously, just on regular visits. I read a lot, you know' and in the same column 'well, thanks to J and Weasel, he's not alive to talk.' And one more: 'The Steele kid got them for me. I didn't buy that trash.'"

"Column three and four are from the other side of the island, I think. The one next to Ruby, 'What's all this got to do with our end of it?' And in column four, 'We're running smooth on our side, but sounds to me like something funny's going on in Honolulu. I don't like it one bit.'

"And in column five, head it attorney and 'I had no choice. Hell, you were on Maui. He knew too much. I had to do something fast. Those goons owed me. Got all that, Pua?"

She turned mystified eyes toward him. "Yes, but what is it all about?"

"One of my secret talents, love. I read lips and am blessed with a memory that won't quit; but I wanted it down on paper while it was clear in my mind. Maybe we can piece together some of it for your dad's use. It's sketchy, but I didn't dare sit there staring at those people all the time. There are other little bits I'll be able to fill in, as well."

"You are incredible!" Pua was reviewing the notes with wonder. "Did you always have that talent, or did you learn it somewhere?"

"I wouldn't call it a talent, but I've always been able to do it--the memory thing, I mean--I learned lip-reading, can you believe, in the Boy Scouts. Got a merit badge for it. Couldn't hack it in knots though. Still can't tie 'em."

"Hmm. It occurs to me that the trash Steele got for Ruby would be poor Prof's pornography."

"That's the way I read it."

At headquarters, Keoki greeted them with a question. "Anything?" he asked. "I hope you got something. Things are at a standstill, here."

"We had a pretty interesting time and when we figure out what it means, I think we have something that may just answer a lot of questions." He tossed the notebook to the major.

"What the hell? You heard all this?" Pua looked smug. "No Dad, Lucky reads lips. He gave me all that on the way back here. Is he amazing, or what!"

"He is for a fact. A talent like this has tremendous potential in detection. I'm glad to see they're wrangling. It's bad for them but good for us. Dissension computes to weakness and that'll help us bag them. Let's go somewhere when we can get away from here and study this out. Okay with you?"

"You bet."

"You're sure they didn't make you? "

"I don't think they even noticed us. But in case they did, we were pretending love talk, while we discussed what was going on. Only one man looked up when Pua went to the ladies' room and that was plain lasciviousness. He was one of the two who apparently came to the meeting together from the Windward side. It proved to us that this thing isn't just over here. They weren't happy, though."

Just then the phone rang. With a now sort of shrug, Keoki answered. "Kanai. Yes, they're here now... No kidding!....Want to talk with...I see. That's great! I'll tell them."

"Your people have had some excitement and we have ourselves a new jail bird."

"What's happened?"

"Your man Bundy got hit again this afternoon. The signals worked perfectly and a half a dozen of the merchants converged on the area. They got reasonably close and nothing seemed to be happening, so Palani decided to check it out. Just as he got to the Package Store door, a young hoodlum came dashing out and Palani tripped him, brought him down hard and sat on him until the police got there. All this time, Bundy was yelling, 'Don't let him go, he's got a gun!' And Palani just kept sitting on him. Can't you picture it? About 300 pounds of Hawaiian plunked down on about a 110 pound weakling?" Keoki was mopping tears of laughter from his eyes; then sobered.

"Bundy identified him as the kid who was in on it, when he got hit the other day."

"That doesn't surprise me," Lucky said. "What was stolen today?"

"Bundy had sold $300 worth of champagne for a

303

party, about an hour before. The cash was still in his till. He'll recover that, of course, but the bottles of Jack Daniels, that the kid had grabbed on his way out, crashed on the sidewalk. Taking them delayed him just long enough to put Palani in position to trip him on the way out. Greed! So many times it gives us the upper hand,"

"Wow! That should make a believer of our friend Bundy!"

"You better believe it!" Palani was standing in the open doorway, a broad grin on his face. "Come on in, Palani. Great job!"

"Mahalo. I'd be lying if I didn't say I enjoyed myself. And I enjoyed my friend Bundy? As soon as they carted the kid away, he began to tell the others that the system works perfectly. Your other clients were all smiles."

Lucky shook his head. "We must all remember that it was you folks' own efforts that really paid off. That's what this system is all about. Cooperation--Kokua. Looks as if our automatic monitor is operating well, too. Hadn't really had a chance to try it out yet."

Keoki was making a beckoning signal through the window. "Come on in, Bundy," he called.

"Hi!" said the little man, his face mirroring both excitement and satisfaction. "I heard you folks were in here. I just want to say thanks for converting me. My neighbors were great! Wish you could have seen Palani do his thing, Major. It cracked us all up."

"I hear you were telling the others how great it

worked."

"I sure did--but I waited until he was arrested and on his way to the slammer. Didn't want to give away any secrets."

Lucky looked worried. "Did the others hang around?"

"Most went on back to work, but some stayed. They were all of them our neighbors--no strangers. We remembered what you said."

"That's good. Did this guy pull his gun on you?"

"No, he just pulled it part way out of his pocket, when he made me open the cash drawer. I couldn't afford that kind of loss, but neither could I afford to take a slug, so I trusted you and the neighbors like I promised and it sure paid off. I feel sorry about being so slow to get the message. In a way, I'm to blame for making it so easy for him the other day. I know better now. Well, I must get back. See you guys at the meeting."

"You will? What about your daughter?"

"I'm going to bring her along. I wouldn't miss this one!" And off he went, a jaunty, confident spring in his step they'd never seen before.

Chapter 29

"That does it for me," Keoki sighed. "Let's get out of here." And in minutes, they were sitting at Lucky Seven's round table, nibbling, sipping and piecing their information together.

"Now then, you're sure that one of the men was Mr. J, right?"

"Right."

"So let's concentrate first on the big man, who seemed to be running the meeting. Pua had the impression that she'd seen him before. Her description of him brings to my mind an old foe by the name of Ferdinand Barnard, a.k.a. Ferdi the Bull, a.k.a the Breaker. But I can't understand how it could possibly be him.

"Several years ago, he burst on the Hawaiian scene. We knew that he was tied in closely with the mainland crime syndicate that had infiltrated the local crime scene, but somehow, he managed to have a scapegoat handy every time the police picked him up. He consistently frustrated us with legal monkeyshines that absolutely negated prosecution."

"That pattern fits," offered Lucky.

"Several years ago," Keoki continued, "he began running junkets to Vegas for Japanese tourists; expensive ones that included a call girl operation over there. He wasn't satisfied with the take, so he added blackmail to his agenda and that was what finally did him in. He put the arm on the wrong tourist, an undercover agent of the

Tokyo Special Forces team, who had been sent over here to investigate. And that was all she wrote!

"The long and the short of it was that he was sent up for ten to twenty in Nevada State Prison. He's still there--or should be--" Suddenly, he stiffened.

He made a brief phone call, gave terse instructions and waited. In minutes, the phone rang. He listened to the message, his face-hardened.

"Just what I suspected," he muttered. 'Subject was released, July 14, 1988, Conditional upon his leaving Nevada permanently. Present location unknown.'

"And so it figures that he went and recovered his stash and moved back to beautiful Hawaii. That's the long and the short of it. We don't even have an active file on him. Could be he settled on a neighbor island when he came back to Hawaii."

"Dad! I remember! When I came home for a week, just before I was assigned to South Hills, I flew to Kona to see Aunty Ilima--my godmother," she explained to Lucky. "It was to attend her 60th birthday luau."

"And mom and I couldn't go because I had a flu bug. Go on. "

"Well, if I'm not mistaken, this man is the noisy big spender on that flight--bought drinks for everyone on board. Claimed he was celebrating something. I don't recall what." She paused, frowning.

"Oh yes I do! He'd just bought a condominium over here--not just an apartment, the whole building--at a steal, he bragged.

"If I recall correctly, he was on his way to get some belongings he'd stored on the Big Island, so he could move back home--I'm sure he said home. Dad, I really think this is the same man."

"And if he is, he's obviously here and back in the rackets. That's all we need--a lousy racketeer like him, operating in Paradise! You say he seemed to be running the show up at Pat's?"

"Definitely! The snatches of conversation that Lucky caught lip-reading certainly bear that out. And from these notes, he was upset that he wasn't getting the cooperation he felt was his due."

"That's true. Now, the pale one you describe as scarred is Harry Peale. He had most of his face scraped off in an accident, some years ago. Runs an electronic game place in Kaneohe. He's been in and out of jail-- mostly petty stuff. May be moving up to the big leagues, huh?"

"Sounds like it. But I don't think the other Windward man has been here long," Lucky interposed. "Grayish papery, skin--maybe prison pallor?"

"Likely. And that brings us to Ruby. More and more she looks to be his operations manager--but Mr. Big is not happy with her, either. That's for sure. And here, it looks as though Mr. J was out of favor, too. Lucky, let me take these notes with me, okay? Or do you need them?"

"We did them for you, Keoki. I'm glad you feel they may help."

Nothing occurred to break the peace of the area

between then and Saturday. But around ten on that morning, there was another incident. It was a first and of all people, it was Mrs. Garcia who triggered it. Lucky and Pua were bringing their case files up to the minute, when a light flashed on the signal board, followed by the triple-ring alert.

"It's the Cantina. Let's go, Pua." By the time they reached the street, they could see Mike and Albie walking together toward the trouble area; and across the street Stella was walking in the same direction with Prof by her side. Bundy was strolling along at a reasonable distance. While they could detect a quiet excitement about it all, there was no rushing. Their people were playing their parts to perfection. They could see Palani crossing the street to the Cantina a block ahead of them. Following instructions, all of the clients were observing the passersby with no more than a reasonable amount of interest.

Suddenly, they saw Garcia rushing out his door, gesticulating wildly as a patrol car pulled up near his restaurant.

Palani reached him first and they could see him urging the agitated Mexican back inside--and then, with a slight wave of his hand, he started back to his own shop.

"That's strange," Lucky frowned.

The patrolmen were entering the cantina by this time; so the rest of the strollers began a retreat, still following instructions by keeping alert to anything of possible significance. But there wasn't anything to see. A boy on his bike caused Stella to stop short, but presently she continued on her way, as she recognized a neighbor's child.

And then the patrol car left.

"What's going on?" Lucky muttered. "That's not part of the scenario."

Pua shook her head, puzzled.

"Let's go in." And as they entered the door, Garcia was spouting a cascade of irate Spanish at his wife, who was sobbing at a table, her head in her arms.

"Hey, hey, what's all this?" Lucky asked.

"My Rosa, she plain stupid," the angry man cried. "We not even open yet today and she has to dust everything, make it just so, so. She dust the register and forget turn off the signal first. So easy, too, like flipping a light button. Next thing I know, here come Palani, police- -Jesu Cristo, I get mad!"

"Why didn't you signal the false alarm? Touch it twice, right away, to call everything off?"

The man's face fell. "I forget," he admitted. "Hey, Rosa, don' cry. I dumb, too. I sorry I yell. Next time, we both do it right." He patted her ample shoulder and she looked up at him, answering his shamed expression with a tremulous smile, as she brushed away her tears.

"Go make more tortillas," she said with a final sniffle. "We gotta open for lunch."

"Don't worry about this, folks," Lucky told them. "No damage was done. In a way it's good it happened. Now we know the other people know how to respond, that's for sure.

As they walked back toward the office, Lucky chuckled. "I really meant it. It was better than our dry run. The others were convinced it was a real emergency and behaved very well, didn't you think?"

"They had the right idea. That patrolman wasn't bad either. He got out of there fast, when he knew it was a false alarm. I'll bet poor Rosa doesn't make the same mistake twice--or Jose either. It was so funny when he realized it was his own fault that the call wasn't canceled."

"It sure put his fire out! Honey, let's take the rest of the day off and go on out to see your mom. I'm ready for another swim in the cove."

"Me, too. I want to pick up some more of my things and I can do our laundry out there, too, if you pack up yours. Why don't I take the Fiat back to the apartment and get ready. You can pick me up in a half hour. How does that strike you?"

"Good thinking. You coming up first?"

"No need. You get your stuff together." And she walked up to the little Fiat, got in, waved, flashed a big smile and was gone.

Lucky was in a pensive mood, as they drove out toward Diamond Head. He pulled off at the view spot beyond the lighthouse and drew her into his arms. "Sweetheart, I'm not too happy about you going back and forth to that apartment. I want you with me. I love you so much. Will you please marry me?"

"We've discussed this before, darling. I want to, you know I do; and some day we will be married, God willing, but I want it to be because we can't stand not to be married, not as a logical out for an inconvenient living arrangement. Do you know what I'm saying?"

"I didn't mean it that way--you know I didn't," he protested. "But yes, I guess what you say does make good sense. Would you consider moving in with me, then?"

"I think that's the best idea for now; but I want to talk about it with mom, first." And at his startled look, "We're always up front with each other."

"Would you like me to talk about it with Keoki?"

"No, when the time comes, we'll do that together." She nestled close to him. Their kisses spoke more clearly than words of the love and understanding they felt for each other and the yearning to be together.

"I'm nervous," he confessed.

"Don't be," she answered. "My parents and I have a unique relationship. I've always been able to talk with them frankly and so will you. Whatever they say, you can count on it to be their honest opinion. Trust us. Come on, dear, let's go swimming."

The swim, the dinner, the music and dancing and the ever-closer companionship were as delightful in every detail as it had been before. Afterward, Pua asked her mother to come with her while she packed up more of her things; and Malia offered to fold the laundry they had done earlier in the afternoon. "There's something important I want to talk with you about, mom," Pua said.

"Somehow, that doesn't surprise me," her mother answered. "I've seen that look in your eyes so many times, when you had a secret you wanted to entrust to me."

"Lucky asked me to marry him today," Pua began, "but I told him it was too soon." Malia said nothing. "I've stayed over with him twice this week," she went on. "Does that shock you Mom?"

Malia smiled gently. "Not really. We know you're very much attracted to each other--and we love you both. Your dad and I have discussed it a little. Lucky is a fine man and you're both adults in every sense of the word."

"You see, my Pualani, we keep remembering a certain young cop from Hawaii and a young crime lab assistant, who met in England. We had the same decisions to make then, that you are facing now. We stayed together for several months and we cherish the memory.

"My reason for not marrying him then, was that I didn't want it to be from pity, because I'd lost my family. I wanted to be sure it was the honest, mutual, lasting love that all people who marry should feel. I can understand, in your situation, how you could have the same kind of concerns. "

Pua hugged her impulsively. "I knew you'd understand that. I don't want to marry him because he worries about my being alone in Alika's apartment. But I do want to be with him. He's wonderful, Mom. I want to marry him some day, but for all the right reasons."

"Well, it worked for me, Pua. Three months after

Keoki left England, I was on my way alone to this wonderful place to become his wife. Those months apart had been an eternity of longing for both of us. I've never regretted my decisions for a minute."

Suddenly she frowned and held up a pair of Lucky's Bermuda's. "Honey, look at this, there's a puka in these. Let me get my needle and thread. I'll mend them in a jiffy."

Both of them understood--that meant this was all that needed to be said. Pua was never to forget that talk, or the equally understanding one she and Lucky had later with her father.

He had listened quietly as they both talked. Lucky found the going surprisingly easy.

"What I really wanted to do tonight was ask your permission to marry Pua," he said. "We are very much in love, but she won't agree to marry me yet and I understand how she feels. But I want to protect her and love her and be with her. However, it's important to me that we do nothing to hurt you and her mother. So please, Sir, be frank with us."

"The way I see it, Son," Keoki said, reaching for Malia's hand, "our Pua and you are both adult people and you have the right to live your lives as you see fit. I admit that a wedding would be much to my liking, but I have to give credit to Pua for her feelings on the subject. You don't rush these women. I tried." He drew Malia's hand to his lips and kissed it gently.

"We seemed to turn out all right and I have confidence that you two will do the same. We can't be

314

hurt by anything that makes our daughter happy; and personally I think she has darned good taste."

On the way home a little later, Lucky said, with a kind of awe, "That couldn't have been easy for them, you their only daughter and all. I'm proud that he put that kind of faith and trust in me and in our relationship. But one of these days, young lady, I'm going to convince you to marry me and we can have a family of our own. I just hope our children will have as wise parents as your mother and father."

"We'll see to it," Pua laughed, snuggling close to him. "May I move in tomorrow? We have a whole Sunday to do it in. "

"I think we can arrange it," he teased. "But Jake, our esteemed manager, may raise his eyebrows, though, huh?"

"Never," said Pua. "That rascal has a live-in housekeeper of his own."

"Now, look here, Pua, you're no live-in " His voice trailed off as laughter convulsed her. "Just for that," he said, "I want my favorite breakfast tomorrow morning, prepared by a little brown gal in my pajama tops and apron! So there!"

By Sunday night, she had moved in; and they were planning to buy an armchair for Pua; an armoire for her things--and found it more than ample for their needs.

"Happy, Pualani?"

"Ecstatic," she said.

Chapter 30

Pua had just started to prepare dinner, when the phone rang.

Lucky answered. "Oh, hi Keoki, what's up?..."What? When? Oh, no! Oh, my God...I'll get there as fast as I can make it."

Pua had turned pale. Is it mom?"

"No, no, sweetheart. I think it is Brenda, the one who talked with me Tuesday night. She's at Queen's. Your dad was called in and he's with her. I have to hurry. They don't think she's going to make it. She's asking for me."

"Would you like me to go with you?"

"I think I'd better go alone. I don't know how long I'll be gone. I'll call you, when I know something." He rushed out the door. Keoki met him at the emergency entrance and led him hastily to an examination room. As he looked at the torn and broken young woman on the table, Lucky felt his gorge rise. He looked away, quickly.

"Is she gone?" he asked.

The doctor in attendance shook his head. "She's still hanging on, but I don't know how. Are you Lucky?"

"Yes."

"She kept calling your name. Speak to her. You may be able to get through, but she's sinking fast. I don't think she can last much longer."

Lucky swallowed hard. "Brenda," he said,

316

"Brenda, its Lucky. You want to tell me something?" There was no response. "Brenda, what happened? Can you tell me? I'm your friend. I want to help you."

The small, battered face twitched and her eyes opened--the blue irises barely visible between the ugly, swollen, purple bruises that distorted her face.

"Lucky?"

"I'm right here, Brenda."

"Purse," she muttered. "I made break." Her eyes closed.

"Brenda, who did this to you? Brenda!" He laid his hand gently over hers and looked inquiringly at the doctor, who shrugged slightly and indicated he should try again.

As he leaned over her, the eyes opened again. "Ruby, Madam, she caught me, --back stairs--with Weasel--he hit me too, so hard. He chops me--." She moved slightly and moaned with pain. "Purse, Lucky, --in--my purse." The bruised and cut lips tried to smile. "See, I almost made it, Lucky. I wouldn't...tell on you...never." Again the voice faded.

"You did fine. You'd better rest now." Again the blue eyes gleamed beneath the swollen lids and the pathetic half-smile formed on her lips. "Find glove, Lucky--an' secret in purse. You get 'em. Glove--seat. I won--! Got away, didn't I?" And as her head fell to the side, those still lips held that rueful half-smile.

"The doctor bent over her--then straightened, shaking his head. "This woman is dead," he pronounced solemnly.

Lucky looked down at her, sadly. "Yes, Brenda, you got away," he whispered, "And we're going to get the people that did this to you." He followed Keoki from the room.

They stopped to give instructions to the patrolman outside the door and went on out to Keoki's car.

"Did she say anything before I got there?" Lucky asked huskily.

"She kept mumbling your name and seemed to be worrying about her new gloves and her purse. Nothing very helpful, I'm afraid."

Lucky rubbed his forehead in frustration. "How did you find her?"

"She was found this afternoon near the edge of a steep bank off the Tantalus road. You know where that is?"

"I know. Pua and I drove up there one day."

"Some residents were searching the area today for their dog. He'd apparently jumped the fence and disappeared some time during the night. About three this afternoon, they finally found the dog, shot to death and were starting to carry him out of there, when they heard a moan and that's when they discovered her. They called the ambulance and the police and she was brought here. It took awhile to bring her up to the ambulance. The doctor did everything he could for her, but she was broken to pieces. She didn't have a chance. Both legs and her right arm were broken; and she had severe internal injuries,

318

from the beating--or possibly the fall--or both. She'd been thrown down a steep hill--twenty more yards and she would have slid over the edge and we might never have found her. That hillside is a mass of giant philodendron.

"Her clothing was wet; and the bloodstains had run, from the rain; but her purse was under her body and was relatively dry. There's nothing in it but a compact and lipstick--no I.D., no wallet, no money. The doctor says she was probably unconscious for hours, which was a blessing."

"What happened to the purse? She seemed sure we'd find something in it."

"Oh, I have it here. I signed for it. Don't know why, really. She seemed to set so many stores by it is all. We checked it for fingerprints--nothing but smudges. No gloves in it."

Lucky examined the black shoulder bag with care, checking the lining, thumping the rigid base of it. "She was a pretty cool person and I can't believe she'd put anything of significance where just anyone could find it. She must have hidden whatever it is, carefully, somewhere in this thing."

"Well, the bottom line is that it's not there now." Lucky looked up, startled. "Wait a minute. I think you said the magic words. Let me see that again." With eager fingers, he reached in, checking around its base panel carefully and found a tiny release spring. He tripped it and the firm bottom panel popped up to reveal an airline ticket and a few bills, hidden in the narrow space beneath it. "That's what I figured," he said, showing it to Keoki.

"I'll be damned!" Keoki exploded. "What gave you that idea?"

"You did, when you said 'the bottom line.' My mother used to have a handbag with this kind of bottom. She carried her extra money down there when she shopped. Called it her emergency fund. That bag, with its hiding place, flashed into my mind." They examined the ticket. "Poor soul," Keoki said.

"She was booked to go out on the ten o'clock flight for L.A. last night, economy class. She got away, all right, but not the way she had it planned."

"There's something else down here," Lucky said, drawing out a slip of paper. "Oh my God, listen to this: 'Lucky, if you read this you know I got caught. Ruby's acting funny and I'm scared, but its now or never for me. I know it. I can't live like this any more, so don't feel bad. I'd just as soon be dead as live like this. Brenda.'"

The two men stared at each other, their faces mirroring pity. Keoki sighed and said in a choking voice, "I've got to get back to the office, Lucky. Her dying statement means we can go ahead and arrest the Ruby woman and this note should nail her good. I left instructions; they may have brought her in already. You go on home. I'll be in touch."

"What about the Weasel? And I wonder what Brenda meant about the glove. Do you have any idea?" Lucky asked.

"Not at this point. We'll have to see what develops."

320

Lucky drove home with a heavy heart for the little hooker who had risked so much for freedom--but at the same time he began to understand that her murder could bring down the house of cards that the extortion ring had built. He just wished he could quit picturing Brenda lying there in the rain, so hurt, so alone, for so many awful hours.

Pua took one look at him as he entered and flew into his arms in an oddly comforting way. "She died?" she asked.

"Yes, while I was there." He went on to tell her the story, and as she listened, horrified, another idea crossed his mind. "That's about it up to now, but I want to call Keoki about something."

"I'll get him for you," she said and dialed. "Major Kanai, please.... Oh, I see, would you have him call his daughter when he returns'? Thank you."

She turned to Lucky. "They arrested Ruby, just brought her in and dad is busy with that so he'll call when he can. Why don't we have martinis and a little something to eat, while we wait?"

"I suppose we should. I just feel rotten about this, Pua. After all, she tried to help us, you know and she was trying to help herself as well. There was good in her. She was trapped in a lifestyle she wanted to escape. I honestly believe that and it makes me sad for her. And I keep wondering if I was respon--"

"Don't even think it, Lucky. She took a risk to gain back her dignity. She knew the odds. But you said her dying words were, "I won." Remember that. She made her choice all by herself. There's gallantry in that."

He held her close. "How perceptive you are, my Pua. Thank you, darling."

A half hour went by and then nearly another before Keoki called. "Pick up your phone so you can listen too, Pua," Lucky suggested. "Go ahead, Keoki. But don't hang up before I ask my question."

"Ruby's in custody and she's been yelling 'false arrest' and denying everything so far. She's scared--scared to death. When her rights were read, she said she didn't need an attorney and she didn't want to make her one call. She hadn't done anything, she kept saying; but she also told us we couldn't prove anything. She'll break, sooner or later. A few minutes ago the boys checked her car, found traces of bloodstains in the back seat. The spots were still damp from a scrubbing."

"They're checking type against the victim's now. Also a good set of Brenda's prints, her whole left hand, as a matter of fact, were found on the inside of the back window of the car, almost as if she'd deliberately placed them there." The rest of the car was clean."

"I believe now that they thought she was dead when they put her in the car and when they threw her out up there. Certainly they didn't figure her to regain consciousness after their brutality. I believe at some point, she came to and managed to take off her glove and deliberately make that handprint. You see we found one bloodstained white glove for the left hand, stuffed under the back seat of the car. She gave us hard evidence."

"I guess its part of our job messing into people's

lives. I'm just feeling low about her losing hers."

"I understand. But remember this, Lucky. She had already begun on escape plans before you ever met her."

"That's true. Thanks for reminding me. So what happens next? I assume you shook down the massage parlor. Anything?"

"Oh, yes, I meant to tell you. We found bloodstains on the back stairs; and a high-heeled slipper that they'd attempted to burn, in the dumpster. The sole and heel were about all that was left, but the lab says it's a match with the one we found on the hillside."

"She made them lose their cool. Damn it, Keoki, all they had to do was let her go on back to Michigan or Iowa, or wherever she came from. There wasn't any sane reason to murder her."

"Criminals so often get paranoid and make senseless decisions. Say, what was it you called about?"

"I have an idea I'd like to explore. Would you mind calling the people who found her and ask them to call me here? It would simplify things if you authorized them to talk with me."

"I don't see anything wrong with that. I'll do it right now. The name is Chesman. Have to get back in interrogation soon. So I'll let you go." When the phone rang again, Pua asked if she could listen in again and he nodded. "Hello," he said. "This is Mr. Chesman. Major Kanai asked me to call you. What can I do for you?"

"Thank you for calling, Mr. Chesman. I was sorry to hear about your dog and wanted to ask you a question or two about it."

"We're pretty shaken about the whole thing. Regis was more than a watch dog; he was like a member of the family."

"What breed?"

"He was a registered Doberman Pinscher, six years old. He'd been well schooled and the only trouble we ever had with him was running after cars up here. I can't figure how he got out, actually. We had just increased the height of the fence by another foot."

"He chased a car last night?"

"I'm afraid he did. We were having a party down in the den and it was a little noisy. We didn't know he was gone until rather late this morning, when we went to feed him, you know. Didn't hear him or any car. That's not much help, I'm afraid."

"Now I have to ask you a painful question. Is the bullet slug still in his body?"

"I imagine so; there was no point of exit. He's at Pet Haven now. I'll have them call you, if you like. Was that poor woman shot too?"

"No, she wasn't. The slug that killed your dog might have belonged to a gun that will figure in another case though and that just could place the girl's murderers on the scene. Would you be willing to arrange for its recovery?"

"I surely will, anything to help. That was a dreadful thing that happened to that woman. Did she make it?"

"No, she didn't," Lucky answered.

"I was afraid of that. I'm sorry. If that's all, I'll make that call now. I'll authorize them to--er--search for it. "

When the phone finally rang again, the man at Pet Haven told him, "I have the slug. It's flattened, but has pretty apparent markings. Will someone pick it up?"

"Yes, an officer will be up there in the morning."

"Fortunate you called when you did. We were preparing the dog for interment tomorrow."

"I'm very grateful for your help. You'll be open in the morning?"

"Yes sir. Someone's here day and night all year round." Lucky shook his head as he put the phone down. "First time I ever talked with an animal undertaker. He had that same doleful voice, so typical of morticians. But he got the slug. It could be a valuable hunk of evidence. We'll see."

"I'm going to try to get dad again," Pua said. "I'll bet he hasn't had time to eat. I could make the three of us salad and spaghetti--what do you think?"

"Go ahead. Won't hurt to try."

This time she got through to her father without delay and offered her invitation. "About an hour? Okay, it'll be ready. And Dad--" but he had gone.

"He's coming. Open that bottle of red wine so it can breathe, will you Lucky? I'll get the sauce on and in

325

case he's too busy, I'll give mom a buzz. She won't come in, but she'll be glad to hear that he's having dinner. She always frets about him missing meals, when he's busy on a case."

It was a tired man who finally walked through their door. He kissed Pua. "Thanks for asking me, honey," he said. "Thanks for calling mom, too. I remembered this time, but you'd already relieved her mind. Well, this thing is beginning to take form."

He took a pull at the beer Pua had placed near him. "Ooh, that's good. How did you know I could go off-duty, girl?"

"Woman's intuition, what else?" she said. "Dinner's nearly ready."

He settled back, comfortably. "Tell me how you came out with the Chessman's, Son."

"It dawned on me that there could well be a tie-in between the dog's death and Brenda's murder. Too much of a coincidence to have the dog shot and the girl disposed of at the same time and place. The slug was recovered and is at Pet Haven. Can someone pick it up tomorrow morning?"

"You bet they can! Good work, Lucky. We were all so busy with the girl we didn't make the connection. When I tried to figure out what you were up to, I began to get an inkling that we'd slipped up. I'm grateful, believe me. With vermin like we're dealing with. I want every bit of evidence we can get."

"Time to eat. Give me a hand, Lucky?" Pua set a

huge bowl of green salad, aromatic with Italian dressing, on the table; and brought in heaping plates of spaghetti, while Lucky poured the wine.

"A lot of things came out today that just may--" Keoki began, then stopped as he noticed his daughter's admonishing stare.

"No business talk now. It will wait until after dinner," she said firmly.

Her father shook his head, laughing, as he told her, "I swear, every day you get more and more like your mother!"

She grinned back. "I should be so lucky!" she said.

Chapter 31

With the last of the breakfast dishes stowed away in the cupboard, Pua called out, "I'm ready; are you?"— The doorbell rings. She runs to open it.

"Kea! This is a nice surprise. Come have a cup of coffee. Lucky will be here in a minute."

"We really haven't time," he said. "Keoki sent me to get you. All hell broke loose during the night and he wants us to meet him in the briefing room. Lieutenant Parkins will be there too. Hi, Lucky, I came to--"

"I heard. What's going on? I could have driven over."

"I know, but he said to bring you. We'll be going in the back way. Kind of a hush-hush thing, I guess. He's been fair with the press, but they still want more; and he doesn't want to jeopardize the case by releasing critical information."

Keoki was mulling over some papers with the lieutenant. "'Morning," he said. "Sit down. We'll be right with you." His face was drawn and lined with weariness.

"Dad, you look awful!" Pua exclaimed.

"I expect I do, honey. I've been here since three a.m. You can thank Ruby for that. She blew up. Insisted they call me.

"When I got here, she wanted to make a deal--her story for protective custody and a safety guarantee until she gets off the island. And I told her she was talking to the wrong man. Her story should go the prosecutor; and she went completely bananas. Screamed a string of filth I wouldn't even repeat.

"No way, I'll talk to that bastard," she shouted after me. "Hell, I'll give you the top man, if you'll deal for me!"

"I walked back to her cell and told her, 'don't bother. We already know about Ferdi.' The color drained from her face and she went down in a dead faint. I called a paramedic. He pulled her out of it--and she kept yelling she had to talk to me; that someone would bail her out and then kill her."

Lieutenant Parkins was grinning sourly. "Good God, Keoki, don't you remember? It was Ruby Pierce who engineered the scandal on Danny Kikomo's personal life, when he ran for District Attorney. Damned near cost him the election and his wife and kids. Ruby left the islands, when he was elected anyway. After the hell she put him through, he's the last person in the world she'd go to for her deal. Old Danny isn't about to let her off the hook and she knows it."

"Holy Mother, you're right. I recall all the fuss, but just didn't connect it with this woman. It's a wonder she came back to Hawaii at all."

Lucky spoke up. "Mr. Big, no doubt and perhaps Mr. J. No one seems to dare to say 'no' to them!"

"And J would scare her even more," Pua said, quietly. "He bailed Steele out and look what happened to him."

The lieutenant slapped his thigh. "Seems to me we have plenty of hard evidence against her to take her to the

Grand Jury. But let's wait a bit. She may just crack the whole thing wide open, in hopes of saving her own skin."

"Kea, why don't you make yourself busy around the desk area. Keep watch. Nobody's to see Ruby without me knowing about it first."

"You got it, Sir."

After he'd left, Pua said, "Dad, you need rest--isn't there somewhere--"

"After while, honey. I'm getting my second wind now. I want to fill you in on the guy I knew as Barnard. We made some calls to the mainland early this morning and found out that his legal name is Ferdinand Benton-- fits neatly with Ferdi the Bull, eh? Anyway, we believe the condo you spoke of him buying, Pua, is the Park Grand; and one of my men saw Mr. J going in there on a couple of occasions--and leaving soon after, apparently very angry.

"We have around-the-clock surveillance on the place. And Benton's been seen going out to dinner with some blonde--the description fits him to a T. That lip reading at Pat's is coming in very handy.

"Oh and one of my surveillance boys saw the Aloha Noe Florist truck bring in a huge bouquet of flowers there. On a hunch, he called the Grand's desk, pretending to be the florist's manager and asked if flowers had just been delivered to suite 217, or something and the clerk told him that the only bouquet that afternoon was delivered to the Penthouse, Mr.Benton's suite."

"Neat!" The phone rang. "What now?" Keoki

muttered. "This is Major Kanai... Oh, Doc, what you got? You don't say. It's a positive? That's outstanding. Good work!"

He turned back to them, triumphant. "Doc, at the lab, just added another biggie to our growing mass of evidence; the prostitute-- the Jane Doe whose body was found in the Iliwai Canal six months ago? She had been shot with a .38;and, of course, the slug had been filed, as they always are. He checked it out, routinely; and it matches perfectly the one taken from Steele--and in every detail possible, the mashed one from the dog, as well."

"How about the guy called Weasel? From Brenda's dying statement, we know he was one of the perpetrators of her beating and death," Pua inquired.

"The Weasel is history. Kea heard about it first, from his cousin out at the airport. The Airport Police caught him trying to get out on a plane to Vegas. He tried to get through the radar gate with a gun, wrapped in wool and plastic, in his carry-on, yet. It buzzed, anyway and he broke and ran out into the parking area and they chased after him. Couldn't shoot, of course--too many people around. There wasn't any need to, as it happened. The poor devil ran smack-dab into a bus coming in to pick up a load of tourists. He was killed instantly."

"Talk about instant justice! Wish I could feel sorry for him, but not for a cold-blooded, heartless killer like that."

"He was a bad one, that's for sure. We sent his fingerprints to Nevada. They confirmed that his name is Peter Brock, with a half a dozen aliases. He was a one-

331

man army for the mob, a 'gun for hire' for at least twelve years. That's a long, long life for anyone in that business. Has an ex-wife and kids in Illinois, but they want no part of him. His parents are dead. There are no siblings. Nevada certainly doesn't want the remains. They're sending us the usual fee for their disposal."

Pua shivered. "It's as if he never existed," she said.

"A lot of people would have been better off if he never had."

"After all the people he's gunned down, it's ironic that he should die under the wheels of a tour bus, that's for sure."

Pua glanced at her watch. "Lucky, hadn't we better get going? It's after noon."

"Oh, golly, yes. First lunch and then touch bases with Mom and Pop."

"What's that?" Keoki yawned. "On second thought, I don't believe I want to know. I'm going to call Malia and then take a long nap on this couch."

They didn't quite make it to Mike's. As they passed the grocery store, they looked in the window; and saw mom beckoning to them, obviously agitated. They hurried in and mom handed Lucky a piece of paper. "Oh, Lucky," she cried. "Look what I just found on the counter."

It was a Crayola-scrawled note and it read, "Tomorro's the day, old lady and you better have more than fifty clams in your till, or you'll have one hell of a dokter bill. You got plenty custimurs. Don't be dum."

"Now calm down, Mom and think. Who might have left this?"

"I don't know. So many come Monday mornings, but I can't think of one who would do such a thing as this.

They're all regulars. Oh, except for the boy."

"The boy?"

"Yes, a young boy came in for cigarettes. I wouldn't sell him any, because he looked so young and wouldn't show me his I.D."

"What was his reaction to that?"

"He just said, 'No big t'ing,' and left. I didn't see which way he went. I was pretty busy and didn't even see this folded paper until I was ringing up an order."

"Well, Mom, he's got to be the one--an errand boy. You'd never seen him before?"

"No. And I almost threw this away. Thought someone had left a shopping list--but for some reason, I unfolded it and read it."

"Okay. Where's Pop?"

"He's got a flu bug. I don't think I'd better come to the meeting tonight. I know he can't."

"Don't worry about that. We'll fill you in later," Pua said, gently.

"What should I do about tomorrow?"

"I don't have to tell you to keep alert to anything-- anything at all that seems suspicious. It won't be the boy, you understand. And when anything seems odd, press

333

your signal. Don't wait to be sure. Better a false alarm than a costly, life-threatening delay.

"He'll probably pick up a bag of groceries, like before. He may be wearing a hat, or glasses, or some other small disguise and maybe a mustache or beard. Look for things like that. Also, he will hang around until there are no other customers in here. That could be a give-away too. Do you understand?"

"Yes. And I expect it will happen right after lunchtime. That's about the slowest it ever gets in here."

"Well, Pua and I will be at Mike's from noon on. If you signal, we'll be here in seconds. Just keep cool, all right? Do whatever he asks."

She frowned. "I worry about Pua. He might hurt her."

"Don't you fret about Pua? She's an expert self-defense, in spite of her small size."

"We're a good team, Mom," Pua said, smiling encouragement.

"Well, should I tell Pop?"

"I wouldn't--but that's for you to decide. He couldn't do anything but worry--right?"

She gave him a somewhat shaky smile. "He's a worry-wart, that's for sure. I can handle it. Is it all right if I don't keep much money in the till? Just in case?"

"What would you do with it?"

A woman had come in and was shopping for frozen foods.

"I put what I don't need in a plastic bag and stuff it down deep in the bulk rice sack," she whispered.

"That's good. Just be sure there's $75 in that till."

"I will."

Mike's was crowded, so they ordered take-out. As he paid for it, Lucky told him, "Call Pua. It's important. You have our number?"

"Sure do. Half an hour soon enough?"

"That's fine," Lucky said. I'll be out for a while, making sure no one has forgotten the meeting tonight. You coming?"

"Wouldn't miss it."

When he called, Pua explained mom's problem and his first response was, "How can I help?" She explained their plan and he assured her he'd keep an eye out for trouble in the morning as well. Anything happens, the neighbors and I will handle it."

At four, mom Hanohano called. "I just thought I ought to tell you--that Mr. Jones came in to shop awhile ago. You may be right about him at that."

"What happened? Are you all right?" Pua was concerned.

"Oh, yes. He acted just the same as always. But when he left, I looked out and a boy was pushing his grocery cart up the hill. It was the same boy that left the note."

Pua hesitated, puzzled. "The same boy came in with him?"

335

"No, no, he waited outside. I just thought it was funny that he'd be out there waiting for him."

"It is. Thank you for calling, Mom."

"No trouble. You said if anything seemed funny to let you know. That seemed funny to me. I won't keep you." And she was gone.

When Lucky came in, she told him about it and he nodded with satisfaction. "She's getting our messages loud and clear now. That's good.

"I didn't mean to be this late, but I stopped by headquarters again--just in case. You'd never believe what's happened over there. Ruby called for the lieutenant and told him everything she had told your dad before was a string of lies.

"So Parkins told her, 'Well, then, we might as well release you.'

She screamed at him, "you can't do that! That's plain murder. Okay, okay! Bring on your steno-typist, or whatever. I'm going to blow the whistle. But you gotta promise to protect me." She was still at it, when I got there. The lieutenant had just left the room to have a smoke. He told me our suspicions of Mr. J were right on--including the safe-house situation. And she was talking about Ferdi, when he left."

"Good grief! And the lieutenant promised her protection? She's such a terrible person!"

"He promised her nothing. She just made demands and started talking. I don't know how it's going to turn out."

"Well, I hope this is going to be good news, not bad--but a letter came this afternoon. It's from Gridley, Wadi and Matsuo, Attorneys at Law, Suite 1727 Alii Towers, Honolulu. Want to face it now?"

"Sure, Pua. You could have opened it. Posh stationery! He slit the envelope and drew out a single sheet of paper. His jaw dropped. Listen to this! "If convenient, we would like you and your associate to have luncheon with us on Friday, at 1:00 p.m. to discuss a business opportunity which may well prove advantageous to us both.

You have been highly recommended to us by our long-time specialist in old and rare books, Mr. Clyde Nello. Feel at liberty to contact him, in advance, for further information and let us know if you are interested. Very truly yours, Malcolm Gridley, President."

This could really be something great, Pua. I'm going to call Prof. We just rode up in the elevator together. He didn't mention--"

"Good evening, Prof. It's Lucky and we received a letter from...yes, today. We want to thank you for recommending us..." He listened with growing excitement.

Pua stood by, her eyes like saucers. "It sounds fabulous, but...Oh, I see...right...Oh, don't worry; we're not about to give that up. Thanks again."

"Pua, Prof is a specialist on old and rare books and has been consultant to this firm for five years. The company's investigator is retiring and Prof recommended us.

It comes with a generous monthly retainer, plus full investigative salary, when we're actually on a case. Prof said he would withdraw his recommendation unless we promised to continue with our merchants. Isn't that great?"

He pulled her into his arms and held her close. "We're on our way, dear heart; we're on our way!"

"But what do we do? What does Prof do?"

He authenticates private libraries and evaluates them for estates and for sales and the like and logs missing items on the inventories. We would be called in to locate missing items, such as books and art works that don't show up when wills are in probate, for example. And involve us in the locating and prosecution of the thieves. He says we're in--he's sure of it. And since we're on call, as it were, we still have time for our present major projects."

"Oh, Lucky! It sounds wonderful!"

"I know that," he said. "Prof says he's positive that we can handle it; and that it's all ours, if we want it."

"I have to get a new dress," was Pua's excited comment. "A new dress!" "To wear to the luncheon, of course."

Chapter 32

Lucky closed and locked the door, with a long sigh of relief. "What a day! --Right, darling?"

"You know it! And weren't those people great? It was almost like a party; so different from the first time. It's hard to believe that such hope and confidence and the closeness among them, could build up in such a short time--and we had eight new people, too."

"It's really amazing, isn't it? And now the key figure is Albie Keach. I'm glad they chose him as their association president. He has surprising leadership qualities. And then, when he nominated Stella to be treasurer, so they could pay us in one check--I got a kick out of that.

"And I'll never forget when Albie said--oh, here it is: 'You've given us back our belief in ourselves and in our ability to meet our problems. But we know we're not at full strength yet. We need you to continue with us.' And they all applauded."

"Yes, attitudes have certainly become positive and it seems-"

The doorbell chimed. Lucky answered. "Mr. Kolinsky, come in, come in," he said.

"I shouldn't bother you, on my first night; but could you give me a few minutes?"

"Of course. Come in and sit down."

"Could I give you a glass of wine?" Pua asked.

"Thank you, I'd like that. You know, I own the

339

little theater up on the next street? Well, while I sat at the meeting tonight, I realized that soon you were going to need a larger place to meet. My theater is dark on Mondays and I'd like to offer it for your use."

"That would be great; but what made you think of it?"

"My friends Herb and Joy Masters told me what a difference you folks are making to our neighborhood and suggested I talk with you. That's why I came to the meeting tonight. I'm not a businessman parse; I'm a teacher and a retired actor.

"I teach and rehearse my students Tuesday through Thursday and we do our plays on Friday, Saturday and Sunday. We have a good attendance, too.

"I'd like to have something going on there Mondays. It's that night that mischievous youngsters seem to pull their stunts--not bad things, a little graffiti, faces drawn on the ticket window glass, a little litter--that kind of thing. It occurs to me that if it were in use, lit up, on Mondays, those things wouldn't happen."

"Now it's not fancy, but the seats are comfortable and it has a nice stage. I don't want to rent it--all it would cost you people is $15 each time, for the electricity, if you'd like to use it as a meeting hall. That's my offer."

"That's very generous and you're right. We are going to need more room and soon," Lucky said. I'd like you to talk with Albie Keach. He's the new president of the association."

"I know Albie. I'll do that; if you approve of the

plan."

"What do you think, Pua?

"It sounds like a perfect solution to our problem. I know that theater--spent many happy hours at the movies there on Saturday afternoons, when I was growing up. I really think it would be a wise move, Lucky."

"Okay. You can tell Albie we approve; Lucky Seven will pop for the electricity. And thank you."

After the dapper little man left, Pua said, "See, I told you! Everything falls into place for you, Lucky. With as many as we had tonight, I was beginning to wonder how we were going to manage."

"Me, too. And if I'm not mistaken, that theater is in the area where Albie wants to build up the membership."

"Somehow, this man reminded me of a more refined Bundy. And by the way, Bundy really capped the climax, tonight--when he said, 'I just want to admit publicly before you folks, that I was a horse's ass to think I didn't need all of you. We need each other and that's where it is. My daughter here, Becky, told me if I felt that way I ought to say so. So I have.' He got a big hand too."

"And Lucky, telling them about mom Hanohano's possible problem tomorrow and how we plan to handle it, was a good idea. They're ready to help if they can."

"I was impressed with Palani, asking to be membership chairman. Let's see, where is it? Here we are. Albie and I counted 52 businesses within eight square blocks of here--and there are only 21 represented here tonight. With some help from a few of you, we can

341

build up a merchants' organization that can make a real difference--like getting the city to put in more and better street lights down here, for example; and giving us the same street-cleaning service as they get downtown and a patrol all our own.'"

"He was right, you know. These people can make it happen."

The next few minutes passed in companionable silence; then Pua said, "You know, tomorrow evening is Uncle Nomana's luau. I hope we can make it. He'd be so disappointed if you weren't there."

"What time are we due?"

"Seven. It's at his place in Lanikai, so it will only take us twenty minutes or so to get there. If we're late, no problem; that's known as Hawaiian time."

"God willing, we'll be there, sweetheart. But we've got a bit of work to do first, remember."

"Piece of cake!"

By noon Tuesday, the two of them were sitting at Mike's counter, slowly eating his special of the day. They were starting on his guava tarts when the signal bell rang. They did their best to achieve a strolling pace up toward the mom n Pop store, but it wasn't easy to be nonchalant. Lucky murmured, as they passed by the store, "There's a man in there all right, did you notice him? Mom's putting money in his bag now, I think."

"And he's wearing sunglasses. Looks jittery to me. I hope he doesn't try something stupid and hurt her. Shall we move in?"

"Not yet, but we move the minute he starts to leave. When I go for him, you go inside and tell mom to crouch behind the counter. I don't think guns will come into play, but just in case. You get down there with her, too. Now!"

As the man reached the street Lucky took a flying leap at him, bringing him down, while groceries and a small stack of bills flew from his broken paper bag. The sunglasses flew into the street to be smashed by a passing car. As the man went down, the wind was knocked out of him and his resistance was feeble, as he tried to clutch at his scattering loot. The battle was over in seconds and Pua appeared beside them, gun leveled steadily at the prone and bitterly swearing culprit. Mike, watching from the Malt Shop, had made sure the neighbors and the police were on the way. The patrol car slipped in at curbside and the arrest was made. It was all over--just like that.

"I'll be at headquarters in a few minutes." Lucky told the officer. "Alert Major Kanai, okay? He's going to want to be in on this, from the beginning."

"Right!"

Lucky and Pua recovered the money and the groceries and returned to the store. Mom was shaking, but smiling gamely.

"I nearly fell over when I saw you go on by. I thought something was wrong, that my signal didn't work or something."

"Sorry, Mom. I should have told you we might do that. To be sure we had a good case, we had to pick him

343

up after he left the store. It's safer for you, too. You did fine. What tipped you off that he was the one?"

"Just what you thought. He had those dark glasses on and kept pushing them up on his nose, like they didn't fit. And he fiddled around until Mrs. Bernstein paid her bill and left. Now you wait right here, Lucky. I'll be back in a jiffy." And she was, with a cloth in her hand. "Let me clean up this shoulder," she said and for the first time, he realized that blood was running down his arm. "I have disinfectant on this. It may sting a little."

As she took care of it, he winced. "You scraped off a big hunk of skin on the sidewalk," she said. "We don't want it to get infected, do we?"

Lucky turned the grimace into a grin and thanked her as she put a neat dressing on his wound.

Later, Lucky and Pua went to see Keoki. They found him jubilant. "We did better than we thought," he chortled. "That damned fool was on the wanted list for Auto Theft right here in Hawaii--jumped his bail. He's in big trouble and he knows it. But, like the others, he seems to look forward to serving time; says his life isn't worth a nickel outside. Say's he botched an assignment and with his outfit, that's curtains."

"You mean the guy they just brought in from the Mom n Pop? We figured him for a patsy."

"When we questioned him, he said, 'they don't give you two chances, That's for damn sure. He says he was going--guess where?" He paused. "To the Makamai Tower, only two blocks away. And who lives there?

344

None other than Mr. J. Kea called the manager after this guy said he had been going there. He asked if they had a Jones in residence. The manager told him no, that the only name starting with a J was Jessup, first name Miles." Ruby gave us all we needed, anyway. The boys are out picking him up as we speak. Ruby couldn't stop talking-- and every car available is out sweeping the area for the rest of them.

"Beautiful! Are you going to be able to land them before they panic?"

"Either before or when, Lucky. They'll be bagged PDQ if they go to the airport, that's for sure."

"Anything new on Ferdi the Bull?" Pua asked.

"No problem there. We won't keep him though. Nevada wants to extradite. He's wanted there on about a dozen felony counts, including suspicion of the murder of the Penthouse Gambler, the one that made headlines some time ago. Far as I'm concerned, Nevada's welcome to him as soon as we get all the information we can out of him."

"And Ruby?"

"Her case will be going before the Grand Jury, as soon as it can be scheduled. We'll pull in Ferdi before that, so she won't try to change her story. Actually, the only ones likely to escape detection are those we don't know about. Ruby said there were about thirty people involved in the actual extortions--though she may not be telling on them ail--and those we don't catch will no doubt be back at it on their own. Your work is still cut out for you, I'm afraid."

345

"We'll keep on it, here. And I think we're going to make a survey on the Windward side too. Albie told us about shopping mall over there that is having a rough time of it."

Pua stretched and said, "Lucky, if we're going to make Uncle's luau on time, we'd better get going. You and mom are coming, aren't you, Dad? Or are you too worn out?"

"Oh, I feel fine--had a nice long nap. Ever known me to miss a luau at Nomana's, Pua?"

"No. Want to drive over with us?"

"You kids better take your own car, in case I have to come back for some reason. You could bring Malia home, if that happened, couldn't you?"

"It would be our pleasure," Lucky smiled. "But I hope you get to have a full evening out. You've been working too hard, Keoki. You need a change of pace."

"We all do," K'eoki said.

The second kalua pig was just coming out of the imu when they arrived and they hurried around to the underground oven, so that Lucky could enjoy the show and the incredible aromas that burst forth as the ti leaves and stones were removed. He watched, fascinated, as three big Hawaiians carefully extracted banana leaf-wrapped sweet potatoes and other packages of mysterious good things, before they lifted the pig to the rack for carving. The aromas were marvelous and even the smoke issuing from hot stones that had roasted the meat to perfection, had an appetite-inspiring richness.

"Lucky! Pualani! Komo mai!" Uncle Nomana had discovered their presence. "Come on to the tent, now and have an elbow-bender or two before the feast begins." He kissed Pua on both cheeks as he placed a lei on her shoulders and handed her another one to present in the same fashion to Lucky. "Lots of folks here to meet kids. You better be ready for a lot of kissing, Lucky. Luaus are kissing affairs." The huge tent, open on all sides to the evening breeze, was lavishly decorated with exotic greenery and flowers, as were the long tables, with dozens of whole pineapples, haupia and other good things to be enjoyed by some two hundred guests.

The time sped by in a whirl of meeting cousins, aunties, uncles and lots of children and babies, all happily playing together, the older ones tending the younger. Pua was surrounded by old friends and relatives and kept pulling Lucky to her side, to meet them. He was; as Uncle Nomana had said, kissed by every woman and child he met. And he felt a part of it all. The warmth of everyone's welcome made him feel at home.

The Hawaiian wear of the guests seemed to make the whole affair a festival of color. And at times, the sound of excited voices nearly drowned out the group playing and singing the Hawaiian music Lucky had come to love.

'Booze 'n beer', as Uncle Nomanu called it, were in abundance, but there was no sign of drunkenness. These people, he thought, really know how to enjoy them selves.

"Well, what do you think, Lucky?" Malia and

347

Keoki had arrived and she kissed him warmly.

"Fantastic! Pua, your folks are here," he called out to her and she ran to greet them.

"It's time to take our places at the table, unless you want to fight the mob. Nomana wants us to sit by him," Keoki said. "Shall we go before we get caught in the rush?" They followed him into the rapidly filling tent and took their places; and when the guests were seated, the rush of sound suddenly ceased and Uncle Nomana, in a surprisingly clear and pleasant voice, sang the ancient Hawaiian blessing.

Lucky lost track of all the dishes presented to him--the wonderfully moist and savory Kalua pig, Chicken Long-rice, Lomi Lomi Salmon, Opihi, fresh crab, Squid luau, Poi, Sweet and Sour Short Ribs, shrimp--the list seemed unending. He ate heartily, enjoying both the familiar and the unusual.

At last, he let out a long, satisfied breath and Uncle Nomana told him. "Eat all you want, Son. We Hawaiians don't just eat until we're full--we eat until we're tired." Lucky laughed. "I think I just did," he said, "and I want to save room for guava cake and that coconut pudding--haupia is that right? --And a bit more pineapple. I swear, Sir, I don't know where I'm going to put it, but I'm going to give it my best shot."

"Don't worry about it, ain't no big thing. We'll send some food home with you. That's Hawaiian style too."

Afterward, Pua danced the hula, on popular demand and her grace was applauded enthusiastically. One by one, others rose from the tables to offer entertainment, as unselfconsciously as children, demonstrating the many talents with which the Hawaiians are blessed.

When the Kanals and Lucky left, bearing 'care packages,' as Nomana termed them, there were still many guests remaining to party on into the night. That too, he was assured, is Hawaiian style.

Chapter 33

Pua had just poured the first cups of coffee for the day, when the call came.

"Lucky Seven. Dad? You sound agitated. What's the matter?"

"Lucky," she called, then heard him say, "I'm on, Keoki."

"There's bad trouble down Kaneohe way. I thought you'd want to know. I'm at Castle Hospital and--"

"Dad. What is it; are you hurt?"

"No, no, no. Not me. I'm sorry, didn't mean to scare you. During the night, there was a big fire at the shopping center near town."

"You suspect arson?"

"You got it. And worse."

"Some one hurt?" Pua asked.

"Yes, seriously hurt. A man by the name of Don Keach is in the hospital with first degree burns over--"

"Keach!" Lucky interrupted. "Any relation to Albie?"

"His cousin. He's in bad shape. Albie called me from here at the hospital; and I came right over. I think you'll want in on this."

"We'll come now."

"No need to rush. Don is undergoing emergency burn treatment right now, but they may have to send him to the burn center in San Francisco. He's pretty bad off. They think he'll make it, but right now it's touch and go."

"Was he able to tell you anything at all?"

"Well, the ambulance EMT did say that he kept mumbling, 'I'm a damn fool. Should 'a just paid up--that kind of thing. Cued me in that what we feared might happen here, has already begun."

"Sure sounds like it, Keoki. When was the fire?"

"About 4 a.m., near as we can figure. Don had a gift shop--flne arts objects--a few tourist-type gift items and some antiques that can't be replaced--things like that. Everything in his place is wiped out. Several of the neighboring shops were badly damaged, too."

"Why was he there at four in the morning?"

"From what I can gather, he had previously had threats of fire and decided to stay there all night, in case someone tried to break in. Whoever it was broke a back window and threw in some kind of a firebomb--perhaps a Molotov cocktail--something on that order. It apparently landed right next to the cot he was sleeping on and exploded.

"The poor guy would have burned to death, or been blown apart, if he hadn't had a thick comforter wrapped around him. Somehow, he managed to drag himself, comforter and all, to the front door and unlock it. The baker, just across the way, was already at work and heard the explosion. He ran across and dragged Reach out."

"Good Lord! We'll come over now. See what we

351

can find out from people at the shopping center, while it's fresh in their minds."

"Fine. Damn it, I've been afraid of something like this, ever since you saw those two men at Pat's. Didn't expect it quite this soon, though."

"Dad, is the victim married?" Pua asked.

"Yes and they have three keikis. She's here at the hospital. The children are with her sister."

"That's good. Do you know if they have adequate insurance?"

"Yes, both health and fire insurance--but a good part of his inventory was antiques and art objects that can't be replaced."

"What a shame!"

"Well, we'll go to the center first, Keoki and see what we can find out; and meet you at the hospital later."

In less than an hour, they were on the fire scene, appalled at the devastation of the store and the blackened shops adjacent. The acrid smell of smoke permeated the air. Police were patrolling and one officer took them aside.

"You're Lucky and Pualani, aren't you? Major Kanai suggested I speak with you. See that little package and gift store down there at the end, beyond the fire area? Well, last week, the owner, a Hapa Haole woman, showed up with black eyes and bruises. Didn't call us, but I finish my patrol here and went in to pick up a six-pack to take home with me.

"I asked her what happened and she said she was clumsy; walked into an open door and fell downstairs at home. Now I know that house and there's no second floor and no basement--in other words, no stairs. And those bruises sure didn't come from a fall anyway.

"I tried to get her to talk; but she told me to mind my own business; to go home and have a beer and forget it. She insisted that she was okay. I had to let it go at that, but she's such a nice lady; and she's scared to death."

"We'll talk with her. Mahalo."

When they walked in, the woman glared at them. "You're Rent-Plus, right? Well, I'm not buying. You can burn me out too, if you like. I've had it with you people! Now get out!"

"Wait a minute, here," Lucky answered, in shocked protest. "What makes you think we aren't shoppers?"

"Shoppers pick up the stuff they want and bring them to the counter. You walked right up to me here-- like--like--" Her face reddened. "You're not from Rent-Plus?"

"No, Ma'am, we've never even heard of Rent-Plus. What is it?"

The woman studied their faces. "I apologize. It's just that the fire frightened me so much and I thought-- I'm sorry."

"Don't worry about it," Lucky told her. "Actually, the reason we're here is to help you if we can. We are private investigators known as Lucky Seven."

353

"Oh, I've heard of you. Don--the man who was burned--tried to talk us into calling you a couple weeks ago; but these are mostly family people and they're too scared to fight. It's hard to blame them, with the little ones and all."

"I'm Lucky Gregory and this is my partner, Pua Kanai." Her face brightened. "Don wanted you to come over and investigate Rent-Plus. I should introduce myself. I am Sylvia Nakana."

"Well, Mrs. Nakana, we're here, now. Level with us. What is Rent-Plus?"

"They send a man--a woman, once--every week, about this time and make me pay extra rent money, for what they call insurance for breakage, shop-lifting and things like that. They say if I tell anyone, the price is double. They want $100 this time and lots of weeks, I don't clear that much, with overhead and all. I'm a widow and this shop is all I have. If they'd just leave me alone, I could make a decent living. My husband left me a little house, that's all paid up. They even said something could happen to that, if I didn't uh--what was it now? --Line up. I don't know which way to turn."

"And when did this start, Mrs. Nakana?" Pua asked.

"Let me think--about two months ago, I believe. It seems like forever!"

"And one of them beat you. Isn't that why you have those sunglasses on?"

Wordlessly, she removed them and they could see

swelling and purplish stains under both eyes.

"Oh, my dear!" Pua cried.

The woman rolled up the long full sleeves of her muumuu, displaying ugly, purple bruises. "All this, because I was short $20 last week. I'm tough, but this thing is getting me down."

Grim-faced, Lucky told her, "Albie Keach is over here, at the hospital with his cousin. When he is free, he'll come over to tell you about the system we developed in Honolulu, to fight this very kind of thing. Will you listen to him?"

Her face relaxed. "Yes, I will. Something has to be done about it. I do have enough money for Rent-Plus this week. Should I give it to the collector?"

"To tell the truth, I doubt if they'll come this week. We believe the fire turned out to be more than they bargained for; and with the center alive with police; and the burned shops closed and guarded night and day, it would be pretty stupid to come anywhere near. Talk with Albie. He works closely with us and he's very good at it. Trust him. He'll advise you. As soon as he can leave the hospital for a while, he'll be stopping by. Don't worry. We'll not forget you. Now, Pua, pick up something we need--so we'll have a package to carry, when we leave."

"Whatever you want. It's on the house."

Lucky grinned. "Not on your life!" he said. "How much, Pua?"

"It's five dollars plus tax. I found a nice holder for our tissue box."

"Big spender!" he teased.

They made several other stops, but an atmosphere of distrust and suspicion in some of the places, made them decide to pass up any further investigations until a later date.

"I think that fire has spooked everybody, today. We'd better let it lay, for now." Lucky said.

"I agree. I've made a note of every store, where that 'wish you weren't here' mood was evident. We can pass it on to Albie, for whatever it's worth."

"Good thinking.

At the hospital they found Albie in a waiting room, staring glumly into space. He brightened, when he saw them.

"How is your cousin doing?" They asked.

"Oh, he's holding his own, they tell me. Looks awful, though. Hair's burned off; neck and back a mass of horrible burns--lower legs and feet the same. God, it made me sick! Dorothea--that's his wife--insisted on staying with him, till he went into the treatment room and now she's sitting outside it. Just won't leave. I feel so damned useless!

Keoki is with her."

"Well, when you leave here, we have an assignment for you, if you're up to it."

"You have; Over here? Tell me about it." As they told Sylvia's story, he listened attentively and they could see the anger building in him. When they had finished, he said, "You don't have to tell me what to do. It's just a new wrinkle on an old pattern I'm all too familiar with. I'll see her this afternoon. Shall we work the same format? I have a man in mind over here. Pretty sure he's having big problems, too. Owns the Brass Lamp shop, next to the store you visited. I think he would be a good choice to lead the fight over here."

"We stopped in there; and he told us to look around, but he was very nervous and followed our every movement with his eyes. We didn't stay. Pua has him on a list of shops that didn't seem to welcome strangers today. It may help."

"Here it is, Albie," Pua said. "We figured they were all likely candidates for a self-help program."

Albie read it and sighed. "I just wish Don had called me. Every one of these shops is just able to make a living. This complex didn't turn out to be the roaring success they had anticipated. They get a fair amount of tourists and some decorators, plus a reasonable number of locals, but they'll never make it, if the racket is bleeding them. The supermarket is the biggest draw. And we can count on it, nobody's moving in on a national chain operation like that--they just feed on the little guys. But if I can get these same little guys to join together, like we did in Honolulu, we can oust them. I know we can. And I'm going to help them."

"Are you sure you want to get in that deep?"

"I sure do, with your help. I know some of them personally and they know my cousin very well. When I heard how the fire started, I thought it sounded too much like what we used to go through on the other side of the Pali.

"It occurred to me that if our group okays it, I'd like Bundy to take over for me over there, while I'm needed over here. He's sort of a rough cob, but boy, is he a convert to our system. What do you think?"

"Won't your shop suffer from neglect without you?"

"I don't think so. Mama is home now and she often helps out in the shop. I've thought it all out, Lucky."

"Okay, Albie, go for it! And count on us for any help we can give."

"Hey, I had no doubts but what you'd work with me. And I can't wait to get started! There'll be no problem about getting police assistance over here, either. They know what's been going on in Honolulu. I know we'll have their kokua. "

Just then, Keoki came in. "Don's doing okay, Albie. He's responding so well that they don't anticipate having to send him to California, after all."

"Thank God for that," Albie said.

Pua was staring at Lucky curiously. "What are you thinking about?" she asked. "You're a million miles away. Lucky!"

He looked up, startled. "Oh, I was just thinking. It occurred to me that, with the big guns gone from the scene, less-experienced people are manning this operation now. Like those two yes-men types we saw at the luncheon at Pat's, Pua. If I'm right, we already have a head start. We've identified two of them and there was certainly no sign of leadership, there."

"I'll buy that," Keoki agreed.

"Now then, Don is doing a lot better than they had hoped. He'll be in the hospital a long time, with skin grafts and the like, but the prognosis is good."

"That's great news," Albie said. "If Dorothea's okay, I'm going to go over to the shopping center, now; and see what I can do."

"She's with her husband, now. The doctor said her presence seemed to give him added strength. So they put her in sterile clothing and allowed her into ICU. She was nodding off in her chair, when I left. Poor lady. It's been an awfully rough day on her."

"I know. I'll check back before I go home. Okay, I'm off to the shopping center."

"Need a ride?"

"No, thank you, I drove over here." And looking much more like the Albie they knew and admired, he waved and left.

Keoki moaned. "Are you two as hungry as I am? I had a sandwich in the cafeteria, but I could sure use a meal about now. "

Lucky and Pua laughed. "We forgot all about eating," Pua said. "We didn't even finish our coffee. Where shall we go?"

"Follow me up to Kailua. I know a great restaurant

that serves all day long--always has good Hawaiian food, too. You game?"

"You bet!"

"Fine. I think we've done all we can here."

The sun was setting as they left the restaurant and drove over the Pali and down toward Honolulu. They were just cruising along. Keoki had passed them and disappeared soon after they left Kailua Town.

"Beautiful," Lucky said, quietly. "What gorgeous colors Hawaiian sunsets display. And look at the city. From here it seems so serene, as if nothing bad could happen there."

"I feel fortunate that we're in a position to do something about the bad things that do happen, don't you? Making a difference is what life is all about. Are you as glad as I am that we chose to live here?"

"You know it, my darling Pua. It's my home too, now; and I don't ever want to leave. It's almost perfect!"

Again, a thoughtful silence ensued. Finally, Pua turned to him.

"Almost?" she asked.

"Well just look at us--launched into a career we love; new opportunities offered; family and friends, whom we love and who love us and we're happy together. Isn't that almost perfect?"

"Almost?" she asked again. "Darling, you know exactly what I am talking about."

He turned off the highway into a view area and

stopped the car. "I know I promised I wouldn't ask--" He got no further, for Pua was in his arms, her lips sweet against his own.

After a bit, she stirred and whispered, "You're right, Sweetheart. I think it's time to make it perfect!"

He looked deep into her eyes, stroking back her hair. "You're sure, my Pualani--very sure? I love you so very much. But we both know that it's no good if you aren't absolutely sure that you want to spend the rest of your life with me, as my wife."

"Now that I have made up my mind, I can hardly wait, kuuipo. I love you with all my heart and soul."

He moved away from her slightly, groping in his pocket and came up with a small velvet box. Taking out a beautiful diamond ring, he slipped it on her finger. I love you, Pualani Kanai--you are and always will be my one, my only great love."

"Lucky," she gasped, "it's gorgeous! Have you been carrying this around in your pocket all this time?"

"I have, indeed, my love. "One of my finest red-head faults is stubbornness," he said. "And there's another ring in this box, which I hope won't stay there too long." There was something very special about the kiss that sealed their promise of life together.

"I want to go home," Pua said, in a small, appealing voice.

"Your wish is my command." He started the car. "But could we take the long way there? I think it's time I had that talk with your father."

"My father!"

"Absolutely. Remember, we both talked with him that other time. This is my turn. I want to tell him everything he wants to hear about me that he doesn't know already--and one big item I know he wants to discuss is the wedding. But first, of course, I am going to ask him, formally, for your hand in marriage. And this time, my knees won't be shaking, the way they did before, when all we wanted was to be together."

Pua was laughing in sheer delight. "Lucky, Lucky, you are too much! It's going to be one grand life, being Mr. and Mrs. Blake Seven Gregory. I know it!"

ABOUT THE AUTHOR

Frances Cook King Kalaukoa (1916 -1998) was a graduate of the University of Oregon. She was a Justice of the Peace in Beaverton, Oregon, founder of the Safe Teen driving program and wrote the Dinning Out column in the Honolulu Advertiser for years. As part of her retirement she wrote two manuscripts that she never managed to get published in remote Hawaii. Fifteen years after her death these two great stories were recovered and are being published by her son, Stan Cook.

Stan Cook as co-author of his mother's book was responsible for formatting, editing and rewrites. He's also the author of: 1920, Shots Fired, Officer Down.

Contact Information:

You can contact the author, Stan Cook via email
stan@stancook.com
http://booksby-cook.com

www.ingramcontent.com/pod-product-compliance
Lightning Source LLC
Chambersburg PA
CBHW061310170626
46817CB00001B/127